Lawful ATTRACTION

A *Crush* NOVEL

ELOUISE EAST

Beta Readers: Emma Brown, Mike Van Eimeren, Jess Waugh-Bacchus, Tammy Basile

CONTENTS

LAWFUL ATTRACTION

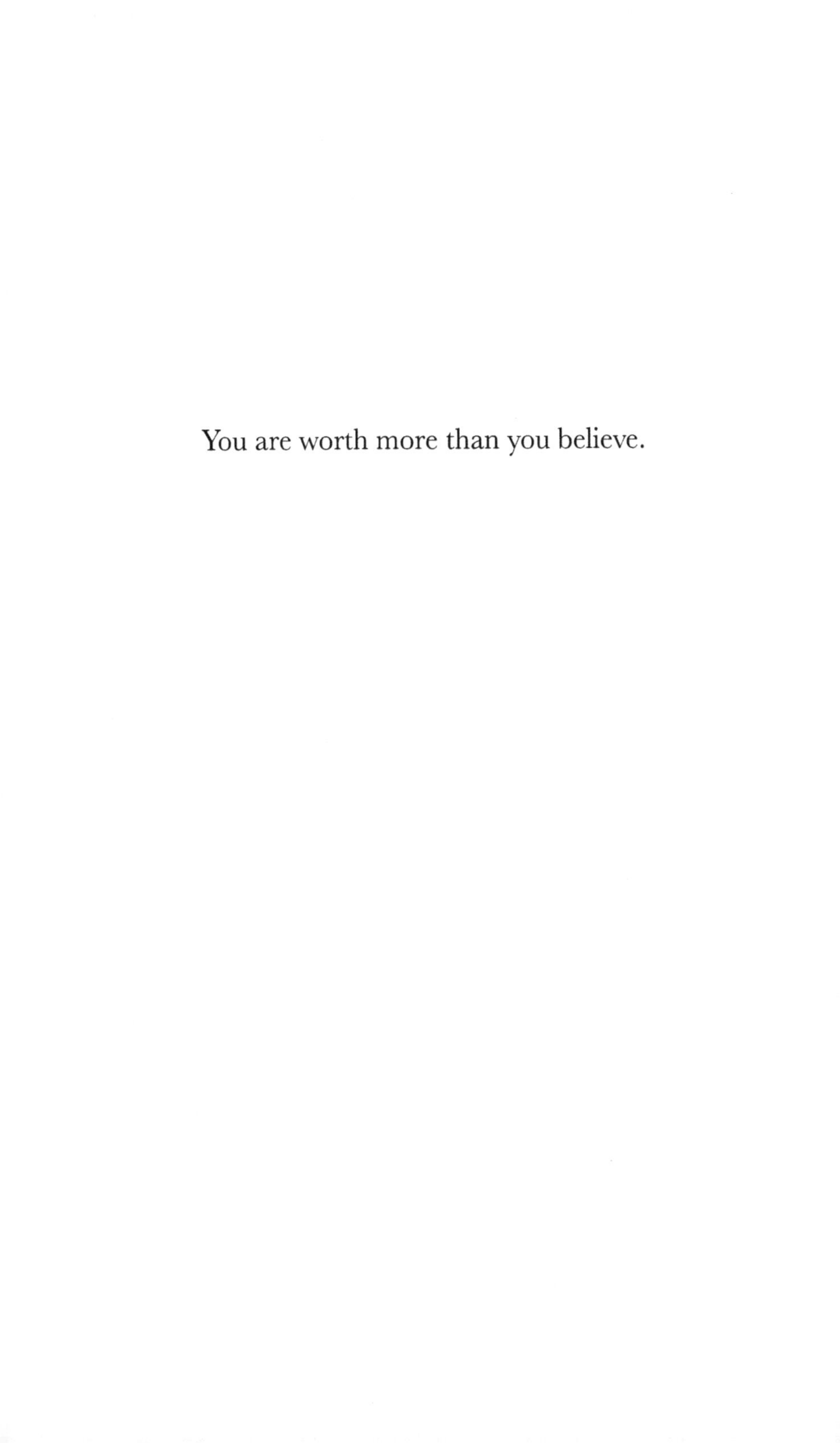

You are worth more than you believe.

Alice, Logan's sister

Amanda, therapist

Analise, Bartender at Crush, Kade's
girlfriend, Friends with Crush group

Asher, Childminder, Sean's boyfriend
(Instant Desire)

Ava, Police officer, Samuel's sister

Barry Jamieson, antique dealer

**Bastien, Stripper, Make-up Artist
and Jewellery maker, only
child**

Brandy, bouncer at the Bone Yard

Brooke, antique dealer

Bryan, Chief of Police, Logan's boss

Casey, Paramedic, Logan's brother,
Luke's boyfriend (Life Support)

Cassidy, dancer at the Bone Yard

Charlie, Bartender at Crush, Josh's boyfriend (First Kiss)

Claire, Logan's sister, Robert's wife

Cody, dancer at the Bone Yard, Bastien's friend

Colton, Woodworker, Ioan's boyfriend (A Crush for Christmas)

Deacon, photographer, Bastien's occasional boss

Emory, dancer at the Bone Yard

Eric, Actor, Samuel's boyfriend (Love Scene)

Ethan, Architect student, Eric's brother, Friends with Crush group

Ginny, Tom's girlfriend

Henry, police officer

Ioan, Carer at nursing home, Colton's boyfriend (A Crush for Christmas)

James, Logan's brother

Joey, Police officer, Friends with Logan and Ava, Kade's police partner

Josh, Charlie's boyfriend (First Kiss)

Kade, Police officer, Friends with Logan and Ava, Joey's police partner

Kat, forensic pathologist

Kenzo, Retired Army, Veteran Centre

volunteer, Zak's boyfriend (Covert
    Strength)
Liam, Logan's brother, Penny's husband
**Logan, Detective Sergeant,
    Siblings: Liam, Alice, Claire,
    Casey, James, Parents: William
    and Christine**
Luke, Personal Trainer, Casey's
    boyfriend (Life Support)
Max, Interior designer, Trent's
    boyfriend (Primary Seduction)
Miles, music operator at the Bone Yard
Mrs Graham, Winona Conrad's
    neighbour
Nolan, bartender at the Bone Yard
Rafferty, owner of the Bone Yard
Rebecca Jarrod, victim
Reed, dancer at the Bone Yard
Samuel, Lawyer, Eric's boyfriend (Love
    Scene)
Sean, Architect, Asher's boyfriend
    (Instant Desire)
Simon, crime scene photographer
Tom, Owner of Crush, Ginny's
    boyfriend
Trent, Teacher, Max's boyfriend (Pri-
    mary Seduction), Samuel's brother

Van, dancer at the Bone Yard
Winona Conrad, victim
Zak, Woodworker, Kenzo's boyfriend
    (Covert Strength)

A pain-filled groan reached his ears, and Logan Taylor's protective instincts flared, halting him in his tracks as he wandered in the direction of home. He tilted his head, trying to gauge where the sound was coming from. The deep sound echoed again, and he stepped closer to an alley next to The Bone Yard, a strip club near the centre of Cambridge. There was no decent lighting in the area, and the moon was hiding behind the clouds, only sending shafts of light as it peeked through.

Placing his feet carefully so as not to make his presence known before he wanted to, he moved further into the mouth of the alley. The sounds continued but changed in tone, becoming more pleasure than pain, and Logan's heart raced as the darkness closed around him, hiding his presence from the carnal get-together.

He was tempted to appear and break up their little party because it wasn't safe, but instead, he chose to check to ensure it seemed consensual, then leave them to it. It wasn't the best place to attend to their needs, but as long as no one bothered them, they'd be fine.

Approaching slowly, breathing through his mouth to reduce the stench of the rotten garbage, he stayed in the shadows until he reached where the noises were louder.

"Just fuck me already! Harder!" The voice had a musical lilt to it but was strained as if stretching for something just out of their reach.

Rhythmic knocking began, and a second deeper and hoarser voice groaned, "Fuck, yeah. That's it. Take it all."

Logan ignored his inconvenient hard-on and peered around the large rubbish bin that was currently hiding his position. The sight took his breath away, taking his cock from semi-hard to fully erect in less than a second.

A slender guy was bent over something, one of his elbows resting on the top of it while the other hand pressed against the wall in front of them as a large man rammed into him. The guy being fucked had his head dropped back, his face towards the sky, which curved his spine and stuck his ass out further. The bigger guy groaned again, speeding up, to which the smaller one appeared to agree.

Goosebumps ran across Logan's skin, which had nothing to do with the chill in the air and everything to do with wanting to be closer, to see more, to be part of it. The thought shocked him but not enough to remove his focus from the two before him. He parted his lips and licked them as a muffled tortured groan filled the alley, flowing over him.

"Fuck, yes! I'm gonna come. Let's fill this ass."

The idea the larger man was going to pump his seed into the slender one had Logan's breathing increasing, light-headedness overtaking him as he stared through the darkness. Bracing his hand against the sticky wall, he took in all the information he could about the scene before him.

A brief flash of moonlight gave him the opportunity to see the smaller man in more detail, and he saw the man push back a little and wrap his hand around his cock. The shadows returned and had Logan cursing silently.

"Oh, fuck, yes! Yessss!"

He could just about make out the jerks of the smaller one's body as he released, and Logan clenched his fists and bit his lip to stop himself from following the man over the edge.

"Fuck!" The larger man shouted his rapture to the sky and held himself tighter to his partner for a second before grabbing the base of his cock and withdrawing, smacking the ass of the other, the sound reverberating through the alley. "That was fantastic. Thanks. I needed that." He took off the condom and threw it aside.

"Glad to hear it because you'll never get it again. No one slaps my ass without permission, asshole."

Logan braced himself as the acidity in the man's voice registered. Narrowing his eyes, he concentrated on the body language of the two men as they righted their clothing.

"No need to be like that, Black. You know I didn't mean no harm," the larger man said.

"Yeah, well, I have to work tonight, and if I have a handprint on my ass, some people, my boss included, aren't going to like it," the man called Black snapped, standing fully upright now that he was dressed. The bigger man apologised, but Black swiped his hand through the air. "No, it's not okay. If I lose money because of you, I'm sending Rafferty after you."

"Oh, come on, Black," he whined.

"Go home, Trevor."

The bigger man, Trevor, hesitated, then leaned forward and pressed a kiss to the other man's cheek before trudging towards Logan, his shoulders as low as his head. Logan stepped back against the wall until the man passed, and his steps faded into the night, then Logan peered around the edge of the bin again. Seeing Black standing with his hands on his hips, staring at the ground had Logan stepping out of his hiding place and confronting the enigma before him.

"That wasn't the safest choice, you know," he said into the silence.

"Holy fuck! Don't do that!" Black pressed a hand to his chest and blew out a breath. "Jesus. You scared the shit out of me."

"Just imagine what could have happened if I had been another man wanting to take something from you that you didn't want to give."

Black rested a hand on his cocked hip and tilted his head. "What? You mean a gang bang? Yeah, let's get to it!"

Logan shook his head, not knowing how to take the words. Was he saving face, or did he really like the sound of it? "I would choose a better place next time if I were you. You might get into trouble you can't get out of."

"Thank you for your opinion. I will keep it in mind. Now, if *you* don't mind, I need to get to work." Black grabbed a bag from the ground and lifted it over his shoulder, then strode past Logan towards the main road, calling, "Besides, trouble is my middle name." He winked, and Logan watched him go, then followed, wanting to make sure he was safe, at least as he exited the alley. He stood on the street, staring as Black headed for The Bone Yard, then the man threw a wave over his shoulder before entering.

"That explains the cocky behaviour," he muttered, shoving his hands deep into his pockets, wincing as the fabric tightened against his groin, and continued his walk home without a backwards glance. It was nearing eleven in the evening, but the traffic was still tearing by as if it was rush hour, the splash of the puddles merging with the other night sounds that had been surprisingly absent in the alley.

Logan shook his head, dispelling the images once more. He had no doubt he would bring them out in the shower later and get off, but for now, he needed to be able to walk home respectably. Being a police officer brought with it certain expectations, and he couldn't be seen to be walking around with a tent in his jeans.

Logan rubbed his face with both hands, trying to ease the throbbing behind his eyes, and rested his elbows on his desk. This case was a shitstorm, and there was no way of making it any better. No evidence had shown up, no witnesses, nothing. More often than not, these were his regular cases. It wasn't as easy as how it was portrayed on TV. The evidence didn't show up at a convenient time and blow the case wide open. Most of the time, they spent hours and days and weeks digging into every little, tiny detail with nothing coming from it.

"Don't tell me you didn't get any last night after all the bar trawling I'm sure you did," Ava said with a grin.

The scene from the previous evening flashed through his head, and his heart sped up. "I didn't, I'll have you know. Not every night is for finding a release." Ava's eyebrows rose. "It's not!"

Ava Walker had been his partner since she graduated as a police officer five years prior. She was fast-tracking herself to detective by working with him, and they found they worked well together. It didn't hurt that they both had large, sometimes overbearing, families, therefore, had a lot in common. She looked a lot like her brothers, but that was where the similarities ended.

It also helped that they were now family. Well, kind of. Logan's brother Casey had started a relationship with Ava's brother Luke. The family dinners had suddenly become a lot larger when they considered the eleven children, four parents and didn't even include the partners and younger children.

"Has forensics come back to you about the Bridgen case yet?" he asked instead of debating his lifestyle.

Ava shook her head, her long brown hair swaying from side to side from the ponytail she pulled it into nearly every day. "No, not a word, but I'll chase them up again this afternoon."

"I don't know how they expect us to close cases when they can't get the bloody results to us," Logan grumbled. He leaned back in his chair, resting his head against the back and staring at the cciling.

"—the woman is clearly trying to cause trouble when there isn't any. How she expects us to find her *stalker* when she doesn't give us any information, I don't know. I'm not going to put her off checking up with me, though, because she's got tits like melons. I could get lost in them. Fuck, yeah." The man groaned, then laughed with several other people joining in.

Logan knew who it was—Henry Ether—and he didn't expect anything less from the asshole who treated all women as second-rate citizens and anyone different as a bug under a microscope. He also knew the guy hated smaller cases and often tried to refuse them. Their chief had no problem giving them to him anyway, but Logan knew Henry's attempts at finding the culprits usually ended up with nothing.

He shook his head and slid his chair back towards his desk again. "That asshole is going to go too far one day. He's going to ignore the wrong person and end up with no job," he muttered.

"I don't know how the chief puts up with him," Ava said.

"Yeah, you do." Logan rolled his eyes. "He has no choice in the matter."

Henry was the chief's boss's son, so there was unlikely to be any firing of the man, even if he didn't do a good job. He might get transferred, but nothing else. The idea had merit. Logan might suggest that to the chief when he saw him next.

"All I hope is that the woman is careful. If she thinks Henry is looking out for her, but he isn't, then she might take risks she wouldn't if she was looking over her shoulder all the time."

Ava was right as usual. The thought dropped a ball of lead into his stomach, and he closed his eyes briefly, wishing he was anywhere but within hearing of that asshole.

"Taylor! Walker! You're up!" their chief yelled from the door of his office. "Homicide."

Logan grimaced but shoved away from his desk, checking that his phone and keys were in his pockets, then grabbed his coat from the back of his chair. They jogged down the cubicles and out of the station into the drizzle, carrying on until they reached Logan's car. He peeled out of the car park and headed towards the address that Ava had immediately brought up on her phone.

"There's not much information on here. Woman, late twenties, found on her living room floor. The neighbour looked through the window after the victim hadn't opened the door for their appointment and saw her."

"Wonderful." Logan clenched his hands around the steering wheel and dropped his neck to the side, a crack easing the tension before repeating on the other side.

They raced their way through the streets until they reached the relevant house, then pulled up at the kerb. Both exited quickly, showing their badges to the police officers on the scene before heading up the path through the well-maintained garden of the detached bungalow. It wasn't a house he would've expected a woman in her late-twenties to own unless it had been an inheritance, but he knew better than to stereotype.

Ducking under the top of the front door—his six-foot-two height unable to fit through otherwise—he headed to the living room, mindful of the low wooden beams dotted around the house.

The living room was comfortable and homely, if old-fashioned, which gave more precedent to the place being inherited. The blonde, slender woman lying on the floor with her clothes askew looked out of place in the room. Several police officers were hanging around, talking, while one of the photographers took photos of the body, the intermittent flashes doing nothing to help Logan's headache.

His gaze examined the scene, not moving any

closer to the body. After several minutes, something out of place caught his eye. "What do you see, Ava?"

Ava stepped to his side and didn't answer, but he knew she was scanning the room. Her breath caught, and he knew she'd seen it. "Why does she have a kitchen knife in the living room?"

"Good question. Simon," he said, getting the photographer's attention, "Could you ensure you get pictures of the knife on top of the mantelpiece, please?"

His eyes widened as he lifted his head. "I didn't even see that. Good catch."

"Just doing my job," he muttered distractedly, still studying their surroundings. "Officer?" The group of police officers turned towards him. "Could one of you give us the rundown?"

The older of the three stepped forward, crossing his arms over his chest. "The neighbour called it in when she came to collect the lady for their usual morning appointment. Apparently, they always go jogging at eleven, so when the lady didn't answer, the neighbour was worried and checked through the window when she didn't hear her coming to the door."

"Does the lady have a name?"

"Sure." The police officer pulled out his notebook and flicked through several pages before saying, "Miss Winona Conrad."

Logan frowned. "Why does that name sound familiar? We've not got any cases with that name, have we?" He glanced at Ava, who shook her head. Staring back at the deceased, he tried to figure out where he'd heard her name before because he didn't recognise her face. Unable to figure it out, he brushed it off and continued asking the officer questions, noting down his responses in his own notebook.

When he had enough information, he stepped closer, continuing his questioning but with the forensic pathologist. She wasn't able to give him many details but enough for him to start gathering facts. It seemed Miss Conrad had been dead for approximately twelve hours.

"Thanks, Kat."

He returned to Ava, who had disappeared into the kitchen. "We need to speak with the neighbour."

Ava nodded and followed Logan to the front door. "Simon, could you please photograph the back door and the knife block in the kitchen. Thanks." Logan raised his eyebrows. "The knife was one from the kitchen. There was a missing spot in the block, and the handles match."

"So, the killer came through the back door, maybe?"

"That's my guess."

"Why?"

"There was a scrape on the back door as if it had

been forced open using something sharp," she answered.

"Good work."

She beamed at him. "Thanks. You've taught me well."

Logan snorted as they left the property and headed to the next-door neighbour's house. He knocked, trying to withhold rubbing at his head any more than he already had done that morning. Paracetamol was the next port of call for him after all this was wrapped up.

"Hello?" A woman in her late-thirties or early-forties answered the door hesitantly.

"Hi, Mrs Graham? I'm Detective Sergeant Logan Taylor, and this is Detective Constable Ava Walker. Could we come in and ask some questions about Miss Conrad, please?"

"Sure." She opened the door wider and indicated for them to enter, closing it firmly behind them. "Come on through. Would you like a drink?"

"I'm fine, thank you." He glanced at Ava, who declined.

"Have a seat. I told the police officers everything I could think of."

"Thank you for that. If it's not too much trouble, would you mind going through it with us again? You might remember something you'd forgotten, but it's completely fine if you don't."

She waved them on. "Sure, go ahead."

"Can you walk us through what happened before you found Miss Conrad?"

Mrs Graham inhaled, then sighed. "I got ready for our usual run. We've been jogging together for the past year since she first moved into the area. Her grandmother, Nettie, had left her the house, and when she passed, Winona came to live there."

Logan made a mental note to check Miss Conrad's likes and dislikes to see whether she liked the house being decorated that way or if there were stipulations she needed to adhere to. It might prove completely irrelevant, but it would be handy to know.

"Her job prevented her from jogging in the early morning, so we came to an agreement to fit it in before lunch. It had been working brilliantly." Mrs Graham studied her hands, her fingers playing. "I got ready as I always did, then waited for her. She usually knocked on my door at eleven on the dot. Like clockwork. I could literally set my watch by her. When she wasn't here by five past, I decided to go to her house and knock for her instead. Everyone is late every now and then."

Ava scooted forward on her seat. "What happened when you knocked, Mrs Graham?"

She cleared her throat. "There was no answer. I remember being annoyed because she hadn't told me our appointment had been cancelled. I was going to leave, but then I realised I was acting bitter, and so I knocked again and called her name. I couldn't check around the back because the fences are too high, and she locks the gate from the inside."

Logan made a note of that information. If the murderer entered the building from the back of the house, there would be some way he'd managed to get in there. He also wondered why Mrs Graham knew so much about her neighbour's back gate.

"I peeked through the window of the living room and saw her lying there." A tear rolled down Mrs Graham's cheek, and Ava patted her hand.

"Did you happen to see or hear anything strange late last night or early this morning?"

Mrs Graham sniffed and shook her head. "I have trouble sleeping, so I take tablets and have the radio on low. It blocks out most of the noise."

"I know this is difficult for you, Mrs Graham, and I thank you for talking to us. If it wouldn't be too much of an imposition, could we come back to you with any other questions we might have?" Logan knew it was an awful ask because most people would prefer to brush it away and never think of it again, but sometimes, all a person needed was some time for the event to sink in, and they would remember more about it.

"Sure."

"Thank you. We'll leave you to your afternoon."

Mrs Graham showed them to the door, but before they left, she held up a hand. "Oh, did you ever find out any information about her stalker? I bet that was who did it."

Suddenly, Logan realised who the woman was: the case Henry had been mouthing off about before they'd been called away. The stalker case.

Logan felt a coldness invade his body, and his chest tightened against the thought of that woman having not been taken seriously and had paid for it with her life. If only Logan had taken the case from Henry and looked into it himself. He could've prevented this from happening. Nausea threatened to send him to the bushes, but he breathed through his nose and closed his eyes until the feeling passed.

"We'll have to check with the officer in charge of the case," Ava stated.

"That'd be the best place to start. He gives me the creeps."

"You've seen him?" Logan snapped his eyes open and raised his eyebrows.

"Not in detail, but I once saw a man standing outside, across the road and staring at Winona's house. It was at night." She grimaced. "One of the nights I'd forgotten to take my tablets, so I was up late. I didn't see very much of him."

"Would you be willing to speak with an artist and try to get an idea of what his body shape looked like and anything else you remember?" Ava asked.

"If you think it would help."

"Thank you, Mrs Graham. Someone will be in touch."

They headed back to the victim's house, needing to see if any more information had been uncovered.

"I bet Henry has no additional info on that case at all. Asshole." Logan's head pounded.

"I wouldn't take that bet."

"Why not?"

"Because you'd be right," Ava said with a frown.

Logan covered his mouth with his palm as he stood near the deceased woman again. His heart broke for her, and his vision greyed as memories of Casey bombarded him. His brother had been kidnapped by the person who had been sexually harassing him for months, and Logan had struggled to find him. Once they had, Logan had been ordered to stay home, but he'd refused, calling on the favours his friends owed him to allow him to attend.

Granted, he didn't take down the asshole who had tried to take his brother from him, but he had been there for Casey, and that mattered more than anything else.

If he hadn't arrived in time…the images of Casey lying like this woman was had nausea roiling through him again. He could hardly face his family with the knowledge that he wasn't there when Casey needed him the most.

"Logan?" He let out a shaky breath and turned

towards Ava, his nostrils flaring to withhold his other reactions. "Shall we head back to the station?" she asked.

Logan nodded, casting one more look at the woman and silently promising her that he would find her killer. He refused to allow another person to suffer the same fate as this woman.

CHAPTER TWO

BASTIEN

"Look at you! You look stunning, sweetheart! Go steam up those photos. You hear?"

Bastien Templeton rested his hand on the woman's shoulders and stared at her in the mirror, smiling widely at her to make her understand his words were genuine. He knew he was damn good at his job, and this just proved it. Perfectly coiffed black hair, smoky eyes, and plum-coloured lipstick stood out from the pale, blemish-free skin.

"I can't believe…" She lifted a hand to her face, but Bastien stopped her before she could touch.

"Don't smudge it. Come on. Let's get you to the studio."

"Thank you so much," she gushed.

"You're more than welcome, sweetheart."

Although it wasn't his job to show the clients to the

main studio area, he always did, wanting to make sure they didn't mess up his artwork before they entered. After that, it was not his problem. No doubt he'd be called in if it was showing too badly.

"Have fun," he whispered to the woman before closing the door behind her, blocking out the noise of the photographer getting the shots ready.

He inhaled and let the air out slowly, leaning against the wall and blinking a few times to clear his blurry vision. That's what happened when he worked so much. Checking his watch, Bastien realised he had another hour to go, then he could have a brief nap before his shift that night.

His trouble was that he was a perfectionist, so each makeup job took longer than it might for someone else. It wasn't his inexperience; on the contrary, it was his need to have every blemish hidden, every shading exact, every line concealed. After years of practising on himself, he was an expert at every kind of makeup anyone could think of. Despite having that ability, he struggled to find jobs that paid more than what these photoshoots did.

Having no relevant qualifications due to his family's wonderful choice of throwing him out at the tender age of fourteen, he never finished school and had no money to pay for college. So, he spent his years learning everything via videos, books from the library and any other way he could think of for minimal cost.

His phone chimed. Pulling it from his pocket, he looked at the ancient phone and shook his head. At least he had one. It was a hand-me-down from one of his acquaintances, but on occasion, he wished he could afford a newer model.

Are you able to come in an hour earlier tonight? Reed called in sick.

Bastien didn't need to know who sent it. It was his boss, Rafferty. He blew out a breath, not wanting to go in earlier but needing the money. He replied in the affirmative, then began packing away his tools of the trade. There would be no nap for him after all.

"B! We need a touch-up!" Deacon yelled.

Grabbing the bag he'd been filling, he whirled around and hustled down the hallway to the main studio. When he entered, the woman was still undressed, and he averted his eyes to show some respect for her. This is what she had come here for: provocative poses for her loved one. "I'm here. Come on, sweetheart. Let's get you sorted."

Luckily, there wasn't much to do. The woman had just sweated a little too much under the lights, so he touched up the foundation and sealed it with some powder, hopefully, to reduce the shine for a little while longer.

"How long left?" he asked Deacon when he'd finished.

"Should only be another fifteen minutes or so."

Bastien nodded and left the room again. "I'll take that to assume another forty-five minutes then," he mumbled.

He sat in one of the chairs outside the studio, crossed his legs and took out a nail file. Gently shaping his nails, his thoughts drifted to the previous weekend. He'd not seen the man who had peeped at him having sex with Trevor since, but he had a feeling it wouldn't be the last time. He hadn't recognised the man, yet he knew how handsome he was. The streetlight had briefly shone on the man's face as they'd exited the alley, and Bastien had been tempted to stay a little longer.

Unfortunately, he'd had to work, and that was the reason for the scene with Trevor in the first place. Bastien had needed to let off some steam after realising he would have to work extra to make sure he could pay his rent. Trevor had been convenient until he'd smacked his ass. Rafferty had not been amused by the handprint he'd been wearing.

If he'd just had several more minutes, he would've been able to find out more about that mysterious stranger. His was a face he wouldn't forget any time soon.

Bastien jumped when the door handle banged

against the brick wall with a thud as Deacon and the woman emerged from the studio.

"All done," Deacon announced. "She was a natural."

"Great. Lynise, would you like to keep the makeup on, or should I take it off for you?"

Lynise flushed. "I would love to keep it on, but I think it would ring alarm bells with my husband as I don't usually wear anything." She grimaced.

"Not a problem. Let's go back to the dressing room, and I'll have it off in no time."

Bastien didn't mind either way. Most women asked to keep it on, but the occasional person requested removal. Lynise's reasoning was sound. It would no doubt cause issues if she came home looking like she'd been on a date.

The removal took around ten minutes because Bastien made sure that he'd removed everything and then rehydrated her skin for her before he bid goodbye. He met Deacon at the front of the building, where he received his payment.

"Thanks, Deacon. You know where I am."

"Sure do. Thanks for today. I appreciate it."

Bastien pushed out of the door and adjusted the bag on his shoulder before pulling his coat closer to his body. There was a chill in the air, and traffic rushing past seemed to make it colder somehow. He needed to go home before he could go to work, so he set a punishing pace that he would regret by the time he got there, but he had no choice. A shower would be essential when he got to the club.

By the time he'd arrived home, he was sweating, and he immediately pulled off his coat when he closed the door behind him. He grabbed a change of clothes, his 'barrel' bag—which was what he called his bag containing everything he might ever need—and his shoes, then threw his coat back on again and left.

The walk to the club was longer, but he knew he'd get there in time to have a shower and sort himself out. Luckily, Rafferty allowed him to keep a locker full of necessities at the club, so he didn't have to haul everything around with him all the time. Without a car, he was limited to how much he could carry. It gave him a good workout, though.

"Hey, Black. How're things?" Brandy, the bouncer, was already in place at the doors, even though the club didn't open for another hour.

"Hey. I'm good, thanks. How're the babies?"

Brandy's smile lit up the world. "Ah, they're growing every day. So quickly. I can't believe the twins are nearly one already."

Bastien raised his eyebrows. "No shit? Wow. Time flies."

"That it does." Brandy lifted his chin. "You're early, aren't you?"

"Yeah, Rafferty messaged. Reed's not in."

Brandy nodded. "Best let you get to it, then. Have a good evening, Black."

"You, too."

"You know it."

Bastien entered the building, glad to be out of the cold but already anticipating the arguments that would happen when he stepped into the dressing room. No one liked that Bastien was called in for overtime first and anyone else only if he couldn't make it. Which was rarely. It made for a simmering atmosphere, which always bubbled over into a shouting match.

"Hey, B!" Cody, the closest he could call a friend, said.

"Hi, Cody." Bastien dropped his bag on the chair nearest his locker and slipped off his coat.

"I see the canary has been called in again." He rolled his eyes as Cassidy spoke in his acidly sweet voice.

Bastien had no idea when Cassidy had begun calling him that or why because it had nothing to do with either his real name or his stage name. "No point leaving gaps in the schedule, is there, Cass?" He used the shortened name because he knew how much it riled the other man up.

"I'm sure we could've managed to cover the slots. There was no need for you to come in earlier than needed."

Bastien turned and crossed his arms over his chest,

smirking. "Unfortunately, I have to do what the boss says." He lifted a shoulder in a half-shrug.

Cassidy's gaze lowered then rose over Bastien's body until he met his eyes, a sneer forming on the smooth, pale skin. He turned around and sashayed off, the move not as elegant as it would have been had he been wearing his heels.

Bastien let out a silent breath and returned to his bag. There were ten dancers in all, but mostly only four or five a night, so it gave Rafferty a chance to alternate them out for nights off. Eight of them, himself included, were nice. The other two needed attitude adjustments.

Heading to the wet room after pulling out his toiletries, he pursed his lips and glanced at Cassidy out of the corner of his eye, then carried on despite his tight chest. Cassidy needed to work on his presentation. He'd get a lot further in the job if he concentrated his efforts on his own performance rather than trying to get rid of his competition.

Bastien stripped off and stood under the warm spray, the pounding water surrounding him with blissful ignorance of those around him. It probably wasn't the safest idea—anyone could come in and knock him out or do something sinister when he couldn't hear them coming, but he needed it. The silence, or rather, the isolation. Contrary to popular belief, he wasn't a social person.

After several minutes of letting the water ease his aching muscles, he stepped back and cleaned up, focusing on bringing back his dancing persona. He smiled into the empty wet room, thinking about his new routine. He had been working on something new for a few weeks now, and he was going to try it out that night. In some ways, being called in to cover for Reed had been beneficial because he could do one of his older routines for Reed's spots, then surprise everyone with his new one for his own.

At this club, each dancer had six sets to dance, ranging from three minutes to fifteen depending on how energetic it was. A slow, sensual number was easier on the dancer's body; therefore, Rafferty scheduled a longer slot. A high-impact routine was tougher to maintain for any length of time—not impossible, but harder—and so those were shorter.

"Black!"

Bastien glanced over his shoulder to see Rafferty standing there with his hands on his hips. He raised his eyebrows in question.

"You were supposed to come and see me when you got here."

He'd forgotten about that. "Sorry, boss. I'll finish up in here, then come straight up."

Rafferty snorted. "Make sure you at least dress first. Don't go giving the early birds more than they paid for." He shook his head and left, leaving Bastien grinning after him. It was true; he had a tendency to give *way* more than anyone paid for. Rafferty knew him well.

Finishing up, he dried off and slipped into the first costume of the night. He'd leave his makeup until he'd finished with Rafferty. The main room had several customers already, and he waved at a couple of regulars as he climbed the metal stairs to the boss's office above the whole building. Entering the small, waiting room type area, he ignored protocol and opened Rafferty's door straight away.

"One of these days, you'll enter without knocking and see something you'll need to acid from your eyes."

"Maybe, but not today." Bastien winked at his boss, a smirk firmly in place. Sliding into the comfortable leather chair opposite the man, Bastien raised his eyebrows. "You rang, my lord?"

Rafferty rolled his eyes and cleared his throat. "Cassidy—"

"Let me guess. Cassidy doesn't want me doing Reed's sets and wants to do it himself. He doesn't like me taking the longer slots, even though I've been here longer than him." Bastien tapped his finger against his lower lip and pretended to think. "What else? Oh, yes! He doesn't want me here and wants you to fire me. Have I about covered everything?"

The expression on Rafferty's face was neutral except for the side-to-side action of his jaw. "Have you finished?" He paused, then carried on, "You didn't get it all, but that covers the majority of it."

"And?" Bastien inhaled through his nose and exhaled through his mouth quietly, unsure of which way his boss was going to go on the subject.

"You bring in more money than Cassidy does. I can't deny the figures. As long as you're happy here, I want you here."

Bastien waved a hand between the two of them. "What was all this then?"

"Being seen to be taking an employee's concerns seriously is what this is."

Pursing his lips to stop a smile from spreading across his face, he sighed. "If there is nothing else, Your Majesty?"

"One of these days, you're going to call me Rafferty and scare the ever-lovin' fuck out of me."

"Only on my deathbed."

Bastien strolled to the door, swaying his hips. Rafferty would never touch an employee; he had made that clear the moment anyone signed their contracts. Shame, though. He was a looker.

"Bring the house down tonight, B."

Bastien glanced over his shoulder with a smirk. "I plan to."

"Oh, shit. B! Bastien! What are you going to do?" Rafferty called after him.

"Nothing that will get me arrested. Unfortunately."

He shut the door, muffling his boss's words and sauntered down the steps slowly, letting his gaze roam across the room to see what customers were around. He wouldn't go out there yet, he still needed to get his makeup on, but he could look.

A lone guy sat at the bar, back to the stage, nursing a drink. Bastien watched, mesmerised, as the man twisted the glass on the countertop, lifted it to his mouth for a sip, then placed it down and spun it again. He didn't recognise the guy, but he was quite a distance away. Maybe he'd get closer when his floor work began and see if the personality matched the body. Pulling his gaze away, he trailed to the dressing room and got ready for his first performance.

It went swimmingly. After his third routine, he sat at one of the mirrors with his bag of tricks. As his hands were busy doing what was in his muscle memory by now, his mind wandered again to the perfect specimen of a man he'd barely interacted with the previous weekend. He hadn't known the guy had been watching, but thinking about it afterwards, the thrill of being stared at while he was fucked had awakened something inside him. He was an exhibitionist when it came to dancing and stripping, but he'd never had the urge to have people watch him while he had sex.

Concentrating as he applied his lip liner and lipstick, he saw, from the corner of his eye, Cassidy come stomping back into the room after his set;

everyone else was either on the floor or on stage. Lipstick in place, Bastien refocused on the man and gathered his items together, placing them back into his bag. He refused to ask Cassidy if something was wrong. He'd tried that once and almost had his head bitten off. Anyway, it probably had to do with Rafferty refusing to fire him.

Putting everything into his locker, he stood in front of the full-length mirror and adjusted his top, ensuring it was straight. The long-sleeved, high-neck, black see-through material was soft against his skin and sparkled in the lights. His black shorts were also highly sequined but had metal chain links as a decoration around the waistband and pockets. His short black hair helped the rest of his face stand out, especially with the bright green eyeshadow and heavily lined eyes. To complete his outfit, he pulled a pair of thigh-high, high-heeled boots from his locker. Slipping his feet into them, he slowly zipped them up, loving the feel of them encasing his legs.

When he was kitted out, he stood, took one final look, blew himself a kiss and sauntered towards the stage area.

"Good luck," Cassidy said into the silence.

"Bitch," Bastien muttered. Everyone knew saying good luck before a performance was not a good thing, but then what did he expect from the evil that was Cassidy.

He stepped behind the curtain, ready to go on when his music started. Keeping his posture straight, he closed his eyes, breathing in and out, clearing his mind of everything except the performance to come. He'd practised this routine enough now to know it by heart, but there was always a slim chance of something going wrong.

"Black, it's time," whispered Miles, the music guy.

Bastien gave a thumbs up, indicating he was ready and waited for his cue. The lights came down, and a roar echoed back from the main area, the customers knowing that another dance was coming. He smiled and stepped up onto the dark stage, tiptoeing so as not to make a sound as he got into place.

Stretching his arms out to the sides, parallel to the floor, he tilted his head to the side and down, bent one knee and kept the other straight. In position, he inhaled deeply and centred himself. He loved this. The anticipation. The tick of the clock. The moment of truth. The silence before the hurricane.

Fixing his smile in place, he gave the imperceptible nod to Miles, and the music began a second before the lights came up.

Silence, then a deafening outburst of noise. Bastien pushed it all aside, apart from the beat of the music. He felt the bass through his bones and began to sway and dip, carrying himself forward towards the raucous crowd. The power that swept through him at the thought of those customers wanting to see him—or what he could do—was like a high from a drug. There wasn't much else that made him feel that way. He loved losing himself in the notes playing through the speakers and his body. Life was carefree and euphoric when he was dancing.

Fifteen minutes later, Bastien stepped from the stage amidst a cheer from the customers. His pockets were decidedly happier with the number of tips he'd received for his dance. The rent might actually be met this month after all.

Rafferty was waiting for him in the dressing room while two other guys dressed for their set.

"That was new." His boss raised an eyebrow.

"I was feeling in the mood to create." Bastien didn't explain further.

Rafferty narrowed his eyes, then nodded. "Good job."

"Thanks."

Several hours later, his aching feet and back told him more than the clock and the empty club that it was time for home. Stepping into the wet room for another shower, he cleaned off quicker this time, wanting to get home. Putting on the outfit he'd arrived in, he said goodbye to those who were still around and exited, waving at Brandy as he took off down the street.

The chill in the air was still present, having not

dissipated through the evening, much to his disappointment. He walked as fast as his feet allowed him, his eyelids growing heavy as his eyes burned and itched. By the time he arrived home, he was frozen and opted out of cooking—or rather heating some pasta—and headed straight for his bed.

Undressing completely and leaving the clothes where they fell, he slid under the cold covers and tucked them tightly around him.

His muffled alarm woke him, and he blearily reached across to his nightstand to turn it off, blinking his eyes open when he couldn't find it. The noise started again but louder, and Bastien sat upright, shivering in the cold room. Throwing himself across the end of the bed, he reached for the trousers he'd worn the previous night and struggled to extract the phone. Finally, it came free, and he switched off the alarm.

Too tired to move, he stayed splayed on his stomach with his naked back exposed. It was only when the cold became too much for him that he shuffled his way off the bed and into some thick joggers and a jumper. Thick socks complimented the outfit, warming his feet as he traipsed into his kitchen. Switching on the kettle, he reached for a mug and the tea bags. He'd run out of coffee already this month and wouldn't be getting any more until he knew whether his rent and bills could be paid.

Holding the heated mug in both hands, he sat down at the kitchen table, staring at his current creation. He studied the design he'd drawn on a piece of paper, then compared it to what he'd made. It wasn't exact because he wasn't an artist, but the bracelet was beginning to take shape. He'd used some of his hard-earned wages to get some special stones to go on these designs, hoping that he could sell them for slightly more than he was currently pricing his jewellery.

Sipping his tea, he stared around the minuscule room he called home. It was a single room with space for a bed, an armchair, a small square table he used for his work and a little kitchenette. The only separate room was a small bathroom with a tiny shower cubicle, a toilet and a sink. It wasn't the best place to live, but he had a roof over his head, which was more than he'd had when he'd been kicked out of his parents' house at fourteen.

He could be optimistic about his situation most of the time, but on occasion, when he'd had a shitty night or a crappy day, he couldn't help the clenched jaw or the sour expression that tightened his face.

His parents were worth millions, but a gay son would've cost them more than they were willing to pay. Having never been good enough, he was used to being alone. What was the point in hoping for more when this was all he would ever achieve?

That hope, though, sparked no matter what he thought.

After he finished his tea, he set it aside and slid the bracelet towards him. Reaching for the next gem in the sequence, he lost himself in the joy of creating something from nothing. This was his passion, his love, his unnamed hope for the future. If he could sell enough jewellery, he would be set.

All he needed to do was get that little extra exposure. The small chance that someone would see his work and commission something that would take him to the next level in his creative dream.

Being a makeup artist or a dancer was not what he wanted to do, but it paid the bills—most of the time. Jewellery was what he wanted to focus on. It was a difficult situation for him to be in. He needed to spend time to create the pieces to sell them, but to do that, it would mean he couldn't do one or both of the other jobs, which meant his bills wouldn't be paid, and he would lose the roof over his head.

Life wasn't fair, and on occasion, Bastien stuck his middle finger up at it.

Most of the time, though, he could weather through the uncertain times, knowing things could be different in years to come. He needed patience, but that was something he didn't always have.

His phone alarm disturbed his work, and he blinked rapidly, trying to make his eyes work properly after focusing on such little items for so long. After carefully putting the unused items away, he pushed everything back to their original positions and stared at them.

One day, he would make this his main job.

It was a promise he made to himself every time he set it aside. Even if it was for only a few weeks, he would take that time and make everything that it was possible to make and throw it all into the ether for the consumers to decide whether he was worthy of their money.

His phone sounded again, and he sighed. Reality returned once more.

Grabbing his phone, he switched off the alarm and cursed when he saw the time. "Fuck, I'm going to be late. Deacon will kill me."

CHAPTER THREE

LOGAN

Logan couldn't get the images of Black out of his mind. Not only did he have the scene from the alleyway on repeat in his head, but now, he had Black's dancing from The Bone Yard. Those fifteen minutes of pure erotic pleasure had brought Logan to orgasm more times than his hand could handle. Even his dick protested when he got hard now.

He hadn't planned on visiting the strip club; it wasn't his usual haunt, but the need to find out what Black did there was something he hadn't been able to cull. Understanding Black was, in fact, Black Magic, the best performer at the club, hadn't gone far enough to make Logan understand what that meant exactly.

Until *that* performance.

Logan shook his head and refocused on the paperwork in front of him. He needed to gather more information about the stalker Henry hadn't bothered to investigate. The deceased woman, Winona, had given Henry some decent details, including places, times and dates, which meant Logan could start visiting those venues to see if they had security cameras.

His nostrils flared as he thought about the callous words Henry had spewed when he'd found out Winona had been murdered.

"I doubt there was a stalker. She probably rejected the wrong man."

Logan had been so angry, Ava had pulled him away and out of the station, even though they still had work to be done. She knew him too well. Henry would've ended up with Logan's fist in his face had he'd stayed any longer.

The only good thing that had come from the situation was that Henry was avoiding him, which enabled Logan to cool off. Even the chief had spoken to Logan in the intervening days to make sure he was all right.

He wasn't, but that didn't need to become common knowledge. Stalking was a tricky case to figure out, for the most part. A lot of it was to do with the feelings and emotions of a victim running high, and so much information was lost as the days progressed. Significant details were made to seem smaller, and insignificant details made to seem bigger. Not always, but sometimes. Unless there were concrete times the police could check, it was difficult to ascertain who the perpetrators were.

Luckily, Winona had kept detailed records, so Logan made a note of all the businesses she'd mentioned and called for Ava to leave.

"Where we heading?" Ava asked as they pulled out of the car park.

"Sorry, Ava. I've been a shitty partner this past week."

"Nah, don't worry. I know this is difficult for you. It's not the same situation as Casey, but it hits too close to home."

Logan didn't reply, concentrating on the feel of the steering wheel beneath his hands and the traffic all around them instead of remembering what he'd seen when he'd found Casey. He cleared his throat. "I made a list of the businesses that Winona said she'd remembered feeling or seeing someone following her. I thought we'd visit them and see if they have any CCTV. It might be a long shot, but we may as well check it out."

"Some of the employees might remember seeing something."

"Not everyone wants to get involved when it comes to other people's business, though."

"True." She was silent for a minute. "You're distracted by something else as well. Care to enlighten me?"

Logan glanced over at her and saw her smirk before returning his gaze ahead. "I don't know what you're talking about."

"It's not just the cases that are making you lose focus. I've seen you with red cheeks more times than I can count this week. Who is he?"

Logan spluttered a denial, "There's no…I'm not… It's…" He blew out a breath. "Fuck."

Ava chuckled, slapping her hands on her thighs. "Lay it on me, babe!"

Logan snorted. "Don't 'babe' me. It sounds ridiculous."

"Aww, come on, sweetie. You know you can tell me anything. Come on. Tell sister Ava."

They both laughed at that, the atmosphere lifting. When they recovered, Logan said, "There isn't anyone as in a bed partner. I met a guy last weekend, and he's…" Logan had no idea how to explain the pull he'd felt towards the dancer.

"Got you all tongue-tied and chasing your tail?" Ava simpered.

Logan side-eyed her. "Your family thinks you are so sweet and innocent. They're in for the shock of their lives when they learn about the real you."

"Yep. Though, it won't be you doing the telling, will it, bro?"

He thought about teasing her, but he couldn't do that. "You know it won't." He pulled into the car park of a bank and stopped the engine, gripping the steering wheel tighter. "I…He's not my usual type, and you're right, I'm all tangled up about it. I've hardly spoken to the guy, but he's everywhere—not physical-ly." He rubbed his head and linked his hands behind his head, squeezing his elbows in to enclose his face, and sighed.

"I never thought I'd see the day." Ava's words were quiet but easily heard.

He dropped his hands. "It's nothing more than curiosity. Once I get to know him, if I get to know him, he'll turn out to be like all the rest."

Ava rested her hand on his shoulder. "A uniform chaser?"

"Yup."

"Maybe you need to stop working all the hours of the day? Rest up a bit in between. You're going to burn out, Logan, and I can't allow a partner, or a brother, to do that."

Logan stared at her, seeing the concern in her eyes. "I'll be fine." He opened the car door. "Come on, let's see what we can find out."

What they found out was next to nothing. Most of

the businesses were smaller ones that had the cameras as ornamental deterrents, but they were not in service. The two larger businesses managed to provide copies of the times Logan and Ava asked for, and those would need to be thoroughly checked for possible evidence. Ava had offered to do that, probably because she knew Logan's concentration levels were at an all-time low.

Taking Ava's advice that evening, he finished at the station at a respectable time and headed home. His house was far too big for just him, but he'd bought it as an investment for the future. His future. Hopefully, with a husband and children running around the place. At the moment, though, it was a difficult place to live with four empty bedrooms, a dining room and two bathrooms that were never used, and a kitchen that was rarely used for more than maybe omelettes, toast or cereal.

His footsteps were heavy on the wooden stairs, the sound reverberating around the large area, making him feel the void even more, but he brushed it off and headed for the bathroom. After a quick shower, he threw on some jeans and a black shirt and slid his wallet, phone and keys into his pockets.

Exiting the house when his taxi turned up—he hadn't been sure whether he was going to drink or not, so erred on the side of caution—he watched the flash of the streetlights as they made their way across the city.

"Going out for the evening?" the driver asked, looking at Logan through the rearview mirror.

"Yep," he said distractedly. He hadn't given the driver his exact destination, but it was only a five-minute walk from the place he'd asked the man to stop. After paying, he exited and began his short trek.

There was a line waiting outside the strip club, and Logan joined the end, pulling out his phone to catch up on some stuff while he waited. He chuckled when he saw the sibling group chat.

CASEY: So, what do you want for your birthdays? @Liam @Claire

JAMES: Haven't you bought anything yet? You're slacking @Casey, get with the program.

CLAIRE: You don't need to get me anything. I'm good.

JAMES: Don't be silly @Claire. You're our sister. You deserve the world.

CASEY: Stop sucking up! Even though he's right @Claire.

CLAIRE: Lol. Idiots. Thanks, but honestly, I wouldn't even know what to tell you to get me.

JAMES: A boat trip along the River Cam?

JAMES: A stripper?

JAMES: A pair of handcuffs? @Logan, can you suggest any good ones?

CLAIRE: @James, stop! Lol!

JAMES: A dildo?

CLAIRE: @James Oh my god! No!

CASEY: How about a boat trip on the River Cam accompanied by a stripper with a pair of handcuffs and a dildo in his bag of tricks?

ALICE: Pink or purple?

LIAM: Are you guys even related to me?

LOGAN: @Liam, yes, good luck. @Casey, get the dildo because I know you won't touch handcuffs. @James, buy the boat trip, I'll sort the stripper. @Alice, definitely purple for our purple-haired sister, no? @Claire, your wish is our command.

By the time he'd caught up, he was next in line to enter, so he put the phone away and crossed his arms over his chest while leaning against the building. The subdued hum of conversation from the people waiting was less energetic than he would've expected at a strip club, but in his research, he'd found the club was one of the better-run ones, not at all seedy from the reviews he'd read.

The bouncer's voice jerked him out of his thoughts. "Go on in."

"Thanks, mate."

"Enjoy your stay." The humorous expression on the bouncer's face had Logan's instincts prickling.

The music bombarded his eardrums the moment he entered, the bass vibrating through his body. His gaze was taken to the dancer on stage, a tall blond, slender man who was doing the splits against the pole as he spun in a circle. The vertical leg slid down and encircled the pole before the dancer lifted his standing leg to follow suit, holding himself in a horizontal position for several seconds.

The strength of the man showed in the positions he held and the precision with which he moved, just like Black did, although Logan could see Black was the more proficient of the two.

"Like what you see?"

A voice dripping with sensuality whispered across his ear, and he immediately knew who it was. He'd been listening to that voice in his head for the past week. Slowly pivoting on his heel, he stared at the man who had been haunting his dreams.

Black raised his eyebrows and leered. "I've not seen

you around here before. I'd remember if you were. What brings you here?"

Black ran his finger down Logan's shirt. Logan watched as Black followed his movement with his gaze, then glancing up at him through his eyelashes. Even in the dimly lit room, Logan could see they were extraordinarily long as close as they were standing.

Another curve of Black's mouth caught Logan's attention to the painted lips, and he realised Black had asked him a question.

"Just wanted to see what all the fuss was about."

His voice was lower than usual, arousal flickering in the depths of his stomach. Logan noticed Black still had hold of his shirt and moved one step closer, their fronts brushing. He felt Black's intake of breath, unable to hear the sound in the noise.

"What are the rules around here?" he murmured, leaning into Black's space to get closer to his ear.

"Rules for what?"

"Interactions. Can I touch?" He felt a shiver go through the man and smiled at the reaction.

Black pulled his head away, meeting his gaze. "You don't touch, except with permission and only after paying for a lap dance. No touching at all out here." Black swirled a finger around, indicating the room they were standing in.

Logan inhaled, his eyes falling shut as the scent of sweat and something sweeter teased his nostrils.

"Have you danced yet?"

Black nodded slowly. "I dance again in half an hour."

"Do you have time for a lap dance?"

Logan knew he was playing with fire, but he couldn't help himself. His dreams would be fuelled for weeks or months to come if he managed to get through the lap dance itself.

Black cocked his hip, resting his hand on his waist and ogled him. "I always have time."

"Lead the way."

Black glanced over his shoulder towards the bar, then whirled on his impressively high heels and, swaying his hips in an exaggerated fashion that Logan would not oppose, sauntered to a set of four steps, leading to a curtained area. Holding the fabric aside, Black indicated for Logan to go first. It led to a short hallway that had several doors leading off it. Opening one, Black stepped inside with Logan following suit. The space held a single soft furnished two-seater sofa, a small table with a sound system on it and a set of shelves full of props. His detective's brain noticed there didn't seem to be any cameras or recording equipment, but that didn't mean there wasn't.

Once the door closed behind them, Black crowded against Logan's back, herding him towards the sofa, where he was spun and pushed into the middle of it with a soft bounce. He rested his arms along the top of it, then quirked an eyebrow at his companion.

Black's mouth curled, and he strode over to the table, fiddling with the sound until some music began, muting the bass from the main club area. Before he'd even faced him again, the man's slender hips had begun to sway to the beat. Logan watched as Black's hands slid up his thighs, hips, sides and around to the back of his neck, where his head dropped back, his feet taking up the beat as he stepped backwards. The mesmerising shift of Black's hips had Logan clenching his fists and jaw. He wanted nothing more than to grab hold of those slim, sleek thighs and spread them beneath him.

Logan cleared his throat at the thought, his jeans already tighter than they had been when they first entered the room.

Black spun around into an elaborate dance routine, bringing him closer and closer to Logan until he was stood with his back to him, undulating his body to the rhythm. So near that Logan could reach if he had been allowed. But he'd not been given permission. Yet.

The lithe dancer whirled to face him, his hand going to the hem of his see-through black top and pushing it higher until his abdomen came into view. Logan's gaze was caught by the sleek skin, coated with a thin sheen of sweat or oil. He didn't care which; he just knew this would be what Black would look like after a hard and heavy session of sex. Logan reached for him, then clenched his fist again and rested it on his thigh. Black curled the corner of his mouth as his whole body rippled with his movements.

The music changed to a lower, more desperate beat, and Black ripped the top over his head, throwing it to the side. He kicked Logan's legs together and straddled him, hovering over his thighs while his hands pressed to the back of the sofa, bringing his upper body closer to him.

Licking his lips, Logan's gaze took in every part of Black he could see, including his half-lidded eyes and bruised mouth where it appeared as though he'd been biting his lips. Black's body never stopped moving, but they were both caught in the heat of their locked eyes.

"Touch me," Bastien whispered, bringing his mouth close to Logan's ear. "Touch me…" He pulled back and raised his eyebrow.

"Logan," he growled.

Black pursed his lips. "Touch me, Logan."

Logan's cock pressed defiantly against his zipper as his eyelids briefly flickered at the sound of his name on Black's lips.

Not moving his hands from where they were on his thighs, he uncurled his fingers, spreading them wide enough to reach Black's legs. The smooth skin surprised Logan, although it probably shouldn't have. His fingers skimmed up Black's thighs until he reached the little mesh shorts he was wearing. Reining in the desire to fist his hands in the fabric and tear them off the man, he slid his hands over the fabric to the back, cupping his ass cheeks as Black surged forward, rolling his hips against Logan's groin.

Black transferred his hands from the back of the sofa to Logan's shoulders, allowing him to take his weight as his ass rose and fell over his lap.

"Jesus," Logan breathed, sweat beading at his temples and sliding down his face. He had not been this hard in a long time.

"No, not Jesus, just Bastien."

The man's rhythm stuttered for a second before he continued, but Logan caught it and knew the dancer had not meant to give out his name.

"Your secret's safe with me," Logan muttered, glancing into Black's—no, Bastien's eyes.

Bastien's gaze roamed Logan's face before he dropped one knee to one side of him and lifted a foot to the other, giving him more room to manoeuvre and tease the hell out of Logan. When Logan was nearing the end of his restraint, Bastien slid his feet to the floor and dropped to his knees, sliding down, skimming every inch of Logan's body as he went. He blew hot air across the zipper of his trousers, then pushed up to standing, resting his hands on the back of the sofa and bringing his face to Logan's once more.

"What is it about you?" Bastien murmured, tilting

his head and closing in on Logan's lips, then pulling away before they met, Logan barely stopping himself from following.

Logan took a chance and slid his hands up Bastien's arms and around his back before resting one hand between Bastien's shoulder blades, his other sliding down to cup his ass. Bastien's movements ceased, and their breathing sounded loud despite the music.

"What is it about *you*?" Logan threw back before tugging Bastien closer.

He knew it was a bad idea. His mind was throwing out all sorts of signs and signals, and still, he knew he shouldn't do this, but he couldn't resist any longer. Pausing minutely to lick his lips, he heard the music die down and knew the moment was gone.

Bastien tensed, pushed free and stepped over to his top, which he quickly pulled back on.

Logan cleared his throat, adjusting his trousers to account for the painfully hard reaction he'd had. There was no doubt it would take a while to cool down.

"Feel free to stay here as long as you need to," Bastien muttered before moving towards the exit.

"Bastien." The man froze with his hand on the handle. The words he wanted to say wouldn't escape. Instead, he said, "How much do I owe you?"

Bastien's head turned to the side, his resident smirk visible, even in the dim lighting. "On the house."

Then he was gone.

Logan rubbed at his face, wiping away the beads of sweat. He stood, pacing around the room, breathing deeply to try and calm his libido and holding his hands on the top of his head.

What *was* it about that guy?

Logan should've been at home or work, trying to figure out the cases he had like he usually was, but instead, he was standing in a bare room in the middle of a strip club with a hard-on that didn't want to abate. What had gotten into him?

When his cock had decided to calm a little, he ventured back out into the main area, noting he had around five minutes before Bastien would be on stage. The bar called his name, and he weaved his way through the crowds towards the stained wooden counter, sliding onto one of the stools.

"What can I get you?"

"Whiskey, any, please."

"Coming right up."

Logan stared at his linked fingers atop the bar as he wandered through the brief but tantalising interactions he'd had with Bastien. His cock was happy with the direction of his thoughts, but Logan pressed against it and willed it away.

"You look like someone who had just been put through the Black Magic wringer," the bartender joked as Logan's drink was placed before him.

"You could say that." Logan threw the drink back and asked for another.

"Did you enjoy a lap dance from our best performer?" the bartender continued.

Logan lifted his gaze, setting his sights on the attractive boy-next-door type man in front of him. "What's not to like?"

The man laughed, holding out his hand. "I'm Nolan."

"Logan," he said, shaking the proffered hand. "He's the best, you say?"

"Hands down. No one has ever come close." Nolan crossed his arms and rested his elbows on the counter to the side of Logan, staring towards the stage. "Many like to think they have, but no one has been able to."

"What makes him so special?"

Nolan raised his eyebrows. "You've just had a lap dance from him, and you can't answer that question yourself? Are you sure you're into men?" He stood.

"I know what he did for me, but I can't relate it to anyone else. That was my first," Logan admitted.

"Ooh, sweetheart. Let me rectify that for you. Black may have some moves, but I have plenty more." A hand slid across Logan's back, leaving a cold feeling in its place. He had always trusted his instincts, and now was no different.

"Thank you for the offer, but I'd like to see the

shows for the rest of the evening. Maybe another time."

The blond dancer who had been on stage when Logan had first entered leaned closer, his breath fanning across Logan's skin as he whispered, "I have plenty of information on Black. I'm happy to *spill* my knowledge to you."

He made a kissing sound in his ear, and Logan refrained from shrinking away. "Maybe another night. I'm going to sit here and enjoy my drink."

The man's features tightened, but Logan knew what to look for when talking with people. It was part of his job, after all.

"No problem. Enjoy your evening."

"Gentlemen and Ladies, if we have any visiting tonight…" A muted cheer sounded from the corner across the room. Logan spun on his chair to view the darkened stage. "Welcome to The Bone Yard. Our next dancer is a regular and favourite here. Let's give it up for Black Magic!"

Music began. A slow, sensual, deep drumbeat that fired all of Logan's senses. The room silenced, his focus directly on the stage where he knew Bastien would soon be visible. His heart pounded in time with the beat, and he licked his lips as his mouth dried up. Despite having just survived a solo dance, he had a feeling this one was about to make him blow.

A spotlight lit from behind the stage, showing

Bastien in silhouette. All Logan could see were high heels, long legs, a cane and a top hat. As the dancer began to move, Logan was mesmerised once more. He believed Nolan when he said Bastien was their best. No one had ever held him spellbound before.

Bastien stepped up to the pole, the spotlight at the back disappearing and reappearing from above him. The hat made it difficult to discern his features, but there was no denying it was him. Logan would know that body anywhere now.

And wasn't that a problem?

CHAPTER FOUR

BASTIEN

Logan had been a constant visitor at The Bone Yard for the past few weeks, and Bastien was having a hard time dealing with his reaction to him. There were also days when Logan didn't turn up, and they confused Bastien even more because he ended up disappointed and grumpy about it. Nolan had picked up on the reason for his behaviour, but no one else had seemed to.

"Why not just find out his number and give him a call? Get the man out of your system, Black?" Nolan said one evening when Logan was absent.

Bastien didn't even know what the guy did for a living, so couldn't think of a reason why except for if he was married. That would be his luck, shacking up with a married man.

"What's the point, Nolan? I'll only have to go and

find another guy when he loses interest. I'm saving myself some future heartache." And wasn't that too close to the truth for Bastien to acknowledge?

After another day working the makeup for Deacon, the man asked Bastien if he wanted to go with him to a party.

"I don't know." Bastien scrunched his nose up at the idea, knowing he'd much prefer to stay at home and work on more of his creations.

"Ah, come on, B! There will only be a few friends, and we're going to drink a few beers and have a chat. It's nothing major."

As Bastien had an evening off, he reluctantly accepted. He had no idea why because it would be the first time he'd ever gone out with Deacon socially. At least it wasn't a date. That, he couldn't have handled.

Standing in front of his mirror, he checked over his outfit for the evening. He'd decided on skinny black jeans; a loose, black sequined shirt, half-opened over a pale purple t-shirt; and heeled boots. On his face, he applied only enough makeup that he would normally do but with extra thick eyeliner. He didn't want to make it seem like he was dressing for a date and make things uncomfortable, but he also didn't want to seem like he hadn't made an effort. Deacon knew what he usually looked like, so Bastien wanted to show him that he wasn't being aloof.

The doorbell chimed, and he hesitantly drifted

across the room to the door, taking a breath and firmly putting his social demeanour in place before checking the peephole and opening it to Deacon.

"Hey! Wow, you look great!" Deacon said.

"Don't I always?" Bastien raised his chin. He grabbed his coat and draped it around his shoulders, knowing he would take it off in the car.

Deacon held out his arm with a grin in place, and Bastien laughed as he locked his front door. As uncomfortable as the gesture felt to Bastien, he slid his hand into the crook of Deacon's elbow and allowed the man to guide him out of the building and to the car.

"So, the house is just on the outskirts of the city, but we'll be there in no time."

"Did we have to bring anything with us?"

Deacon shook his head. "Nope, just us." He grinned at Bastien again, steering them onto the main road.

"Work seems to be picking up for you." Bastien glanced over at the man before twisting back to the passenger window.

"Yeah, it is. I didn't expect so many people to enjoy having those types of photos done, but it's getting more and more popular, especially with word of mouth getting around. My previous clients are talking to their friends and so on, and I'm getting recommended more. It's amazing."

"That's great." Bastien wished the same thing would happen for his jewellery business.

"And more work for me means more work for you. If you want it, that is?"

Bastien cocked his head and pursed his lips. "I'm happy to have more work. I have to make sure it doesn't interfere with my other job, but it should be fine."

"Great. How is the dancing going?"

"Good, thanks. I'm slowly climbing the ladder, so it's a bonus for me."

"Why?"

He exhaled. "Well, if I become more popular, then I will also get more tips, and I will be requested more often for dances. Both mean I earn more money, which is certainly not a bad thing at the moment."

"Sounds like you'll be the star of the show before long." Deacon glanced over at him, a small smile in place and a look in his eye that Bastien couldn't interpret.

Bastien chuckled. "They need more than just me to make a profit, but it works out for me. I'm not complaining."

They chatted about inconsequential things for the rest of the journey, and Bastien became more and more uneasy as the direction they were heading became clear. As with all cities, towns and villages, there were areas that were better and some that were…

not. This was a place he would not have considered coming to had he been given a choice. Not wanting to upset his companion, he inhaled slowly and tried to settle his stomach.

They pulled up at a tiny, terraced house, identical to several around them, and Deacon smiled before exiting the car. Bastien closed his eyes, trying to push down his panic at being in a place where drug deals, drive-bys and dead bodies were frequently recorded in the news. When his door opened, his eyes startled open, meeting Deacon's bright gaze.

"Come on. The fun is inside the house, not outside." He chuckled at his joke, but Bastien didn't find it amusing.

Swallowing hard, he painted on his smirk and climbed out of the car, fussing with the front of his shirt before sliding his arms into the coat. All the actions were trying to delay the inevitable, but he couldn't for long.

Deacon grabbed his hand and dragged him towards the door, swinging it open before Bastien could say anything. Cheers greeted their entry, and Deacon lifted his hands high, taking Bastien's with him.

"Come on, let's grab a drink."

Bastien didn't bother to nod, knowing Deacon wouldn't see it with the high-fives and back-slapping he was doing, all the while squeezing Bastien's hand as if his life depended on it. There was a hell of a lot more people than Deacon had said there would be, which Bastien was not happy about. There was a whole lot of difference between a few friends having a beer and a huge party with close to probably fifty people.

When they entered the kitchen, Deacon let go of Bastien's hand, and he gently rubbed the circulation back into it. Glancing around, he saw bottles upon empty bottles of alcohol strewn across the counters, on the floor, piled up next to the back door, pretty much everywhere he looked. He wasn't sure if those bottles had been emptied that night or not, but either way, it didn't bode well for the outcome of his night. Bastien didn't drink alcohol. It wasn't because he didn't like the taste or because he didn't like what happened to him when he was drunk, it was more because he couldn't afford it, but it meant his tolerance was a whole lot lower than other people's. Plus, he preferred being in control in places he didn't know. Especially this one.

Deacon passed him a cup, and Bastien could tell, just by the smell, that it was full of alcohol. He smiled, though, and thanked the man before lifting it to his mouth and pretending to sip at it. After faking a swallow and licking his lips, Bastien smiled again. Deacon grinned and downed the drink he'd made himself, whirling around to make another one. Seeing no one looking at him, he tipped a little from his cup into a beaker near him, so he could show that the liquid was reducing if Deacon became anal about checking.

Deacon came back to him and linked their hands together once more before shuffling in the direction of the living room. There were even more people packed in that small space with people sitting on top of other people or standing against the walls. There was no way anyone else would be able to fit without it becoming uncomfortable. All Deacon did, though, was pull Bastien's back to his front and rest their linked hands over Bastien's shoulder.

It was at that point that Bastien knew he'd made a terrible mistake. Deacon thought this was a date.

Bastien was tempted to down the drink when the knowledge swept over him, but he wanted his wits about him. He needed to figure out how to get himself out of the mess he'd gotten himself in.

"Deke!"

A tall, overweight man of indecipherable age came over, making Deacon let go of Bastien's hand. Bastien stepped to the side, allowing the men to embrace.

"Spike, man! How are you?"

"Doing good, thanks." His eyes darted appreciatively over Bastien, who inwardly cringed at the expression. "Who's your friend?"

Deacon slid his arm around Bastien's shoulder, which he was more than grateful for at that moment.

"This here is Bastien. He's the artist who does all the makeup for my clients. He's a gem!"

"I can see that." The man licked his lips. "Nice to meet you, Bastien."

"You, too," he managed to croak.

"I never thought I'd see the day you managed to catch a fly in your trap, Deke."

The two men laughed, sliding glances across at Bastien, which made his stomach churn more than it already was.

Bastien needed to get out of there. "I can't stay too long, Deacon. I have an appointment in the morning."

Deacon's eyes narrowed, but he grinned. "Sure thing." Then he went back to talking to the other man.

Bastien's gaze took in the room. More and more people were making out, humping each other, feeling each other up, and it was making Bastien queasy. Not the displays, but the knowledge that Deacon expected the same from him. He couldn't think of a single thing he could do to stop it from happening apart from leaving.

He watched as lines of drugs were laid out on the tables and other flat surfaces and plenty of people taking part. He never had and never would take drugs. Ever.

After a very long half an hour of listening to Deacon talk to other people and ignoring him except when he wanted to drape his arm around him, which

Bastien reluctantly let him do to keep the peace, Bastien decided it was time for him to go. Keeping up his social persona was wearing him out.

"I'm going to head out, Deacon." He kept his voice level and a slight curl to his mouth as he normally would and met Deacon's gaze, crossing his arms and tapping his finger on his biceps.

"I don't think so, babe. You haven't danced for us yet." Deacon grinned, and Bastien's stomach dropped.

"I never agreed to dance." He cocked his hip and set a trembling hand on his waist, raising a haughty eyebrow at the man. If Bastien had more people around that he knew, he could've done more, but he had to be careful.

"You don't need to agree; you're a stripper, for god's sake. When Spike gets back, it's time for you to earn your time here." Deacon crossed his arms over his chest, a smirk gracing his face, making Bastien withhold a shiver.

"I don't think so, Deacon. I only dance at the club, nowhere else." Bastien mirrored the man's posture, loosely wrapping his arms around his waist and trying to project his usual confidence.

"I think that will change." Deacon narrowed his eyes, straightening from where he was perched and making Bastien lift his chin to keep eye contact.

"Thanks, but no thanks. I'm heading out." Bastien pulled his coat tighter around his body and stepped forward. Deacon grabbed his biceps and held him firmly.

"Jer! Close up, will you? We don't want our entertainment going missing."

Laughter flowed around him as a guy headed towards the front door and stood with his back to it, and Bastien began to panic. He had no issues with dancing for them if that was what it took to get himself out of here, but he was under no illusion that dancing was the only thing Deacon wanted. Where had he gone so wrong with the man? He'd thought the guy was nice, but underneath it all, Deacon was an asshole.

Heat warmed Bastien's back, and he tensed, glancing to the side and watching from the corner of his eye as Deacon moved in closer.

"You're my prize tonight, babe," he whispered, his hands sliding down Bastien's front and cupping his crotch.

Bastien refrained from saying anything and, instead, chose to twist in Deacon's hold, putting their faces nearer than Bastien wanted. He slid his hands into Deacon's hair and gripped tight. "I need to freshen up if I'm going to dance for everyone," he murmured, bringing Deacon close as if he would reward him with a kiss, then pulling away.

"All right. The bathroom is up the stairs on the left."

Bastien could see Deacon's eyes had dilated, and as

he stepped back, the evidence of his arousal tented his trousers. Swallowing his disgust, Bastien sneered and headed to the bathroom.

Locking himself in the small room, he sat on the closed toilet seat and rested his head in his hands.

"What the fuck am I going to do?" he whispered. For a brief second, he'd wished he'd taken Nolan's advice and found out Logan's number, although he probably wouldn't be any help against so many others.

As soon as the thought crossed his mind, he knew what to do. He pulled out his phone, then paused to turn on the tap, hoping to mask his voice. Dialling, he waited, his eyes fastened on the door in case someone tried to enter.

"Emergency, which service?"

"Police, please."

"Hold, please."

He waited then answered the new person's questions, giving his personal details, "I'm being held against my will, and there are drugs and drinking," he whispered.

"Can you give me your location?"

"Not exactly, no. I know I'm in the slums of Cambridge," he muttered.

"All right. I have your location via your phone. We should have a car with you shortly. Are you in danger?" the operator asked.

"Not in so many words. I'm going to go and dance

like they've asked me to. It will keep them occupied while you guys arrive."

"If that will put you in danger, I would strongly advise against it."

"I'll be fine as long as I dance. It's when I stop there will be issues, so get here fast."

He hung up just as someone banged on the door.

"You can't stay in there all night, babe," Deacon crooned.

"Yes, I could," he whispered.

Standing, he checked his reflection in the mirror, seeing his usual social expression absent and the hidden façade plain for all to see. He shook his head, closed his eyes and pushed everything away except the need to dance. It didn't matter who his audience was; he would dance his ass off and hope he could keep going until the police arrived.

Turning off the tap, he lifted an eyebrow at his reflection, then opened the door. "I'm ready. Can we go into the living room? I think a tabletop dance would be good for starters."

Deacon's eyes blazed, and Bastien pursed his lips, lowering his eyes and looking up at Deacon from underneath his lashes. He'd had plenty of practice; it shouldn't be too hard to make-believe for a short time. He just hoped the audience wanted to see more dancing and less touchy-feely stuff.

Deacon wrapped his arm around Bastien's shoulder and guided him to the living room.

"Yeah! Let's get this party started!" Deacon announced, dropping himself on the centre of the sofa between two other guys.

Bastien knew the coffee table would hold him as light as he was, but it was smaller than he'd realised, so moving would be problematic. He tilted his head. He could improvise though, making his movements smaller and more seductive might work to keep him on the surface and not flat on his face on the floor. If necessary, he'd dance towards the kitchen where there was a bigger table.

"Come on! Get started, B!"

Bastien inhaled and slid off his jacket, stuffing it under the table; his phone was inside, and he would need it. "Do I have a choice of music, or are you choosing?"

"Hit the sound!" someone shouted, and music blared from speakers somewhere close.

It was not something he had danced to before, but he let his body find the beat, then stepped onto the small table. Normally, he would've closed his eyes for part of the dance and allowed himself to get lost in the sound, but he couldn't do that here, mainly due to who he was surrounded by, but also because he had such a small space to work with. He would have to keep an eye on where he placed his feet.

Despite his reservations and fears, he allowed himself to relax enough to dance. He reminded himself of all the clandestine lessons he'd taken when he was younger. Knowing that his parents wouldn't allow him to do such things, he'd become efficient at dancing quietly and in small spaces in his bedroom so he would never be found out. Having to do that here brought back all the memories from that time of his life.

He didn't lose himself in the dance as much as he would normally but instead kept an eye on his surroundings through a narrowed gaze. The people around him appeared to be mesmerised, leaning forward or straining to see him. Deacon, he could see, had braced his elbows on his knees and stared with wide eyes.

He had no idea how long he danced for, but he didn't stop. He spun, stretched, bent, twirled and moved over and over. He didn't stop until a large crash sounded.

Jumping off the table, he crouched, rummaging for his coat, which he gripped.

"Police! Stay where you are!" a voice shouted as the lights were flicked on. He winced and closed his eyes briefly.

People began scrambling to get out of the house, knocking into or tripping over him. He didn't care. Staying where he was until there were fewer people around, he then stood, slipped on his coat and held his hands up in surrender. A police officer headed towards him.

"Bastien Templeton?"

He nodded. "Yes, sir."

The officer smiled, stepped around him and shut off the pounding music, leaving the house slightly quieter, except for the shouts of police and partygoers. "Thanks for this."

Bastien exhaled and glared at Deacon, who narrowed his eyes at him. "The pleasure was *not* mine, I'm afraid."

The officer placed a hand on his shoulder, making him flinch. "Sorry," he said. "I'm Detective Kade Stirling. I'm sorry for what you've been through. We need to take a statement from you before we do anything else. Are you happy to go through it now while it's still fresh in your mind?"

Bastien nodded. "May as well. I have no place to be."

"You'll pay for this, asshole!" Deacon shouted, and Bastien glanced to see him being taken away in handcuffs.

"Hopefully, we can get something on him, and he'll be a figment of your past," Detective Stirling said.

"I highly doubt that. He seems too organised."

"What do you mean?"

Bastien pulled his coat tighter around him. "This

seemed to have been organised in advance. My being here, I mean. I haven't been at a social gathering like this in years. I usually keep to myself, doing my jobs then heading home. I work with Deacon on occasion, doing makeup for his photoshoots. That's how I know him. When he asked if I wanted to go to a party tonight, I agreed despite not feeling right about it."

"What made you agree?"

He hesitated, listening as the noises around him petered out, leaving them in silence. "I've had a shit few weeks. Few years, really. I thought it would be nice to get out and meet some new people." Bastien shook his head. "Yeah, won't be doing that again."

"What happened after you accepted the offer?" Stirling glanced down at his notepad, then back to Bastien, a neutral expression on his face.

"He came to pick me up, then we drove here. As soon as I saw where we were going, I knew I'd made a mistake. I didn't know how to get out of it, though. Therefore, I came in." He peered around the room. "There were a lot more people than he had led me to believe, and some seemed really sleazy. I stayed for a short while, then told Deacon I was leaving."

"How did that go?"

Bastien huffed a self-deprecating laugh. "He told some others to block the exits, and they complied as if this had happened many times before."

"Shit."

"Yeah. I made the excuse that I needed to freshen up in the bathroom, and that's when I called you guys."

"Why didn't you stay in the bathroom?"

"I thought it would be easier for you to catch more of them unawares if I had them occupied. He brought me here so I would dance for them." He shrugged. "So, I did."

"Dance? Why would they want to see you dance?"

Bastien sighed. "I'm a stripper at The Bone Yard."

"Ah."

Bastien shivered, pulling his coat closer again and crossing his arms over it to keep it in place. He had a bone-deep chill in his body and couldn't stop his extremities from trembling.

"So, Deacon managed to get you here, made you dance for them, but what was he hoping for?"

Bastien lifted a shoulder. "I don't know. There was a lot of drinking, drugs, humping and fucking going on in all areas of the house from what I could hear and occasionally see. I'm assuming he wanted to fuck me."

Stirling blew out a breath. "Are you okay?"

"Not really, if I'm honest with you," Bastien answered, his voice soft. "I'm worried about the repercussions this will have when Deacon goes free."

"You're so sure he'll go free?"

Bastien raised his eyebrows and nodded. "Aren't you, Detective?"

"Kade, please. And I have no idea. We'll try and get more information out of the people we managed to grab, but they might have to be sobered up before we get anything of use."

"It's fine, Detec—Kade. I'll be fine. I certainly won't be working with him anymore, but maybe I can find something else."

"Come on. Let's get you home. Do you have everything?"

Bastien nodded again, checking his pocket for his phone, then following Kade out of the house. Blue lights flashed in the darkened sky, lighting it up like a light show they'd have at the club. In his glazed mood, he told himself to ask Rafferty about doing a police show with a few dancers all in one. It would certainly get the customers going.

Kade opened the passenger door of the unmarked police car for him, then closed him in, stopping to chat to another police officer before circling the car and climbing in beside him.

"What's your address?"

Bastien gave it, then settled in for the journey home. Kade didn't ask any more questions, except when they were finally outside his house.

"Would you please contact me if you need anything?" Kade held out a business card. "I know you probably think you're fine, but you might need something or remember something that could help."

"Thanks."

"I would like to check on you tomorrow if that's okay?"

Bastien stared at the officer, concern apparent in his expression. "All right."

"Get some rest."

Bastien climbed out and headed to the building, letting himself in and slowly ascended the three flights of stairs to his apartment. Once he closed the door behind him, he slid to the floor, closing his arms around his legs.

"Why does this shit happen to me?"

Tears flowed down his cheeks, but he refrained from sobbing. He knew better than most people that it wouldn't help.

CHAPTER FIVE

LOGAN

"Come on, Chief! There has to be something more we can do to get this case blown open?" Logan paced from one side of the small office to the other while Ava sat patiently in the chair opposite their boss.

"I'm not sure what to tell you, Logan. The evidence you have here doesn't point to anyone. I can't bring a suspect here out of thin air, you know," Chief Bryan Anderson said from his perch in his chair.

Logan rubbed his hands over his cropped hair. "I know. I just…"

"We just need something to make sense," Ava finished. "All these little things add up, but it's as if there is still something we're missing that makes it all link together."

"Look, if you've exhausted all the avenues you

have, put it to one side for a few days. Catch up on one of the other cases you have, then come back to it. I will even have a quick look over it myself during that time if you want or ask one of the others for their opinions."

Logan scoffed. "What's the point in that. They already wasted time by ignoring the woman when she came to us for help." His chest felt tight, and he flexed his fingers, wanting to watch something smash to the floor as if that would help him exhume what was inside him.

Bryan sighed. "I know you don't like him, Logan, but you also know my hands are tied at the moment." He glanced out of the small window to the main area where the officers sat. "Be patient is all I ask."

His cryptic words bounced around Logan's brain, and he narrowed his eyes. Meeting the chief's gaze, he read between the lines, and his heart eased a little; Henry would be getting his comeuppance soon if his guess was any good. Logan nodded once.

They exited the office, the noise rising considerably just by opening his boss's door.

"I'm going to grab some coffee. Do you want one?" he asked Ava.

"Yeah, go on then. I need to keep myself awake somehow." She hid a yawn behind her hand.

"Something kept you up all night?"

"Bloody neighbours are having their kitchen and

bathroom refitted. It started late last night for some stupid reason. You would've thought they'd be more aware of noise disturbance being next door to a police officer. Had to go around and tell them to quit it at eleven."

Logan squeezed her shoulder in camaraderie, then split off to head for the coffee machine. The coffee was awful, but it kept them alert in some ways and burned off their tastebuds in other ways. As he filled their cups, Logan's friend and fellow officer Kade entered.

The man had an athletic build, though Logan knew from when they worked out in the gym together that his muscles were hidden beneath his clothing. He was a good-looking guy with full lips, bright blue eyes and short black hair. If Kade had been gay and single, Logan would've looked twice, even if they did work together. Analise, a bartender at Crush, would have his nuts in a vice if Logan ever thought about trying something, though, since she was Kade's girlfriend.

"Hey, Logan. What's up?" Kade reached for a cup, and Logan moved out of the way.

"Same old shit," he muttered.

"Hey, Kade? Heard you had some fun with a stripper yesterday?" one of the younger officers remarked with a hip wiggle before laughing and walking off.

Kade rolled his eyes and huffed. "Immature assholes."

Logan's heart had started pounding at the word "stripper," but there were plenty of them around—men and women. It wouldn't have anything to do with Bastien, but he couldn't help but be curious. "Strippers?" he chuckled, raising an eyebrow.

"Yeah. We received a call from a stripper about a party that was happening in 'slumville.' At first, we weren't going to do anything about it, but then he said he was being kept against his will and that there were drugs around. We thought we'd check it out, even if for nothing else than a potential drug bust."

"What happened?" Logan's pulse raced, and he swallowed hard when Kade confirmed it was a male stripper.

"The stripper told the operator that he was going to dance for them to keep them occupied until we got there. Pretty ballsy if you ask me."

Hardly daring to breathe, he waited for Kade to continue, knowing exactly one person who would do something that stupid. He ran a hand over his mouth.

"Anyway, Joey and I took a few of the other officers and went in quietly. We busted the door down and managed to nab a few of the bastards."

"And the stripper?" he croaked.

"Fine and well, although a little shaken. I took him home after taking his statement. Apparently, he'd been invited to attend by a work friend. That friend had thrown him to the wolves by telling them he was a stripper." Kade shook his head. "Assholes."

Logan sipped his coffee, his gaze on the floor as he tried to figure out how to ask who it had been without giving away more information than he wanted anyone to know right then. Then he frowned. "How did he manage to call if he was being held against his will?"

Kade laughed. "The guy told them he was going to freshen up for the dance and rang while in the bathroom. I can't believe they fell for it."

"Will he be in danger?"

Kade gulped his coffee, shaking his head from side to side. "Possibly. I'm going to catch up with him later today and check in a few more times to make sure he's safe, but he has my number in case something happens."

Was he feeling a bit jealous, even though he knew Kade wouldn't stray? He pushed the feeling down as far as he could, not having time to dissect his emotions. Short of asking Kade outright who the stripper was and therefore giving away his interest, the only other thing he could think of was swiping the details from the file. He concentrated on the bitter taste and the burnt scent of the coffee, swirling the remnants around in his cup.

He'd been back to The Bone Yard several times in the last month or so, each time seeking out the man who he'd thought about more than he probably should have. Bastien had never offered a lap dance again, and Logan had been the object of the blond-haired guy's advances many times, much to his discomfort.

A kick to his foot brought his attention back to his companion. "What?"

Kade quirked his mouth. "What's got you all tied up? Or should I say who?" He winked and chuckled, dodging the empty plastic cup that Logan had thrown his way.

Pushing off the wall where he'd been leaning, Logan bent down to pick up the cup and throw it in the bin before answering, "No one. I'm just fed up with all the dead ends I'm finding in my damn case."

"Do you want me to have a look through it? I'm not saying I'll find anything you didn't, but a fresh pair of eyes…" He shrugged.

Logan nodded. "Yeah, definitely. We can swap cases for a few hours. I need out of my head." He half-heartedly chuckled.

"Deal. You best get Ava a new coffee if that was supposed to be for her. She won't be happy if you bring her a cold one."

Logan rolled his eyes but dutifully threw the cup in the bin and filled a new one.

"You took your sweet time," Ava said, cradling the cup in her hands and closing her eyes as she inhaled the aroma, scrunching her nose a bit in the process.

Logan's mouth twitched, knowing the scent was

less than appealing, but he refrained from commenting. "Kade offered to look over the Conrad case for us. He might see something we missed."

"That's good. Maybe we can check over the Trainor case instead?"

"Would you mind having a look at that? I'm going to look at Kade's case first, then I'll come on board with Trainor."

Ava nodded. "Sure."

Kade came whistling his way, and Logan's heart rate increased. He had no idea whether he wanted the stripper to be Bastien or not, but he needed to find out one way or another. The noise of the surrounding officers dimmed as Kade handed him the file, his entire focus on the words hidden within the cover.

"Let me know what you think," Kade said, and Logan nodded absentmindedly.

He stared down at the pale-yellow card, hesitating to open it now it was in front of him. Inhaling deeply, he flicked it open, his throat convulsing, trying to swallow the lump. When Bastien's name jumped out at him, his breath caught, and he felt sweat gathering on his forehead. His eyebrows drew together as he read the statement the man had given, and icy tendrils slid along his spine at the thought of Bastien being in danger.

Scanning the other documentation, he found out that Bastien's friend—and he used that word loosely—

was already out. Logan's muscles tightened, and without thinking more on it, he noted down Bastien's home address and was out of his seat, jogging to the exit. He had more than enough work to do, but he needed to check on Bastien first. He needed to warn him. Climbing into his car, he peeled out of the car park, turning the vehicle in the direction of Bastien's apartment.

Logan had no idea what he was doing. He tried to reassure himself that he was only doing his job, but it fell flat every time. Somewhere along in their interactions, the man had become important to Logan, and he didn't know what to do with that knowledge. What he did know was that he couldn't help his instinctive reaction when it came to Bastien; he had to help, no matter the consequence.

Stopping the car outside the apartment building, Logan studied the dilapidated brick housing, noting several broken and boarded-up windows, graffiti and overflowing rubbish all around the area. He clenched his jaw and headed towards the entrance, shaking his head when he realised the lock was broken and anyone could walk in. Just like him. The idea had his nostrils flaring, and he bolted up the stairs towards Bastien's home, passing several shifty-looking people who, undoubtedly, would love to wail on a police officer if they knew he was one.

Breathing hard, he knocked on the door, not even

considering the repercussions of his actions before he faced a decidedly pissed-off-looking dancer.

"How did you find me?" Bastien asked through the chain-locked door, part of his face shielded by the less than sturdy front door.

"I'm a police officer," Logan muttered under his breath, not wanting Bastien's neighbours to hear their conversation. He didn't want to take the chance that Bastien would receive problems if they knew he was associating with cops.

Bastien's eyes widened, staring at him for a second before closing the door. Logan panicked for a moment until he heard the sound of the lock releasing, then Bastien reappeared, holding the door wide and indicating for Logan to enter.

"I'm not happy that you're here without checking in with me first," Bastien said when he'd closed them inside the apartment.

The dancer was tiny when he wasn't wearing his heels and barely came up to Logan's shoulder. His demeanour overshadowed everything, though, making him appear larger than life, especially when his cocky attitude came to the forefront. That day, he appeared softer, the casual blue joggers and a purple t-shirt under a black hoodie seemingly out of place on the body Logan had always seen in revealing clothes.

When Bastien crossed his arms over his chest and

cocked his hip, Logan knew he'd been staring for too long. He tried to recall what Bastien had said.

"Oh, I, um, I'm sorry. I should've called, but I wanted to check on you. When I found out from my colleague that it was you, I couldn't help it." Logan felt his cheeks burning, and he clenched his jaw again, fighting the urge to look at the floor.

They stared at each other for several moments, the only sound came from the neighbour's loud conversation clearly heard through the door before Bastien's shoulders lowered, and his arms dropped to his sides.

In an uncharacteristic show of nervousness, Bastien pulled the cuffs of his hoodie over his hands and asked, "Would you like a drink? I have…" He wandered to the tiny kitchen area, consisting of two base cupboards, a small fridge, a sink and a cooker. "I have milk? Or water?"

Logan didn't think the water from the taps would be the best choice, and with the few deductions he'd made while looking around the place, he knew Bastien would be better to keep the milk for himself. "No, I'm good, thanks."

Bastien sighed and leaned against the counter, once more crossing his arms over his chest, spearing Logan with his bright green gaze. "What can I help you with? I'm assuming you came to talk to me about last night?" He snorted. "You being a police officer should not have come as a surprise. Now that I think about it, you have that demeanour about you."

Moving a few steps closer, Logan pursed his lips. "Well, we didn't really have much of a conversation before now." He hesitated. "Deacon's out already."

Bastien dropped his gaze, but Logan could see his breathing increase and the trembling that he was trying to fight against. Logan wanted nothing more than to close the distance and enfold the man in his arms, protecting him against anything that might try to hurt him. It was a similar feeling he had for his family, but that hadn't gotten him anywhere. It was the reason he didn't reach out, no matter how much he wanted to. Logan might be a police officer, but apparently, he was shit at protecting people.

He called on his years of police work and managed to collect his thoughts. "I wanted to warn you. You need to be careful, especially if that Deacon guy is likely to follow through with his threat. Do you have someone you can stay with?"

Bastien let out a small laugh, his hand covering his mouth. "Do you really think I'd be living here if I had someone I could stay with?" He whirled away from Logan, resting his hands on the counter and lowering his head.

The pain constricting Logan's chest weighed heavier than ever before. He could hear Bastien's panicked breathing, even over the noise of the neighbour's ranting. There was nothing in this place that would protect Bastien if that asshole came for him, and that scared Logan.

"I'm sorry. If you want, you could—"

Bastien twisted around to face Logan. "Do you know what? I'm good. I'll sort it out myself. Thanks for letting me know." He headed to the front door, then waited with his hand on the handle, raising his eyebrows at Logan. "Thank you. I'll be fine from here."

Logan hated the idea of leaving the dancer in that place by himself with nothing or no one to protect him, but it was his choice at the end of the day. It didn't matter how much Logan prodded; the man would push back. He had a feeling Bastien had been on his own for a lot longer than Logan originally thought, and that was both a blessing and a curse. It meant he wouldn't accept any outside help, but it also meant he would have survival skills other people didn't.

Clenching his jaw, Logan stepped towards the front door, Bastien opening it when he was close enough to exit. Before he left, Logan whispered, "Please, *please* call Kade if you need anything. I know you probably don't want to hear from me, but please call him if you need anything at all."

Bastien nodded once and pursed his lips, his body tense and rigid.

Logan gazed at him for a second longer than he

should've and left. The door closed firmly behind him. Resting a hand on the wall beside the apartment, he breathed deeply before lifting his head and resuming his trek back to his car. Luckily, it was still in one piece when he got to it.

He would've preferred not to have to return to the station, but there was still plenty of work left to be done, and besides, he hadn't told Ava he was leaving, and she was going to be pissed with him. Bracing himself for her anger, he headed back.

As expected, Ava gave him the evil eye when he sat at his desk. Diverting her gaze to the papers in front of her, she ignored him. It was a similar trick Logan's mother used on him to get him to tell her all his secrets, and it worked wonders—for both his mother and Ava.

"I'm sorry," he said, linking his fingers on top of his desk and sighing heavily. She didn't say anything, and Logan's mouth twitched with the need to smile. Although he knew what she was doing, he couldn't help but succumb every time. He hated having her cross with him. "I know the victim in Kade's case. I went to check he was doing okay."

"Why didn't you tell Kade?"

"I wasn't sure it was him until I read the file. The man who had held him against his will has already been released. I wanted to tell him face to face."

Ava nodded slowly. "Next time, regardless of who

or what it is, let me come with you. I was worried sick, Logan." He studied her and saw the strain in her features. "I know I'm not a full detective yet, but I can still help."

"I know you can, Ava. It wasn't about that. I just didn't think."

"Well, think next time. Otherwise, I'm sending our mothers after you."

Logan winced. "Ouch! That's harsh."

"Yeah, well, maybe you should've considered the punishment you'd get before doing it."

Grinning, he waggled his eyebrows. "Punishment? You've been talking with Trent and Max too much." Ava's face flushed as she spluttered a denial, and Logan took pity on her. "I will make sure I let you know what's going on next time."

"Only because you know there *will* be a next time." She pursed her lips and narrowed her eyes.

"Oh, definitely. You've been with me long enough, Detective Walker, to know that what I say is the truth, the whole truth, and nothing but the truth."

Ava snorted and shook her head, picking up a piece of paper from her desk. "Leave me in peace, Detective Taylor. I have work to do."

Logan screwed up a piece of paper and threw it at her, laughing when it hit her forehead. "*We* have work to do."

"Get to it then." Ava threw the paper back, and

Logan unfolded it, smoothing it out as much as he could when he realised it was something he needed.

They worked together, going over the Trainor case with a fine toothcomb, trying to think of different aspects they may not have thought of before. Having found a couple of small areas they could re-check, they set them aside and focused on the other cases weighing down their desks. As Logan had said to Ava earlier, they had been working together for so long, they knew each other well. They knew how each other worked, and it was a good and bad thing sometimes.

Having been able to distract himself enough that he barely thought about Bastien for the last few hours of his shift, he finally allowed the man to invade his thoughts once more. He tried to decide whether he should swing by The Bone Yard and see if Bastien was working or not. Bastien would be safer around a lot more people, but Logan wasn't sure if he liked the idea. Shaking his head, he pointed his car towards his home.

Three minutes later, he turned the car around and headed to the strip club. What was it about that slender, cocky, gorgeous dancer that made Logan lose all sense? He had no idea whether Bastien was even working that night. Pulling the car up in a parking space outside the building, Logan hesitated. He drummed his fingers on the steering wheel and stared at the line of customers waiting to enter the building.

He could easily bypass them now—all he needed to do was state police business—but he didn't want to bring attention to himself.

Heaving a sigh, he pulled back out of the space and headed away from the place he wanted to be. What was he doing? There was nothing he could do to help Bastien, and if anything, he would make life more difficult for the man.

Turning his thoughts to Casey, he felt his mood plummet. Casey had kept the sexual harassment quiet for over four months before it had come out, and the only reason Logan had found out was when someone had thrown a brick through Luke's—his boyfriend and Ava's brother—window. Other than that, he knew Casey would've kept it quiet to make sure it didn't cause any problems with his family.

When Logan had found out, he was furious. Not at Casey, although he was a little angry that Casey hadn't told him, he was mad at himself for not realising Casey's behaviour had changed and for not checking in with his brother. It had made Logan wary of making promises of protection when he knew he couldn't guarantee it.

Finding himself dawdling in his driveway, he switched off the engine and went inside the house. After a quick shower to wash off the day's grime, he laid on his bed, the covers covering his lower half with his hand behind his head, staring at the ceiling. Sleep was a million miles away from Logan, but he didn't get up. He went back over every little detail of Casey's behaviour to try and find the little nuggets that should have clued him into something being wrong, and then when that was enough torture for him, he went through every interaction with Bastien to see what clues he could find there.

Sitting upright, he realised something he should've seen earlier.

Bastien had no one.

CHAPTER SIX

BASTIEN

"What can I do you for, B?" Rafferty asked from behind his desk, though his attention was still on the computer screen.

"I wanted to ask if you had any more shifts I could pick up?" He tucked his hands into his pockets and clenched them tightly, not wanting to show exactly how screwed he was.

Bastien hated asking for more work, especially from Rafferty, who already helped him out so much, but he had little choice. In the last week and a half, every single contact he had used in the past few years for makeup gigs had declined or just plain ignored his messages or calls. He knew it was Deacon's doing, but it still rankled that they would choose Deacon over him, especially because they probably knew what he was like. Or maybe they were the same as Deacon, in which case, Bastien was probably better off not working with them.

His rent was coming due at the end of the month, and so far, he didn't have even close to the amount he needed to pay for it. Which was why he was there begging for more work.

Trembling was a constant companion of his at the moment, and he hated the feeling of being unable to sit still and enjoy the moment. His jewellery design had suffered because he hadn't been able to stay in one place long enough to complete something. The excessive energy that seemed to flow through his body was becoming tedious, as was the tightening in his chest and the increased heartbeat whenever he thought of his money situation.

Rafferty switched his focus to Bastien, who tried not to squirm under the narrowed gaze. The silence was deafening, whereas usually, it was calming to be able to sit in the soundproofed office and not hear the music.

"What's happened?"

Bastien cleared his throat. "There's not much makeup work going around at the moment, and I need to make my rent money. That's all."

He hoped he sounded honest enough, but he doubted Rafferty would buy it.

"Sure. I was going to search for another dancer to cover for Reed's extended absence, but if you want to take his sets for the next few weeks or however long you need, then that's fine with me. Just don't work yourself into a grave. I'll be keeping an eye on you."

Relief coursed through him, though he tried not to let it show. "Thanks, Boss. I appreciate it."

"Not a problem. But I will be mentioning it to the bouncers and bartenders, and if they see you looking less than stellar at *any* point, you will reduce back to your usual hours. You hear?"

"Absolutely." Bastien wasn't a makeup genius for nothing; he could hide pale skin and a few bags under his eyes with some lovely foundation and concealer.

Rafferty rummaged in the papers on his desk and found what he was looking for with an, "Ah-ha! Here's Reed's schedule." He passed the paper to Bastien.

Bastien checked through it and saw that even with adding Reed's sets onto his, he still managed to have a night off. It just meant he'd be dancing for six out of seven nights instead of five and doing eight to ten sets a night instead of four or five. It was a lot of dancing, but he could do it. He would need to use some of his hard-earned money on some food, though, or his energy levels would suffer.

"Perfect. Thanks again."

"You're welcome. Keep healthy, B." Rafferty raised his eyebrows and pointed a finger at Bastien.

"Yes, sir."

Leaving the office, he closed the door behind him,

giving himself a moment to breathe deeply. His whole life was now in the hands of the customers because his wages would not be enough to cover his rent, bills and food. The jewellery design would have to be pushed aside for the time being, and he would have to be conservative with everything he bought, but he could manage.

A final breath escaped him, and he set his shoulders and descended the stairs. He could feel his legs trembling from the lack of food—he was down to having one packet of noodles or pasta a day to make it last. Hopefully, things would pick up, and he'd be back to the way things were before.

Three weeks later, things were still the same. He'd managed to just scrape enough together for his rent and bills, but food was scarce, and he could tell he'd lost weight he couldn't afford to lose. There was nothing he could do about it, though. He was back to being the scared little boy he had been when he had first been kicked out from his childhood home, and he didn't like it one bit.

Every time he felt himself go down that rabbit hole, it took more and more to climb his way back out again. He felt bad for Rafferty because Bastien had been able to hide everything from him so far, but he didn't know how much longer he could.

Gulping the cold water from the bottle he'd been given at the bar, Bastien rested his hand on the counter when a wave of dizziness swept over him. He focused on a spot on the floor and waited until his head stopped spinning before glancing up and breathing deeply.

"You need to rest."

The voice, coming from directly behind him, made him jump, and he knocked over the second bottle that had been resting next to his hand as he spun around, almost losing his balance until warm, gentle hands stopped his momentum. Gripping the man's arms, Bastien paused with his eyes closed before opening them and staring up at Logan.

"When was the last time you ate, Bas—Black?" Logan asked, his hold firm but escapable.

"I ate before I came to work," he whispered. It was the truth. He made sure every meal he did have was before he had to dance; otherwise, he would have no energy at all.

"And the time before that?" Bastien kept silent. "Hmm, I thought so. You've lost too much weight. You'll be too thin to dance if you're not careful. What's going on? I thought you were going to ask Kade for help if you needed it."

Bastien pulled away, taking a step back. "I was going to ask him for help if I was in trouble. Not eating enough is not trouble; therefore, I do not need to speak to him."

Logan cocked his head and narrowed his gaze. "Semantics. You've been in here more than usual, according to the bartenders. What happened?"

"Nothing has happened. You don't need to check on me," Bastien lowered his voice, glancing around to make sure they were not garnering any attention from those around them. When Nolan raised his eyebrows at him, he held out a hand to say he was fine. "I'm not getting as much work as I did before, so I've picked up a few extra sets here instead."

He didn't know why he was explaining himself, but he couldn't help it. The man seemed to be able to get him to spill his guts with just a look.

"Will you give me a lap dance?"

Bastien frowned. "What?"

"I'd like to pay for a lap dance. How long until the end of your shift?"

He glanced at the clock. "An hour."

"How much for an hour's lap dance?"

"Lap dances are usual like fifteen minutes maximum," Bastien scoffed.

"All right. Four times the price for the last hour of your shift. Done."

He had no idea what the detective was planning,

but he nodded and leaned over the bar to tell Nolan what was happening. Nolan grinned and waggled his eyebrows, but he knew Bastien would never have sex with a customer. At least, not on the premises.

Trailing towards the back room, they passed Cassidy, who curled his lip at Bastien before smiling serenely at Logan. Chancing a glance at Logan's face, he found the man's gaze on him rather than Cassidy. A small thrill went through him at the thought that he was Logan's sole focus, not the asshole who made Bastien's life a living hell.

They entered the same room they'd used the first time, and Logan immediately dropped to the sofa. Bastien strode to the player.

"Put something soft on," Logan said, making Bastien pause in his movements.

Bastien pursed his lips, then switched the channel to something else, and soft, flowing, relaxing music came through the speakers. Taking a deep breath, he began to sway his hips to the sounds, learning the beat before turning to the man who was paying for an hour of his time.

Logan was positioned on one side of the sofa with his leg curled underneath him, his elbow resting on the back and his head resting in his palm.

"Come sit down, Bastien," Logan whispered.

"What? I thought you wanted a dance?"

"I wanted you to have time to rest and recuperate. If I have to pay for that to happen, I will."

Bastien stared at him, and he felt his walls begin to crumble. "I…I…"

"You can."

He hesitated. He didn't know what to do. Logan confused the hell out of him, and Bastien wasn't used to it. The need to be in control and know what the plan was pushed at his insides, making him twitchy as hell, but the want that pulled him towards Logan was visceral. He had never felt it for any other man.

Stepping closer, he studied Logan as the other man watched him. The ease at which his body relaxed against the cushions settled him. There was no pretence in Logan's demeanour, no deceit showing. Bastien inwardly rolled his eyes. Deacon didn't show that either, and look what happened there.

He sat as far away from Logan as he could get—which wasn't far—and crossed his legs and arms, hiding how much they were shaking.

"Take your shoes off," Logan mumbled.

Bastien hesitated, then leaned forward to remove them. Logan was paying for the hour so he could potentially ask Bastien to do whatever he wanted, within reason. Once his shoes were pushed to one side, he scrunched his toes into the grey carpet, surprised by how soft it was. He smiled, making a note to mention it to Rafferty.

A tickle at his neck had him leaning forward and twisting to see what it was. Logan's hand was poised in the air where he had been.

"Sorry, I just wanted to massage your neck a little. You look tense."

"Yeah, maybe because this is weird. I don't usually just sit here. I normally dance around."

He studied Logan's face once more before returning to his position, allowing Logan to rest his hand on his neck and gently press his thumb into the area. It was nice, but it would be better if he had his back to Logan. He wasn't going to ask for it, though, but Logan must've been reading his mind because, after a few moments, he told Bastien to twist away from him.

Bastien did as he was instructed, bending one knee to keep him on the sofa easily, and propped his hands in his lap. He groaned and dropped his head forward when both of Logan's hands kneaded the muscles of his upper back and neck. Losing himself to the feeling, he closed his eyes and gave in. Magic hands released the tension that had been resting on his shoulders for weeks, and Bastien couldn't have been happier.

Logan stopped the movement and gently pulled Bastien back against him until he was resting against Logan's chest. The heat from the man seeped into Bastien's body, and he found himself turning and burrowing closer, allowing Logan to tuck Bastien's head under his chin and wrap his arms around him. Bastien had never felt more cared for.

The next thing he knew, Logan was shaking him softly and talking to him, though it took him some time to figure out his words.

"It's been almost an hour, Bastien."

Bastien blinked open his eyes, then realised he was cradled in Logan's arms still. He pulled away, staring up at him. "Sorry."

"Don't be sorry. I'm glad you rested. You obviously needed it."

"I—"

"Go and get ready to leave. I'll take you home."

Bastien reached for his shoes, not wanting to put them back on but also not wanting to get the jeering and laughter he knew he would if he left the room without them on. The dancers would assume he'd gotten laid. Sliding them on, he grimaced at the thought, then removed the emotion from his face and stood, facing Logan.

"Thank you for that. But you don't need to take me home. I'll be fine."

"I want to take you home, Bastien."

Bastien firmed his jaw but nodded. The music in the room had stopped at some point while he'd slept, and the main area music had turned lower, indicating it was closing time. "I need to get back out there."

Logan nodded and stood. "I'll wait in the car park."

Bastien swallowed at the nearness of them but managed to stop himself from falling into Logan's arms again. Pivoting away from the temptation, he exited the room, leaving Logan to find his own way out like he did last time. Entering the main area, he strode over to the bar, checking in with Nolan before going to the dressing room to get changed. There was only Cassidy and Cody left by that point, and the former sneered at him when he entered.

"Wow, the prodigal son returns. Did you get your kicks while being in there *for an hour*?" Cassidy leered.

Bastien drew himself higher, needing to shore his defences from where Logan had torn them down. Dealing with Cassidy required more than he had at that moment, but he refused to back down. "I don't do anything except dance in those sessions, Cass. I'm sure you know that's against the rules. But, oh, yes, you would know that since you'd been caught giving a blow job yourself." It was catty, but it was also true, which Cassidy's clenched jaw and narrowed eyes proved. Bastien stepped closer. "Don't mess with the prince, Cass. You'll get taken down quicker than briefs in a strip show."

Cassidy slammed the locker closed, grabbed his bag and left.

A slow clap brought Bastien's attention to Cody. "Go, you! What brought that on?"

Bastien stalked to his locker. "I'm sick of him thinking he's god's gift. He needs to be taken down a peg or two." He pulled out his trousers and top, quickly divesting himself of the dance outfit he'd been wearing the latter part of the evening.

"I agree. Just be careful. I don't want him causing problems for you."

"Thanks, Cody."

They finished getting changed, said goodbye to the bartenders and Brandy, and headed to the car park.

"Do you want a lift home, B?" Cody asked, pulling his keys from his pocket. Bastien glanced over at the man waiting patiently by his car, and Cody chuckled. "I'll take that as a no. Have a good night."

"You, too, Cody. Get some rest."

Bastien examined the police officer as he drifted closer. His muscles were barely contained within the coat he was wearing, but Bastien knew Logan would never use those muscles to cause harm. Not only because he knew Logan was a police officer but also because of the way he had held Bastien while he slept. There was no way a man who could cause intentional harm would also be able to hold him so gently.

Coming to a stop in front of him, Bastien lifted his gaze to look in Logan's eyes and saw a fire burning brightly.

"What's happened to make you need to work so much? I know you said you'd been struggling to find work. I'm assuming that has to do with that asshole, but couldn't you—"

Bastien didn't want to explain anything else about the situation that night. So, he did the only thing he could think of to keep Logan quiet. He kissed him.

Lifting to his tiptoes, he grabbed the back of Logan's neck and pressed his lips against Logan's. The initially hard mouth softened beneath his, and Logan rested his hands on Bastien's hips. A tongue came out and caressed Bastien's lips, and he immediately opened, his eyes closing and a moan leaving him when Logan took control of the kiss. Logan didn't wait. He plundered and explored. He tasted and took. Eventually, Bastien had to pull away to breathe, and he rested his forehead against Logan's. Their breaths mingled in the cool air, steaming away into the night sky.

Logan pulled back, lifting Bastien's chin to look at him. "Come home with me," he whispered.

Bastien didn't need to think twice. He closed his eyes and nodded. Logan guided him into the passenger seat, and he clicked his seatbelt closed. He had no idea if this was a good idea or not, but he no longer cared. For once, he wanted to do whatever he wanted, regardless of the outcome.

The journey was made in silence, although Logan threaded their fingers together during the trip, except when he needed to change gear. Bastien found he loved the little touches that had always seemed so sleazy from other people. Logan made everything different, and if that started a niggle of doubt to form, Bastien pushed it aside to think about another day. He was determined to just enjoy their night together, under no illusion that it would be more.

Tomorrow—or maybe earlier, depending—he would leave and look back on the evening fondly.

They pulled onto the driveway of a small, detached house in a nice neighbourhood. The outside had been painted white at the top with the brick exposed on the ground floor. From what he could see in the dimmed streetlights, the front garden was mainly grass with a few bushes.

His car door clicked open, and he jumped, shaking his head when he focused on Logan.

"Sorry, I was studying your garden."

He climbed out, and Logan shut the door behind him. The man grabbed his hand and tugged him towards the house, unlocking the front door, then locking it behind them again. Logan stared at him in the darkened hallway, barely any light from outside illuminating his features.

"Are you sure about this?"

The gravel that had entered Logan's voice was new but sent goosebumps all over Bastien's body. A full-body shiver wracked him, and he stepped closer.

"Definitely."

As soon as the word was out of his mouth, Logan removed their coats and shoes and slipped his arms around Bastien's waist, lifting him off his feet. Bastien instinctively wrapped his legs around Logan's hips as the man moved through the house.

"Let's get something to eat before we relax, shall we?" Logan said.

Ignoring everything except the man holding him, he held the back of Logan's head, pressing kisses to his face and neck and tugging on his earlobe with his teeth. "I'm fine. I want you."

"I want to make sure you eat."

"After. Promise."

Bastien had no idea how far Logan had carried him when Logan laid him down and rested on his elbows over him. He lost all track of thought because Logan took his mouth in a blistering kiss that made their first kiss back in the car park of The Bone Yard seem like a peck on the cheek.

They twined their tongues, stole each other's air and gripped each other tightly as Bastien's arousal rose, flowing over him like the relaxing music they listened to earlier, but with more fire. Their panting breaths and smacking lips were the only sounds in the quiet room, and Bastien loved it. He lived for music, but these sounds meant more than anything else.

Logan pulled away and rubbed his nose over

Bastien's as they locked gazes, a small amount of moonlight or the streetlights shining through the open curtains. He could feel Logan pressed tightly against him, his hips cradling Logan's body, his legs wrapped around Logan's thighs, his feet against Logan's calves. They were twined together, and neither seemed to want to let go.

"You are gorgeous," Logan murmured, nipping at Bastien's jaw when he tilted his head to the side.

The kisses skimmed across the skin of his neck and down towards his collarbone. Shivers wracked Bastien's body at the tenderness Logan showed, and Bastien slid his hands over Logan's head, scratching at the soft, short strands.

When Logan licked at Bastien's Adam's apple, Bastien groaned and gripped at Logan's shirt, pulling it further up until it was bunched under his arms. He needed to feel him, needed their chests to rub against each other. Logan pulled back, yanking his shirt over his head before resuming his caresses.

It wasn't enough. Bastien pushed at Logan's chest, and when he moved back, Bastien pulled his own shirt off, throwing it somewhere to the side before grabbing Logan's shoulders and bringing him close again. The moment their naked chests met, both groaned, and Logan took Bastien's mouth.

Bastien's hands roamed across the soft skin that encased such magnificent muscles, feeling the valleys and hills of his back. As his hands caressed lower, Bastien smoothed his fingertips along the skin just above the waistband of his jeans, causing Logan to shiver and pull away with a gasp. Bastien watched as his eyes fluttered and pleasure rippled across his face. He filed the sensitive spot away for later.

"More," Logan growled, pushing to his knees, his very alert cock pressed against the zipper, giving Bastien more of an idea of how much Logan wanted him. "You are too fucking sexy for your own good, Bastien. I don't know if I can go slow," he admitted, his forehead creasing.

"We can go slow later," Bastien said, lifting to his elbows.

Logan cocked his head, staring at Bastien as if to discern all his secrets. "You sure?"

"Fuck me, Logan. Fuck me hard and fast."

Logan groaned and reached for Bastien's zipper at the same time Bastien reached for Logan's. Their hands collided, but they fumbled around until their jeans laid somewhere else. Logan lowered to his body once more, moving their brief-covered cocks against the other as their kiss inflamed Bastien's nerves.

Logan grabbed hold of Bastien's head, gripping his hair and moving him to where he wanted him. His other hand slid between the mattress and his ass, squeezing his cheeks and pushing their groins closer.

"Stop!" Bastien gasped as he pulled away. "Fuck. I'm gonna come if you keep doing that."

"Isn't that the point?" Logan replied, kissing down the column of his neck.

"Not yet. I want you inside me."

Logan's rumble vibrated against his chest, and then he moved. Bastien's skin pebbled at the cool air that flowed over him with Logan's retreat. Within seconds, Logan was back, dropping lube and a condom beside them. Then he pulled his briefs down, and Bastien's eyes widened at the sight of the purple-headed shaft pointing at him. It wasn't overly large as he'd been expecting, but it was long. Bastien knew that would hit him in places many others had never tried to reach, and he licked his lips. Logan's hand encircled his cock, stroking up and down, the foreskin covering the head, then revealing it again.

"Take them off," Logan growled.

Bastien scrambled to do as asked, then returned to his position until Logan told him to get onto all fours. As he did, he gripped the sheets below him and lowered his head to rest on the mattress. His back bowed when Logan's hand skimmed down his spine, and he could feel the goosebumps lifting in his wake. His body was sensitive, but he needed…

"More!"

Bastien heard the distinct click of the lube container and felt the cold gel slide between the crack of his ass. Logan's finger, when he rubbed it against his skin, was warm in comparison. As Logan prepared him with a gentleness he was beginning to believe was second nature to the guy, Bastien bore down and pressed back, encouraging Logan to go faster.

"I'm ready. Fuck, please. I'm ready. I promise."

Logan rested the head of his cock against Bastien's entrance, then paused. Gripping his hips to stop him from impaling himself, Logan growled, "Are you ready? You wanted fast and hard."

"Yes, god, so ready!"

As soon as the words were spoken, Logan sank into him, not stopping at all until he was balls deep. Bastien's mouth was wide open, though no sound was exiting. He was full. So fucking full, and it felt delicious. He hadn't felt this for such a long time. Logan waited until Bastien caught his breath, then withdrew and drove in over and over.

Bastien had been right; Logan hit every nerve ending that was inside of him and had him whimpering into the sheets from the first thrust. His cock leaked profusely, and he wrapped his hand around it, stroking it in time with Logan's movements.

"Oh god!" he cried as Logan increased his speed. "Fuck, yes. Right there."

Logan held tighter to Bastien's hips, pulling him back as he slammed forwards, their skin slapping together loudly. "Come on, Bastien. Come for me."

Bastien stroked faster, twisting at the top to rub against the sensitive nerves and came within seconds. His vision whited out, and all he could do was feel the pleasure coursing through him and exploding out of him. Distantly, he heard Logan shout, then his arousal spiked when he felt Logan tremble against him, holding him close.

When his arms wouldn't keep him up any longer, Bastien dropped his upper body to the mattress, uncaring of the wet spot, and breathed heavily, trying to regain some semblance of control. His whole body tingled as Logan withdrew, and Bastien wanted nothing more than for Logan's body to cover him as he slept away the hours. But he needed to get up and leave.

He stayed still for a little longer, jumping when Logan began wiping his ass with a warm, wet flannel.

"Thank you," he croaked into the silence.

A kiss to the back of his neck was what he received.

CHAPTER SEVEN

LOGAN

Logan climbed onto the bed behind Bastien and dragged him towards him, so they were spooning, and Bastien was out of the mess he'd made. He'd get up and change the sheets in a bit, but first, he finished cleaning Bastien's front, then threw the wet cloth on the floor.

They'd both needed the release they'd strived for. He had a feeling that Bastien would attempt to go home now that it was over, but Logan planned on keeping him there for the night. He didn't like where Bastien lived, and it worried him. At least for that night, he could give him a safe home.

Feeling Bastien stir again, Logan pulled the covers from beneath them and dropped them over them both. The wet patch could wait for tomorrow. Luckily, it was on the top of the covers, not on the sheets they'd be sleeping on.

"I'd better—"

"If the next words out of your mouth aren't 'I better get some sleep,' then you should think again," Logan growled in Bastien's ear.

Bastien tensed for several seconds, and Logan wasn't sure which way he was going to go, but then he relaxed and gripped Logan's arm, tugging him closer. Logan breathed out slowly, relief softening his muscles.

"Sleep, Bastien," he whispered, pressing a soft kiss to the back of his head.

Logan knew when Bastien had fallen asleep because his body went completely lax, and the grip he had on Logan loosened. Despite being exhausted, he couldn't find the same peacefulness that Bastien had. His mind was warring with all different thoughts about keeping this man from ever being hurt again and how he could do that with the stubbornness that was ingrained in Bastien. He knew Bastien would never accept help if he thought it had to do with pity, but what could Logan do to show him that he cared about him without actually exposing his soul with that knowledge?

Then a thought crossed his mind, and he smiled.

Bastien was still fast asleep when Logan had woken that morning, so he decided to make an English breakfast. They had both worked through a lot of calories the previous night, and if Logan had his way, they would exercise some more later.

His plan for the day was tenuous at best, but no matter what Bastien decided once he knew Logan's surprise, Logan would adhere to his wishes. He hoped he wouldn't mind, though.

He had just finished adding the sausages to their plates when soft footsteps padded into the kitchen. Glancing over his shoulder, he smiled at Bastien's sleep rumpled form draped in the pyjama bottoms that he'd left for him. Luckily, they could be tightened; otherwise, Bastien would've never fit in them.

"Something smells delicious."

Bastien's morning voice was husky and unused but also sexy as hell, and Logan found his cock perking at the sound.

"Good morning. I've made a full English for us." Logan finished piling the plates and carried them over to the table.

Bastien's eyes widened. "I don't think I'm going to be able to eat all that."

Logan shrugged. "Just eat what you can. I wasn't sure what you liked, so I did a bit of everything. Leave what you don't want."

Bastien sat on the seat Logan held out for him, then Logan went to the fridge for orange juice and milk.

"Do you drink tea or coffee?"

Bastien's cheeks tinted. "Coffee would be great if it's not too much trouble."

"Not at all." Logan flicked the switch on the kettle, taking the juice and milk over to the table. "Help yourself. The coffee will be ready in a minute."

"I can do it. You eat your food before it gets cold."

"Bastien? Sit down and eat. Please."

Bastien gnawed on his bottom lip but nodded and sat back down. Concentrating on making the coffee, so he didn't seem like he was hovering, Logan relaxed his posture and breathed deeply. He could get used to mornings like that. The silence felt a little heavy, and he asked Bastien if he wanted some music.

"Sure."

Logan switched on the radio, turning it up enough that they could hear it, but it would not overwhelm their conversation. When Logan sat down again, bringing two cups with him, Bastien was tucking into his food.

"Did you sleep well?"

Logan knew he'd slept fine because every time

Logan had woken with the fear that Bastien had left, Bastien had been sleeping contentedly next to him.

"Yes, thank you. Your mattress is very comfortable."

Logan chewed the bacon, then said, "It is. It was one of the few expensive purchases I've made. My back would've never forgiven me had I bought a cheaper one."

The words, meant to make Bastien smile or laugh, instead made him stare at his plate, and Logan could've smacked his head at his insensitive remark. How could he have forgotten that Bastien hardly had anything, and what he did have was possibly "cheap and cheerful" as the saying goes? The food turned to ash in his mouth, but he continued to eat.

Hopefully, his surprise would help Bastien to relax more. Either that or push him further away.

They made small talk while they ate, and Logan found out a few small things about his guest: Bastien enjoyed reality TV and reading. When they had finished, Logan piled their plates in the sink, ready to wash later, and turned to Bastien, who looked decidedly uncomfortable now he had nothing to do with his hands.

"Come on." Logan held out his hand to Bastien, then pulled him to his feet. "Time for a bath."

"A bath? Don't you mean a shower?"

"Nope, I think we both could do with a long soak in a bath."

Logan tugged him along behind him up the stairs and into the guest bathroom. He didn't take baths very often, hence why he had a shower in his master bathroom, but the guests had a bath with a shower overhead. Letting go of Bastien's hand, Logan pushed the plug down and turned on the taps. He reached for some bath bubbles he knew he kept under the sink and emptied a hearty amount into the water. A giggle had him examining Bastien.

"What?"

Bastien tried to withhold his smile, but it spread across his face, although slightly hidden by his hand. "Do you want some water with your bubbles?" He laughed, his eyes sparkling with merriment.

"I might not want any water with my bubbles." Logan grinned, then shrugged. "I might have put a bit too much in. Never mind. If we drown, they may have to have a bubble party first to find us."

Bastien's mouth curled. "Definitely a possibility."

Logan held out his hand to Bastien when the bath was ready, holding him tight, so he didn't slip as he climbed into the tub. As his body descended into the bubble mountain, Bastien giggled again, batting them away to be able to breathe. Once Bastien was situated, Logan ensured there were flannels and soap within reach and stepped in behind him, groaning as the warmth from the water seeped into his body. He didn't think he had used that many unusual muscles the night before, but he hadn't had sex in a while and must've been out of practice.

When he was seated, he pulled Bastien back against him, moving the bubbles out of the way, allowing him to see his companion.

"Are you okay?"

Bastien moved his head to look to the side and up at Logan. "Yeah, I'm good. It's nice to just relax for a bit."

Logan slid his hands up and down Bastien's arms. "Kade told me you worked with Deacon. That was how you knew him. Is he the reason you can't work?"

Bastien was quiet for a moment, then nodded. "He's blacklisted me from being able to do makeup for the people I used to work with. It wasn't just him. I had several contacts I did makeup for when they needed someone. As soon as it happened, I wasn't being contacted. I called a few of them up asking if they had anything, and they all declined, saying they wouldn't need my help anymore."

Bastien shrugged, although Logan could see he was hurt. He pressed a kiss to Bastien's forehead.

"It's why I've been picking up more shifts at The Bone Yard."

Logan nodded. "I figured as much. You need to take care of yourself, though. You'll end up fainting if you don't eat enough. I know food can be expensive, but you still need to eat."

Bastien sat upright, the bubbles sliding down his back. "I know that! It doesn't make it any easier when bills come first; otherwise, I won't have anywhere to live."

Logan dragged him back against him. "I'm sorry. I know you're trying. I apologise." He clenched his jaw, then added, "Do you not have any family around who might help you?"

Bastien shook his head, and Logan thought that was the only answer he was going to get until Bastien said, "My family threw me out at fourteen, and I've been on my own since. I'm fine. I've been able to live how I want to live, and that's all that matters. I refused to hide then, and I refuse to hide now. I wouldn't be true to myself if I had hidden it and lived in shame."

They both sighed, then laughed, lightening the mood. Bastien threaded their fingers together, resting them on his stomach, and they sat in silence. All Logan could hear were the small breaths coming from each of them and the quiet pop of the bubbles. It was serenity at its finest.

"I suppose we should get clean," Logan said when the water started to cool.

"If we have to," Bastien replied in a sleepy voice.

"Now that most of the bubbles have gone, do you

want to stand up, and I will rinse you off with the warmer water from the shower?"

"All right."

Bastien stood, the water cascading off him. Logan had never seen a more beautiful sight than that of his dancer standing wet and naked in front of him. Unable to resist, Logan pulled himself to kneeling, splashing a little bit of water over Bastien's lower half, then encircling his dick. By the time he'd stroked twice, Bastien was hard and getting harder by the second. Fingernails bit into Logan's shoulders as Bastien trembled.

"Shh. Let me take care of you," Logan whispered, licking across the tip of Bastien's cock.

He lapped around the head, making sure to flick at the underside, which made Bastien's shaft stand taller. Tasting the remnants of the bubbles, he sank down until his nose hit the skin, and then he rose again, marvelling at the smoothness of Bastien's body. His hand slid across the man's skin, feeling no hair along any part of it. As he continued his ministrations, Bastien's whimpers of need were music to his ears, increasing whenever Logan plucked at his nipples or squeezed his ass. Bastien's hips bucked against his mouth, and Logan grabbed hold of his waist and stared up at him. When Logan stopped moving, Bastien's forehead wrinkled until Logan pulled at his waist, indicating he wanted Bastien to move.

Tentatively at first, Bastien thrust his hips into Logan's mouth, Logan providing suction where needed. After several strokes, Bastien increased his speed, grasping at Logan's head as he drove forward over and over again.

"Fuck, Logan. I'm gonna come!"

Logan blinked up at him, hoping he'd understand that Logan was completely on board with that idea, and seconds later, Bastien released into his throat, moaning and shivering as he cradled Logan's head in his hands. Logan swallowed every drop, licking Bastien clean again and held him tightly to keep him upright.

"Right," Logan said hoarsely, "Now to get you showered off."

"What about you?" Bastien asked, pointing at his cock.

"I'm good for the moment. I'm happy to take a rain check for later?" He raised his eyebrows and grinned.

"Sure." Bastien laughed.

The shower warmed them up again, and then they headed back to the bedroom. Logan's plan was either going to fall apart now, or it was going to go as planned.

"I have a surprise for you if you are willing to trust me a little?" he said once they were dressed.

Bastien stopped with one arm in his t-shirt and one

arm out, staring at Logan through narrowed eyes. "I'm not a huge fan of surprises."

"Are you willing to try? For me?" Logan gave his best puppy dog expression and grinned again when Bastien rolled his eyes and continued to dress.

"Okay. But don't make it a regular thing."

Bastien paused after his words, and Logan thought he knew what had crossed his mind—he'd made it sound like they were going to do this again. Logan would love to, but it was up to Bastien. He wouldn't force him into anything. Even what he had planned today would only work if Bastien agreed once they arrived.

"Agreed. Do you have a jumper or anything to keep you warm? We have to drive there."

Bastien shook his head, and Logan headed to his drawers to see what he could find. After rummaging around, he pulled out a jumper he hadn't worn in years because it was too small for him. It was still likely to drown Bastien, but at least it was warm.

Raising his eyebrows, Bastien took the jumper and held it out, smirking as he read the slogan out loud, "'A fairy good detective.' Interesting." He slid it over his head and mussed up his hair again.

His stomach fluttering from the sight of Bastien in his jumper, Logan ignored the need to wrap his arms around the man and headed to the door. "It's time for a field trip."

They descended the stairs, where Logan found his phone, wallet and keys, then passed Bastien's coat to him before donning his own. He was nervous, surprisingly. Locking the door behind them, he opened the car door for Bastien, receiving a smirk in return.

"Such a gentleman."

"I try. Plus, my mother would kill me for not doing it."

Bastien laughed as Logan had wanted him to, breaking the tension a little so that when he climbed in, they were able to begin talking as usual. He pulled out of his driveway and pointed the car towards his destination, fingers gripping the steering wheel tightly.

"Are you not going to tell me before we get there?" Bastien asked, his hands clenched between his knees.

Logan could tell he was nervous, too; therefore, he decided to explain and hope Bastien was still willing. His chances were slim, though.

"We're going to my parents' house for Sunday dinner."

Silence met his proclamation, and Logan waited with bated breath. He didn't have to wait long. They were five minutes from Logan's parents' house when Bastien told him exactly what he thought of his brilliant idea.

"What the ever-loving fuck! Logan, stop the car right now! I'm not going to your parents' house!"

Logan inhaled. "Why not?" he asked calmly. "They

are happy to have extra people visit them. They won't mind at all."

Bastien huffed, "I'm sure they won't, but we're hardly at the stage to meet the parents, and besides, I'm not dressed for it."

"You look amazing." Logan glanced at him, loving the feeling that flowed through him when he saw him in his jumper.

"Thanks, but I look a mess. What will they think?"

"They will think that you are a nice man who needs feeding up."

"So, that's why you're taking me there. To make sure I eat more. Well, no, Logan. I want to go home."

Logan sighed and pulled onto his parents' driveway. "Can I ask a question before I turn the car around?"

Bastien gaped at his surroundings. "This is where your parents live?"

"Yes. They've had this house for years. The house has everything we needed as a big family—lots of room and space to play outside where we couldn't get into too much trouble."

Bastien raised his eyebrows. "Really? I can't see you being a troublemaker at a younger age." He squinted.

"You'd be right. I wasn't. I was the one making sure the others behaved." Logan snorted. The front door opened, and his mother came to stand on the porch, a towel in her hands and a frown on her face.

"I can see some similarities between you," Bastien murmured. "What did you want to ask?"

"Why do you not want to meet my family? Really?"

Bastien inhaled deeply, staring across the stone driveway to where Logan's mother waited. "They might not like me," he whispered.

Logan's heart broke at the tiny voice, and he grabbed Bastien's hands with his. "They will love you. What's not to love? You're snarky, cocky, sassy, opinionated, loud and more." He went on quickly before Bastien got the wrong idea, "Everything we are."

Bastien glanced at him. "What are your family like?"

Logan knew instinctively what Bastien was asking. "I came out to my parents when I was thirteen, and Casey followed a few years later. Neither of us were condemned in any way. In fact, my father said that we were brave for being open about it and that we should be proud of ourselves. Casey is now in a relationship with Luke, and they have been together for several months. Neither of my parents are bothered about the fact that we are gay. All they care about is that we're happy."

Bastien bit his lip and transferred his gaze back to Logan's mother. "Okay," he murmured. "No guarantees I'll last long, though."

Logan wanted to kiss him, but he thought that might set him off, so he squeezed his hands instead.

"Thank you. You won't regret it. Hmm." Logan paused. "You might actually." He laughed before climbing out of the car, leaving a mumbling Bastien behind. Jogging around to the other side, he opened Bastien's door and held a hand out for him.

Bastien hesitated then placed his hand in Logan's, exiting the car. Logan slammed the door shut and threaded their fingers together, pulling Bastien close. The brave man beside him trembled a lot, Logan was concerned his legs wouldn't hold him up, but he managed to step closer and closer until his mother was in front of them.

"Hi, Mama." Logan bent to press a kiss to his mother's cheek.

"Logan. I'm so glad you could make it. I was worried you had been called into work."

"No, not today. I'm having a day of rest. May I introduce Bastien? Bastien, this is my mother, Christine Taylor."

Bastien side-eyed him and held out his free hand to his mother. "Nice to meet you, Mrs Taylor."

"Oh, please, call me Christine. I'm too old to stand on ceremony." She pulled on Bastien's hand and hugged him before transferring the hug to Logan. "I'm glad you're both here. Lunch is almost ready."

She spun and headed back into the house, and Logan stayed where he was, turning to Bastien. "Are you okay?"

"Nope. No. Not at all. No way. But, yes, I'm fine." Logan snorted, and Bastien frowned. "I said all of that out loud, didn't I?"

"You did. It's your choice. We can leave if you want to. I don't want you to feel unwelcome."

"That's just the thing. Your mother made me feel… like a person. Like I mattered, even with that short embrace." It was more than he'd received from his blood family.

Tears pooled in Bastien's eyes, and Logan stepped in front of him, shielding him from the undoubtedly shrewd gazes of his siblings. He cupped Bastien's jaw in both his hands, wiping the overflowing tears with his thumbs.

"You do matter, Bastien. You matter a hell of a lot more than I expected you to," he whispered, dropping a kiss on Bastien's bruised lips. He couldn't believe he'd spoken the words he'd decided to keep to himself aloud.

Bastien clung to his coat and burrowed his head under Logan's chin before letting go and breathing deeply. "Okay. I'm ready."

"Good job because we couldn't wait any longer."

Logan groaned at his sister's words. "For god's sake, you guys. At least let us get through the door!"

"Nope. Now, who is this gorgeous piece of eye-candy?" Alice said, smacking her lips together.

Logan slid his arm around Bastien's back. Even

though he knew Alice was messing around, he made it clear Bastien was with him. Catching the smirks on his siblings' faces, he knew the message had been received.

"Bastien, these are some of my siblings." He pointed to each in turn. "Alice has the potty mouth, Claire pretends to be angelic but is not, and James is a troublemaker."

"Liam, Penny, Robert, Casey and Luke are inside," Claire said.

"Yeah, they are the patient ones!" Logan grumbled.

"You have eight siblings?" Bastien whispered to him, gripping Logan's hand tightly.

Logan chuckled. "No, I have five siblings. The others are partners. You'll be fine. Come on. Mum and Dad will save you if I can't."

They headed into the house, and the smells of a beef dinner wafted down the hallway, making Logan's stomach growl. Bastien giggled beside him, and Logan smiled at him as they walked into the kitchen. His mother had placed the plate of meat in front of his father to slice and waved at them to sit. Logan pulled a chair out beside his father, indicating for Bastien to sit, then took the seat next to him.

"Dad, this is Bastien. Bastien, my dad, William."

"Nice to meet you, sir."

His dad waved a hand, which unfortunately had a knife in it at that moment and had Bastien flinching away. "Now, don't go calling me sir or Mr Taylor. We don't go on titles here. William is just fine by me." The knife returned to the meat, and Logan breathed deeply, sending an apologetic look in Bastien's direction. "Do you like beef, Bastien?"

"Yes, sir—uh, William. I love it."

"Fantastic. You can have first dibs as you're our guest today."

Logan squeezed Bastien's hand, wanting him to know there was nothing to worry about. Everyone else came into the room and settled down. The table had been extended to fit everyone since their family was growing significantly. "Bastien," he whispered. "I'm going to introduce you to everyone else, but don't worry if you don't remember their names. You have lots to remember; they only have one. Okay?"

He saw Bastien swallow hard and nod.

"Right, everyone, this is Bastien, Bastien, this is Liam, my brother, and Penny, his wife; Claire, you've met, but this is her husband, Robert; Alice and James you've met; Casey, my brother and his partner, Luke."

Luke smiled. "Nice to meet you, Bastien. It's a lot to take in, but I was in your shoes not long ago. You'll get used to us all."

"You wait until both their families get together," Claire said, pointing at Casey and Luke. "Then, that's a lot."

"There's only fourteen of us then, not including the parents," Casey argued.

"Yeah, but it's probably thirteen more than he needs to worry about," Liam groused.

"Ah, quit ya grumbling." Claire threw a napkin at Liam. "You're spoiling our fun."

Logan could feel Bastien trembling, thus kept hold of his hand, even when their plates were served. When everyone was settled down, they thanked their mother and father for providing their lunch as they had been taught from a young age, then dug in.

"So, Bastien, what is it you do?" Alice asked.

Bastien's hand reflexively clenched on Logan's. "I'm...um, I..."

"Take a breath, Bastien," Logan murmured. "He's a dancer," he intervened, not wanting Bastien to feel uncomfortable.

CHAPTER EIGHT

BASTIEN

Bastien had never been around so many people who were intent on finding out about him. He was used to the scrutiny when he was dancing, but all the customers cared about was whether or not they could see more than they should. This was different. These were people who wanted to know about his personal life. These were people who were staring at him, waiting for his answers. He couldn't let Logan answer all the questions.

"I also do makeup, though not as much at the moment."

"Really? Mama, did you hear that? Maybe Bastien would do our makeup for the charity event?" Claire gushed.

"Claire! Why not ask him yourself instead of talking as if he isn't present."

Claire's cheeks reddened, and she apologised to him, "I'm sorry. I didn't mean that the way it sounded." Bastien nodded in reply. "We have a charity event next weekend, and none of us are brilliant at doing makeup. We do okay, but we're not professionals."

"Oh, I'm not a professional. I don't have certificates or anything like that," he stammered, getting flustered.

Christine chuckled. "We don't need certificates, Bastien. We need someone who can make an old woman like me look twenty years younger."

"You don't need to look twenty years younger, Christine, but I can do that if you so wish."

Christine flushed, and Logan squeezed his hand again, making Bastien realise they were still holding hands.

"Suck up," Logan murmured under his breath with a smirk on his face.

Bastien nudged his shoulder with his own and smiled.

"That would be amazing, Bastien. Do you really not mind?" Claire asked.

"Not at all. Oh, it would depend on what time you need me, though." His heart clenched at the thought of missing his shift at the club.

"We could do any time, really. The event starts at eight, so it would need to be before then, obviously," she said.

"Yeah, that's doable."

"Woohoo!" Claire shimmied on her seat, her husband rolling his eyes at her. "What? You know I hate wearing makeup just as much as putting the damn stuff on."

"I do, yes. I also know you love wearing it despite what you say." His grin softened the gruff expression he sported with his thick salt and pepper beard. Claire's cheeks pinked again, and she glanced at her food.

The conversation continued throughout the meal, where Bastien ate more than he should've, but he didn't care. He was more content than he expected to be and even managed to let go of Logan's hand to cut their food. Logan's family was amazing. They hadn't blinked at Bastien being brought into the fold, but with a family that size, an extra mouth was probably not a problem.

This was the type of family Bastien had always dreamed of. He would've loved to have his family support him unconditionally, but the moment everything became "real" to his parents was when it ended. They were able to hide his "eccentricities," as they called it, while they pretended to be ignorant, but as soon as the words had been spoken, that was it.

Bastien rolled his lips inwards and stared down at his food, moving the remainder from side to side as he recalled the awful names his parents had called him.

"You okay?" Logan's voice made him jump, and his fork clattered against the plate.

He tried to smile. "Yes, I'm good."

"Liar," he whispered in his ear. Bastien shivering at the warmth of his breath. Louder, he said, "Well, I think I've given Bastien enough of a taste of my family for one day. We're going to head off."

"Hold on one second, Detective. Where do you think you're going?"

Logan grimaced when his mother spoke. "Come on, it was worth a try!" he whined, winking at Bastien before standing.

"Get your backside over here."

Bastien watched with a small smile as Logan joined his two brothers to wash the dishes. He began to stand so he could help when Christine placed her hand on his arm.

"Can I have a quick word, Bastien?" she murmured.

"Of course." His heart raced at the thought of what she would want to talk to him about, his thoughts immediately going to what his own parents had said, and he braced for whatever she was going to throw his way.

"Logan is a very protective man. He loves nothing more than taking care of people, especially when it comes to those in his family." She turned her gaze from Logan's back to Bastien. "I can see you mean a lot to him, which means you mean a lot to us." She slid her arm around his shoulder. "If you ever need anything at all, you come to us. If you can't get to Logan, you find one of the others or us. Understand?"

Bastien swallowed hard, trying to stem the tears that threatened to leak. His nostrils flared as he tried to thank her, but nothing came out.

"Oh, sweetheart." She pulled him into a hug. "You have us now. No matter what happened to you before, you have us. Let us be your family because I can tell you never had a good one," she whispered.

Bastien closed his eyes and let his tears flow quietly as she held him, rocking him side to side until he stopped trembling. He couldn't believe that she'd figured him out so quickly when he'd expected her to tell him to leave Logan alone, that he wasn't good enough for him. Which he wasn't.

Christine pulled back, and he wiped at the tears on his face, smiling tremulously. "Thank you," he croaked.

"You are very, very welcome, my dear." Christine smiled at him, rubbing her palm against his cheek. "I can tell you're going to be good for him."

He didn't have to heart to tell her that they weren't anything more than sexual partners. It seemed too crude to mention that to Logan's mother.

"Everything okay?" Logan asked.

"Yes. We're all good, aren't we, Bastien?" Christine stood and embraced her son, whispering something in his ear. His mouth twitched, and his cheeks darkened with a hint of a blush, which made Bastien curious as to what was said. Maybe he'd ask Logan later.

Logan released his mother and held out a hand to Bastien. "Time to go, if you're ready?"

"Sure." Bastien gripped Logan's hand, not wanting their day to end but knowing he shouldn't get too close to the man. Logan could easily break his heart, and then where would Bastien be?

They said goodbye to everyone and climbed back into Logan's car. As he reversed out of the driveway, Logan said, "It wasn't too bad, was it? I wasn't sure if I'd made the right choice for you."

"It was amazing," Bastien whispered, his emotions too close to the surface again.

"I'm glad you had fun."

"Your family is fantastic. Huge but fantastic." He chuckled. "I can see where you get your sense of humour from."

"Yeah, Dad has a lot to answer for, or that's what Mama always says." Logan laughed.

They lapsed into a companionable silence for the remainder of the journey back to Logan's. Bastien had left his bag there; he intended to grab it and head home. However, when they pulled into the drive, Logan cut the engine and glanced over at him, the heat in his eyes unmistakable.

"When are you working next?" he asked, his voice deep, vibrating along Bastien's spine.

"Tomorrow night." Bastien swallowed, trying to wet his dry mouth.

Logan nodded once, then climbed out of the car, circling the vehicle to open the door for Bastien. Gripping his hand tightly, Bastien followed him to the house, his bottom lip burning with how hard he was chewing at it.

Once the door was closed behind them, Logan backed him towards it, his hands resting either side of Bastien's head. Their mouths were separated by only a few scant millimetres, and Bastien's breathing increased as desire coursed through him. His chest heaved, his head dropped back to rest on the door, and his eyes locked with Logan's as he tilted his head minutely to the side, wanting what Logan was advertising.

He lifted his hands, which had been hanging by his sides, and gripped Logan's belt loops to stop himself from falling due to light-headedness.

"Stay with me," Logan whispered across his skin, the heat from the words caressing his lips. "Not just now. Move in. I have space."

As if a bucket of cold water had been thrown over him, he shivered and pushed Logan away. He'd been stupid to think that Logan wanted *him*. Instead, what Logan wanted was the chance to 'save' someone. He'd seen Bastien's living arrangements and had decided that Bastien was his next project. Just what Bastien needed.

He crossed his arms over his chest and lifted his head. "Sorry, but no thanks. I'm managing just fine where I am."

"I know you are, but if you stayed here, it would make things easier for you. You'd be able to save some of your money if you weren't paying rent."

Bastien snorted. "And how would I be paying you? In sexual favours? I'm a stripper, not a whore."

He darted around Logan and headed for the stairs, intent on grabbing his bag and leaving. Entering the bedroom, he spared a glance at the state of the bed, then turned his head away, focusing on finding his bag and all his belongings. He hadn't taken much out of it, but he threw everything that he had back into it. He would return Logan's jumper at some point.

Turning to exit the room, he jumped when he saw the man leaning against the doorframe.

"You going to stop me from leaving?"

"Of course, I'm not! I don't *want* you to leave, but I won't stop you if you want to." His voice had lowered at the end, his gaze shifting to the floor.

"I want to. Thank you for everything. I appreciate you taking me to see your family. It was nice."

Bastien tested the waters and stepped forward, releasing the tension in his muscles when Logan moved to the side. He carried on along the hallway and down the stairs, pausing with his hand on the door handle.

"I'm assuming you won't let me walk, so I'll wait by the car."

He headed out of the house and waited by the car as he said he would. When the car beeped open, Bastien got in, slamming the door behind him and waited for Logan. The detective locked his house, climbed into the car and started the engine without saying a word.

The silence this time was deafening. There was nothing comfortable about it, and Bastien itched to fill the void, but there was nothing he could say to make this any better without getting angry. He didn't under-stand why Logan would ask such a thing of him. Every time he thought about Logan's words, he felt his pulse trip and increase and his stomach harden. He thought they had become friends at least, but apparently, Logan just saw a charity case.

When he pulled up at Bastien's apartment building, Logan left the car idling, for which Bastien was grate-ful. He swung his legs out of the car, then hesitated before saying, "You don't need to save me, Logan. I'm fine as I am."

He stood, closing the door with a soft click, and headed home.

After entering his apartment, he threw his bag to the side and wandered to the kitchen for a glass of water. Downing the whole glass in one go, he put the glass down and rested his hands on the counter, lowering his head between them. He wanted to know why people kept letting him down. Did he have too high expectations of the human race? He'd thought his belief in others had been knocked enough when his family let him down, but maybe he'd begun to raise them again when he'd brought others into his life.

That was a mistake he would not make again. There was no one but him in his life, and that was how it was going to stay.

Bastien lost himself in the music, spinning, swaying, gyrating to the music as he tantalised the customers into tipping him more. He was exhausted, but he didn't show it. His dances were the highlight of his night, and he'd even managed to create a couple of new ones that he would be learning over the next few weeks. He couldn't do the same ones all the time; the customers would soon get bored.

After having left Logan outside his apartment, Bastien had done nothing but work, eat and sleep, and not necessarily in that order. He'd been trying to think of a way to get out of the job he'd inadvertently agreed to do this weekend but couldn't think of anything that wouldn't sound awful.

He didn't want to spend any more time with Logan's family than was necessary, but he also didn't want to let them down at the last minute. It was two days until he was supposed to be making them up for their charity event. Every time he thought about it, he felt sick that he would have to spend time with Logan again. He'd not even seen him in the club since that weekend.

"That was one heck of a performance, B," Rafferty said, catching him as he returned from the stage.

"Thanks," he puffed, his breathing heavy and sweat dripping off him. "Definitely worth it." He held up the tips the customers had thrown his way with a small smile.

"I'd say."

Bastien opened his locker, tucking away the money before grabbing his toiletries. He needed a shower, which he could fit in before his final dance. It seemed pointless having a shower before dancing again, but Bastien preferred feeling clean, and if it meant showering six times a night, he would.

"You never told me that guy had so much stamina, B," Cassidy drawled from behind him, and he glanced over his shoulder to him, raising his eyebrow in question. "You know, that guy you gave an hour-long lap dance to. His stamina is…wow."

Cassidy fanned himself. "I could barely walk afterwards."

Bastien's stomach threatened to bring up the water he'd drunk after the show, but he refrained by breathing through his nose and facing his locker again. Clenching his jaw, he ignored the words.

"What? Can't we compare?" Cassidy's silky-smooth voice grated on Bastien's nerves, and he turned and crossed his arms, pursing his lips.

"Compare what?" He feigned ignorance.

Cassidy licked his lips and moved closer, lowering his voice, although not nearly enough for it to be a private conversation. "Compare the size of…you know."

"You can compare what you like, Cass. He's nothing to me except a way to make money." The words had bile rising, and he forced it back down, refusing to rise to Cassidy's attempt to rile him.

Cassidy's eyebrows rose. "Really? Well, in that case…all the more for me." He rubbed his hands together, a look of glee on his face. "I bet you couldn't keep him entertained anyway. That's why he's had to look elsewhere." Cassidy spun around and headed back to his locker.

"You know nothing," Bastien spat, wishing immediately after that he had kept his mouth shut.

"Oh, don't I?"

The calculation in his eyes had Bastien instantly

worried, but he couldn't do anything about it. He was at his wits' end.

"No, you fucking don't, Cassidy. You pretend to know everything, but in fact, you know nothing. You pretend like you're the queen bee around here, but guess what?" He stepped closer until he had Cassidy backed against the lockers. "You're just a minion. I'm queen around here, and I will continue to be while there is still breath in my body. You are nothing. Do you hear? Nothing. No one will miss your cattiness when you get too old or tired to do this anymore. No one will miss how you treat them. No one will miss anything about you because…You. Are. Nothing. You're worthless. If Logan gave you any bit of his time, you should be immensely grateful because I'm telling you, it won't happen again."

Bastien's temperature was through the roof, as was his heart rate. He needed to cool down, so he turned away from Cassidy to grab his toiletries. Unfortunately, Cassidy had other ideas. A hand gripped his hair and yanked him backwards, sending him to the floor. His hands immediately gripped the wrist to try and keep his hair from being torn out.

Cassidy pulled and tugged, dragging Bastien across the floor. He finally stopped the momentum and crouched down beside Bastien, still holding his hair.

"I'm worthless, am I? What does that make you then?"

"Better than you," he gritted out, unwilling to give in. His rage exploded out of him, and he let go of Cassidy's wrist, wrapping his hand around Cassidy's neck instead, rearing up to take Cassidy to the floor.

There was a commotion around them, but Bastien was too engrossed in trying to stop Cassidy from tearing his hair out. He had no intention of killing the guy, but he couldn't think of any other way to get him off him. His whole body was trembling and vibrating with anger, mainly due to the images his mind had conjured up of Logan with Cassidy. He knew it was unlikely to be true, but he couldn't help his traitorous heart from feeling hurt by the possibility.

"What the hell is going on in here?"

Hands grabbed at Bastien, and he let go of Cassidy's throat, scrambling to his feet when the person behind him pulled him up. Cassidy had been left on the floor, coughing and looking mightily messed up. Bastien tried not to smirk too much at that. He failed if Cassidy's glare was any indication.

"What the hell, B?" Rafferty yelled, and Bastien glanced at him. "What the fuck happened?"

"Ask him," Bastien said, lifting his chin towards Cassidy.

"Cassidy?"

"He called me worthless."

"I also called you nothing, don't forget." Bastien knew he was digging his own grave, but he couldn't have Cassidy feeling like a winner. "It might have had something to do with him trying to bait me."

"I succeeded; I didn't try." Cassidy smirked.

"Right, Cassidy, Bastien, into my office now. Emory and Cody, I want you to finish up your dances and then come and see me. I want to know what went on here. Tell Van to see me as well before he leaves, please."

The guys nodded, and Cody's wide eyes met his. Bastien shrugged. He had no idea what kind of trouble he would be in. He'd never made a step wrong before this. Cassidy went in front of Rafferty at his request, and Bastien took up the rear. When they arrived at Rafferty's office, Rafferty pointed Bastien to the chair outside and took Cassidy inside. He had no idea how long he sat there, but when the door opened and Cassidy stomped his way to the stairs, Bastien smiled.

"B! In here, now!"

He entered, seeing Rafferty leaning back in his chair, looking at him with a shake of his head. "Your turn. Tell me what happened."

"Cassidy was shooting the shit. Pressed a button I'd held in check for far longer than I should've. He got what he deserved, although he started it."

Rafferty sighed. "Talk me through it."

Bastien went through everything in as much detail as he could remember, wincing slightly when he recalled the words he'd said to Cassidy. They reminded him too much of the words his family had flung at him.

Nothing. Worthless. Perverted. Evil.

He blinked away the memories of his mother's voice, clearing his throat and focusing on Rafferty again.

"I know what I should do." He stared at Bastien. "I should suspend you, but I know how much you need the money."

Bastien sat taller. "If you think I should be suspended, so be it. I'm fine."

"Stop talking shit, B. I know you need the money. Stop pretending that you don't. Cassidy has been suspended for two weeks, but…" he continued before Bastien's glee became too apparent, "as far as anyone here knows, I will be docking your money for this and giving it to Cassidy for loss of earnings. You will not tell anyone that *I* am paying him. This stays between these four walls. Do you understand?"

Bastien couldn't believe what Rafferty was offering. "Why?" He felt pressure behind his eyes.

Rafferty leaned forward, resting his arms on the desk. "Because you need a break, kid, and Cassidy had it coming. I'm not blind or deaf to what goes on here, no matter what people think. I know everything that happens, and Cassidy is a prick." He winked at him. "And you're too good for business to let go."

Bastien chuckled, looking down at his hands,

grateful for the attempt to lighten the mood. He breathed deeply, trying to stop any emotions from leaking out. That wasn't how he rolled when he was working, although Rafferty had seen more of it than most.

"Go and get a drink from the bar, then head back to the dressing room. I believe you'll have just enough time to change and tidy yourself up before your final dance."

"Yes, sir."

Rafferty winced. "Don't sir me, B. You make me feel old."

Bastien grinned and stood. "You're only as old as you feel, Rafferty."

"Holy fuck…" was all Bastien heard as he closed the office door behind him. He grinned again and descended the stairs, heading to the bar. He'd have to get Nolan to check on Rafferty later to make sure he hadn't had a heart attack like he said he would. Bastien had never said his full name to his face before.

"Hey, Nolan."

"Black! What was all the drama? I saw Cassidy fly out of here like there were hellhounds on his heels."

"A little disagreement. Can I have an orange juice, please?"

Nolan went about getting his drink, saying, "A *little* disagreement? Only a little? It looked much worse than that."

"Well, there was a little hair pulling, a little choking, a little tumbling. Not much to say, really." Bastien smiled when Nolan turned to him with raised eyebrows.

"Not much to say, he says. You're no good as a gossip."

"If you want to find out, ask the boss. I about gave him a heart attack before I left his office. He made need resuscitation." When Nolan frowned at him, Bastien bit his lip. "I called him Rafferty to his face."

"Jesus, Black! Why'd you do that?"

"Because I could."

He grabbed his plastic glass full of orange and headed to the dressing room. His locker had been closed for him, and hopefully, the money was still inside. He wouldn't put it past Cassidy to swipe all his tips as penance for losing out on work.

Sitting on one of the wooden benches, he sipped his drink, the sweetness tasty on his tongue. For the next two weeks, he would have an easy time at work without that bitch around. Now, if he could just sort out the rest of his life, he'd be good.

CHAPTER NINE

LOGAN

Logan had not made much progress in his cases. He hated it when that happened, but there always seemed to be a short window where nothing seemed to go anywhere: no lead, no evidence, nothing. Then all of a sudden, something would click, and things would get moving again.

Unfortunately, they were in the stalemate section right now, and Ava was as pissed off with it as he was.

Nothing had turned up in the stalker case, and Henry had fun making them the butt of the jokes in the station because they had believed her story, when in fact, there was no stalker to be found. Henry didn't have proof that there wasn't a stalker, but Logan didn't have proof that there was. It was frustrating.

He stared at the computer screen, wishing the information would change to something he could work with when his name was called. Lifting his head, he saw Anita wave him over. Hustling to her, knowing not to keep her waiting when she was working at the front desk, he stopped in front of her.

"What's up?"

"Chief told me to give this case to you. A woman has just come in off the street claiming she has a stalker. Chief thought it might relate to your case."

Logan's heart rate picked up. "Where is she?"

"Room six."

"Thanks, Anita. I'll just grab Ava, then we'll be there."

He hurried away to the coffee machine, knowing Ava was picking up a couple of cups for them. "Let's grab another one. We have someone to talk to."

Logan explained what Anita had said, and they stopped at their desk to get what they needed and strode to the interview room the woman had been placed in. He knocked on the door first, announcing his presence before entering, holding it open for Ava, who walked a cup of coffee over to the woman.

"I didn't know if you drank coffee, but I thought it might help your nerves a bit," she said, sitting opposite the woman.

Logan took a seat to Ava's left and studied the slender woman. She appeared to be in her mid-to-late twenties with long blonde hair with blue eyes. Her face was round, and she dressed in what Logan would have called an outfit his grandmother would've worn. It reminded him of something from Winona Conrad's case, and he made a mental note to check it out.

"Good morning. I'm Detective Sergeant Logan Taylor. This is Detective Constable Ava Walker. Our colleague mentioned you think you're being stalked. Can you expand on that a little?" He opened his notepad to a clean sheet and waited for her to talk.

"I believe I am, yes." Her hands wrung together as if she couldn't keep them still. "I can feel the hair on the back of my neck lifting when there doesn't seem to be anyone around. I hear footsteps behind me, but when I turn around, no one is there."

"Okay. Can you tell us about one specific incident, Miss…?" he prompted.

"Um, Rebecca Jarrod, and yesterday, I finished work as normal at five o'clock and walked to my car in the car park. I work at a women's clothing store in the shopping centre. It was still light, and I thought I'd be fine." She cleared her throat. "As I got to the multi-story car park, I heard footsteps behind me, speeding up, sounding like they were getting closer. I didn't want to turn around, so I walked faster until I was jogging to my car. I got in and locked the doors, but no one was there. No one walked past the car or anything. Then while I was driving home, I saw the same car behind me most of the way until I turned onto my street." She raked her fingers through her hair. "It sounds stupid, saying it out loud, but I swear, it's not my imagination."

"It's okay. What I need you to do is give us as much information as you can about what you've experienced, and if you can remember any significant details about times or days or the car make or model. Anything at all, no matter how small."

"All right."

"We're just going to step out while you get the information down, but be assured, no one will harm you here."

"Thank you."

They left her writing down the information, and Logan led the way to the chief's office. He knocked on the open door and explained to him the basics of what the woman said.

"It doesn't give you much else to work with, does it?"

Logan shook his head. "It all depends on what information she can remember. Even one small detail might give us a clue."

"It seems too coincidental to have two stalker cases within such a short period," Ava commented, a frown on her face.

"I agree," Bryan said. "Keep on it. See what comes about."

When they retrieved the information from Rebecca Jarrod, they showed her out and gave her their contact details in case anything happened. Checking through the information she had provided didn't net them anything straight away, but they began the investigation into the different times and places she mentioned, seeing if there were any CCTV cameras in the area. If they could get some footage, they might be able to compare it to Winona Conrad's case and see if any of the people show up on both feeds.

By the end of their shift, they were no closer to finding any information.

"You're going to the charity event tomorrow, aren't you?" Ava asked as they trailed towards the exit and their respective cars.

"Yeah, Mama insisted."

"Me, too. I guess I'll see you there, then. I'm glad to have a Saturday off for a change."

"Are you going to come out with us tonight?" he asked.

Ava shook her head. "I have plans."

"Same old story." He grinned. "I hope whoever he or she is, they are worthy of your time and secrecy."

Ava grinned, waving her finger in his direction. "You're not getting any kind of information from me that way, Detective Taylor. You've taught me well."

Logan laughed, shaking his head at her. "Damn. It was worth a try."

"Good night, Logan."

"Night, Ava."

He watched as she climbed into her car and went on her way before he carried on to his car. There was just enough time for a shower and change of clothes before he headed to Crush. Tonight was the owner's birthday, and it was set to be amazing. Tom had only recently come clean about being the owner of the bar, having not wanted anyone to treat him differently, which Logan could understand. It had finally come out when Charlie had taken over as manager at the ripe old age of twenty-one.

Charlie deserved the promotion, having worked extremely hard as a bartender for three years before being awarded the position. It had helped Tom out at the perfect time, too, because his girlfriend had given birth to their second child.

Crush had been the epicentre of their group for the past couple of years, and Logan loved it. The whole place was welcoming and growing from strength to strength with every day that passed. He didn't know what he'd do without the place.

When he entered the bar an hour later, the party was already in full swing. Often, when there was a party, Tom or Charlie would close the place down to make it a private affair, but on occasion, the birthday boy or girl would request it be kept open to the public. Tonight, Tom had kept it open to the public, and it proved how popular the place was because it was heaving.

The roar of conversation was louder than the music that played, but he didn't mind. He headed towards the usual place their group congregated and saw several of his friends already waiting.

"Logan! Hey, man, nice to see you again," Charlie said, standing for a half hug.

"Where is the birthday boy? Don't tell me, he's working?" Logan only half-joked.

"He wouldn't dare today." Charlie nodded with his head towards the other guests, and Logan saw Ginny, Tom's fiancee, sitting next to Tom and Josh, Charlie's boyfriend.

Logan chuckled. "Ah, I see. She's not going to let him out of her sight then. I bet it was difficult for them to leave the kids with a babysitter." He sat next to Charlie, resting the gift bag between his legs until Tom was free from his current conversation.

"Tom didn't want to. He threatened to cancel the whole thing. The only way he would agree to come was if the babysitter and the two kids were upstairs." Charlie pointed a finger to the ceiling.

Tom had a small apartment above the bar, which various people used on occasion. It made sense that the parents wanted their kids close, especially as their youngest was only two months old.

"Ginny obviously put her foot down."

"Naturally." Charlie laughed, then glanced over his

shoulder. "Oh, I've got to check on something. I'll be back in a few."

"Hey, just the big brother I wanted to see," Casey drawled from beside him.

Logan whipped his gaze around, his stomach churning. He loved his brother, but it was always hard to see him after what he'd been through. He saw Casey a lot at their family dinners and social responsibilities, but it was still difficult. He had to forcibly push everything down and try to act normal around him when, in fact, he wanted to run so Casey wouldn't have to deal with him. "Hey, I didn't realise you would be here."

"And I bet if you did, you would've avoided me." Casey stared at him, hardly blinking.

"Of course, I wouldn't. I wasn't expecting you to be here because you have new additions to your family. How are the beasts?"

Casey backhanded his shoulder. "They are not beasts!"

"Bet you won't be saying that when they don't listen to you." Logan snorted.

Luke piped up, "We already say that when they don't listen."

Casey glared at his boyfriend. "They're loveable. They are learning to relax in their new home. There is bound to be a period of adjustment. They'll be fine."

Logan raised his hands. "Okay, okay! They're adorable. How's that?"

"Much better." Casey sipped his water. "Are you looking forward to tomorrow night?"

He grimaced and rolled his eyes. "Not really. These events mean I have to wear my monkey suit, and I'd prefer not to. I don't know why they're so uncomfortable," he complained.

"Maybe you need a bigger size," Casey quipped.

Logan pressed the palm of his hand against Casey's forehead and pushed him backwards, laughing when he knocked him into Luke. "The suit fits just fine, asswipe."

"So you say."

"Hey, guys. Thanks for coming." Tom sidled up beside them, giving each of them a hug and thanking them when he was passed gifts. "I appreciate you being here."

"I hear you have the little ones upstairs," Logan said with a smile.

Tom curled the corner of his mouth. "Why not have everyone I cherish close by?" He glanced across at Ginny. "It's not a complete celebration if you can't have your family nearby."

As the minutes turned into hours, Logan began to acknowledge what had happened to their group of friends. Most had paired off and found their other half, leaving very few of them single. He slumped into his seat, staring off into the crowds and sighing. He hadn't realised how much he'd been missing until he found

Bastien. Or at least, he'd thought he'd found something with Bastien.

He'd thought he was acting kind, offering Bastien a place to live without the fear of being turned out if he couldn't make the rent payment, but Logan hadn't realised how Bastien would take his words. He certainly hadn't meant them as anything more than trying to help, but he supposed he could see how Bastien would think he was only interested in saving him. His mother probably hadn't helped with that, no doubt telling Bastien how protective he was of everyone.

An apology was needed, but Logan had no idea how he was supposed to give Bastien one when he hadn't summoned up the courage to speak with him.

His visits to The Bone Yard had been carefully done to ensure he'd stayed in the shadows when Bastien had been on stage, and he'd taken off before the man started his floor circuit. He wasn't trying to protect him, but he also didn't want to see him hurt. The thought reminded him of what he'd seen the previous night.

Bastien had gone off stage, and Logan had seen several staff members run backstage after a few minutes. Shortly after that, Cassidy followed by the owner, and then Bastien had traipsed up the stairs to the second level, where Logan assumed the owner's office was. Unsure what had happened, he sat at the bar, nursing a glass of orange juice, waiting to see if anything would transpire.

Several minutes later, Cassidy had stormed down the steps and into the back area, then a few minutes after that, marched out of the club with an angry expression. When he'd seen Bastien start down the stairs, he'd quietly slipped off the stool, leaving his money under his glass, and hustled out the building.

He was none the wiser as to what had happened, but he was curious enough to consider approaching Bastien tomorrow and asking.

"Earth to Logan. Come in, Logan." He flicked his focus to Casey and raised his eyebrows. Casey nodded in the direction of Tom and Ginny, who were standing at the head of the table, talking.

"—everyone for coming tonight. I really do appreciate you taking the time to celebrate with us. It's not every year you turn forty-one." Tom glanced at Ginny, who grinned. They didn't have a care in the world that there was nineteen years difference between them and wasn't that the best way to live?

Ginny wrapped her arm through her fiance's arm. "If you could all raise your glasses, bottles, cups, mugs, whatever you're holding—no, Max, that does not include the plate of food you have." Everyone chuckled. "Let's wish my amazing fiancé a wonderful birthday."

"Happy birthday!" cheered the whole group.

Logan was happy for the man, but he also felt envious. Not only of Tom but the whole group. With a tightness in his throat, he worked his way through the crowd to grab Tom into a hug, wishing him well, then said he was heading home.

"Already? I expected you to be one of the last standing," Ginny said.

"Nah, I've grown up now," Logan joked.

"I'll believe that when I see it," Tom quipped.

Logan laughed, waved goodbye and grabbed his coat before leaving. The air was fresh with a warmth that had been hovering all day. He hoped it held until after tomorrow because he would hate to have to escort his family to the charity event in the pouring rain. He made a mental note to check the weather forecast in the morning in case he needed to figure out a different solution for if the heavens opened.

Thankfully, the weather did hold, and the following day dawned bright and clear. Logan knew he was anxious about the day, not only because he hated the events which required him to dress up smartly, but because he knew he'd potentially see Bastien again. He couldn't figure out the best course of action, and that, for a police officer, was frustrating.

He hung his suit by the front door, ready for when he would leave for his parents' house and wandered to the kitchen for breakfast. Despite having been awake on and off throughout the night, he was alert enough to go without his usual morning coffee. He might regret the action later, but he'd prefer not to feel jittery after having several cups. No doubt, there would be plenty at the house if he needed a pick-up later.

His phone pinged as he was buttering his toast. Using his pinkie finger, he unlocked it and scrolled to the group chat.

JAMES: Why the hell do we have to wear these suits. It makes me look ten years older. That's not a good thing for a twenty-two-year-old!

A bubble came up saying someone was writing, so Logan waited until he'd finished getting his breakfast together before checking it again. When he sat at the table, he propped his phone in front of him and opened it, grinning before taking a bite.

CASEY: It's to make us look smart for our parents' sake. By ourselves, we just look like fools playing dress-up.

ALICE: You guys look cute. Stop worrying.

JAMES: Cute, she says. I don't want to look cute, Al, I want to look hot! How else am I going to find someone?

CLAIRE: What happened to what's-her-face? April? Andie?

JAMES: *Apparently, I wasn't cutting it as boyfriend material. She broke it off last week.*

ALICE: *Why didn't you tell us?*

CASEY: *What the hell, James! You should've rung.*

CLAIRE: *I'll kill the bitch!*

LOGAN: *No talk of killing when your police officer brother is on the chat.*

CLAIRE: *You'd get me off the hook.*

LOGAN: *Not on your life, missy. You do the crime, you do the time.*

CLAIRE: *How unfair is that? What's the point of having a brother who can help if he won't help?*

JAMES: *It's fine everyone. Just means I can start looking where I hadn't been before. If you know what I mean.*

ALICE: *Just be careful. Don't fall into the single man's trap.*

JAMES: *What's that?*

CASEY: *What trap?*

LOGAN: What?

ALICE: The single man's trap? When a man has just come out of a relationship and wants to hump everything that has legs.

JAMES: Hmm…

CASEY: Hmm…

LOGAN: Yeah, that's about right.

CASEY: That's what I was going to say.

JAMES: Yeah, I'm feeling it. I'm gonna say…I'm going with it!

CASEY: LMFAO.

LOGAN: Jesus fucking christ.

ALICE: James! I didn't say that so you would go and do it! Idiot!

CLAIRE: Go sow your seeds, little brother. Just keep those seeds in their casing.

JAMES: Oh my god!

CASEY: I'm dying here.

LOGAN: Claire, that was priceless. LMAO.

At that point, Logan had to sign off. He could barely eat his toast because he was laughing so hard that tears were welling up. He was very glad his parents weren't on the group chat. They'd be both freaked out and happy there was talk of safe sex.

Finishing off his juice, he took his plates to the sink to wash them off, then headed to the living room. He had time to catch up on some of his programmes before he had to leave for his parents'.

Wanting nothing more than for the time to move quickly so he could get to see Bastien again, he started the first episode he needed to watch. If he was lucky, he could watch at least five episodes before his mother started calling him about where he was.

He was more than lucky. It was six hours before his mother called him. He had around twenty minutes left of the final episode, and then he'd be caught up. He told his mother he would be there within the hour.

Once the show finished, he closed everything up, made sure he had everything he needed to take with him—not that it was a huge distance to drive if he forgot anything—then headed to his parents' house where six cars were already parked in the driveway. He parked behind Casey's car and grabbed his belongings, carrying them carefully into the house, shouting a greeting as he entered.

"Finally!" his mother said. "What took you so long?"

"Mama, it's fine. We have plenty of time."

"But Bastien isn't here yet."

His heart jumped at the name. "He will be. He said he would, and he will." As soon as he said the words, he heard a car pull up. "This is probably him now."

"Go greet him. I'll take these." Before he could protest, his mother had taken what was in his hands and waved him away. "Go! He might need help carrying stuff."

At that, he exited the house again, seeing Bastien climbing from a taxi. Logan wished Bastien had called him for a ride, but then, he probably should've offered to pick him up. Striding over to him, he smiled as he said, "Hi."

"Hey."

"Do you need help carrying anything?"

"I'm good. I only have this case and a small bag."

"Let me carry the case for you," Logan offered.

Bastien hesitated, then handed it over. "Thanks."

They headed to the house, Logan indicating for Bastien to precede him, then winced when his mother's exuberant greeting reached Logan before her physical presence came.

"I'm glad you're here. I can't wait to see what

magic you can create. We've set up in Claire's room since it has the best natural light. It's not every day we get dressed up nice and pretty; this is a special occasion. Oh, I'm glad you could help."

Her mutterings continued as they all ascended the stairs to Claire's bedroom. Logan followed them into the room, noting the space that had been made around the room—it wasn't technically Claire's room any longer because she lived with her husband, but his mother wouldn't dream of changing anything about any of their rooms. He still had some of his high school posters on the walls, and he made a note to get rid of them at some point.

He waited for direction about where to put the case, then stood there mighty uncomfortable as they began talking about makeup colours and foundations and something else that sounded very much like they were building something rather than putting makeup on.

"Right. Time for you to shoo," his mother said, waving her hands at him. "We need the space to do our thing. The boys are downstairs somewhere."

Logan backed out of the room, sparing a glance at Bastien, who was too busy talking to Claire to notice, then his mother shut the door in his face.

"Charming," he muttered.

He trudged down the stairs, heading for the noise at the back of the house, letting himself onto the back porch. James, Casey and Liam were throwing a rugby ball between them while his dad and Robert, Claire's husband, were sitting enjoying a cup of coffee if the smell was any indication.

"Logan! Come join us!" James shouted, ducking when the ball flew towards him. "Hey, I wasn't looking!"

"You snooze, you lose," Liam taunted.

"I'm good. I'll sit here with the sensible folks."

"I don't know if I like the idea of being sensible. Maybe I should go and play some ball," his dad said, a twinkle in his eye.

"You're sensible only because you have coffee," Logan replied.

"Good save," Robert stated with a smirk. He'd been with their family long enough now to know how they were with each other.

"How are things with you and your boyfriend?" his dad asked.

Logan's eyes widened, and he cleared his throat, unsure how to answer the question. "A little rocky, but we're still finding our feet," he hedged.

"Well, you make sure you hold onto that young man because he's perfect for you."

"I'll try, Dad. I'll try," he murmured.

If only it were that simple.

CHAPTER TEN

BASTIEN

"Oh my! How do you do that?" Claire leaned forward, inspecting her face in the mirror, lifting her hand to it but stopping just shy of touching. "I look flawless."

"You're beautiful, even without makeup," Bastien said, squeezing her shoulder.

"Thank you. It hardly feels like I'm wearing anything. Whenever I do this for myself, all I can feel is something thick and uncomfortable against my skin. This feels…light."

"Sometimes, less is more, but it also helps to have the right makeup, too. I can leave you a list of what I used so you can get yourself some if you want to."

"I know what you should do!" Claire turned, a smile breaking out across her face, making her look radiant. "You should do makeup tutorials for people—

either online videos or face-to-face ones. People love learning how to do things like this. You'd make a fortune, and that's just from the people we know." Claire laughed, her mother joining her.

"You're not wrong, sweetheart. It's an idea if nothing else, Bastien."

Claire turned to the mirror again, and Bastien's heart swelled at the joy on her face. This was why he did makeup. This right here. The happiness, joy and euphoria that swept across people's faces when they saw what he could do.

"Who's going next?"

"Alice," Christine said.

"Mama, I thought you wanted to go first so you could get yourself ready?" Alice said.

"I've changed my mind. I want to see both my girls have their makeup done first. Everything else can wait. I'm enjoying myself."

"As you wish."

Bastien waited until Alice had settled herself in the seat, pulling her robe tighter against her neck. He glanced at her reflection in the mirror and guessed at the colouring he'd need. Searching through his case, he found a couple of similar colours, then squirted some onto the back of his hand. Holding them up to her skin, he chose the nearest, then set out a few more essentials he needed.

"So, Bastien, how are things going with Logan?"

Bastien's hands trembled at the man's name, and he turned to his case to hide his face, which was no doubt filling with colour despite his own makeup. "Um, we're all right."

"*All right?*" Claire sighed. "What has he done?"

"What?" He glanced over his shoulder, forgetting about hiding his face. "He hasn't done anything," he said, wincing when his voice sounded less than convinced.

"He's my brother. I know when he's being an ass."

"Claire! Maybe Bastien doesn't want to talk about it with us. We are Logan's family, after all."

"No, it's not that…um…" He blew out a breath. "I've not really talked to him since we left here last weekend."

"So, I ask again. What did he do?"

Bastien concentrated on moisturising Alice's face and gathering his thoughts before having a huge debate with himself over whether he should be discussing this with Logan's family. He didn't have anyone else he could use as a sounding board, and if he mentioned it to Cody, the man would just persuade him to move in with the guy.

"Logan knows my…situation and asked me if I wanted to move in. He meant well, but…"

"His execution could use some work," Logan's mother finished.

Bastien caught her gaze in the mirror and nodded minutely.

"As I said to you last weekend, he's very protective of his family and friends and not only because he's a police officer. He takes far too much on his shoulders, especially now."

Bastien cocked his head. "Why now?" Christine inhaled and blew out the breath, and Bastien could tell her emotions were simmering beneath the surface. "Sorry, it's none of my business."

"But it is," she replied. Claire wrapped her arm around her mother's shoulder, and Christine stared up at him as she explained what Casey had been through. When Christine stopped, placing a hand over her mouth, Claire continued the story. "When Casey was kidnapped, Logan lost control. He overturned every stone, he called in favours, he sent out feelers. He did everything he could to find Casey."

"Was he okay?"

Bastien wasn't sure which man he was talking about and had given up doing Alice's makeup while they were telling the story.

Alice continued the story, "Casey was mostly unharmed, thankfully, but Logan hasn't been the same since. He's distant, barely sees us some weeks. It's as if he's withdrawn within himself."

"Until you," Christine said, a smile lighting her

face. "The Logan we saw on Sunday was the Logan we'd been missing since that happened."

Bastien cleared his throat, trying to swallow the lump. "I don't know if I can be that for him. We are so different and come from completely different backgrounds. I don't know—"

"You don't have to know, Bastien. Just follow your heart."

He stared at the floor. "But my heart has led me wrong so many times before. I can't trust it anymore." He glanced up at Logan's mother, her features swimming before him.

She stood and stepped towards him, enfolding him in her arms. "And that's fine. Do what you must. What is best for you. If it's meant to be, it will be. You just may need to do some healing yourself before you can help someone else heal." She smiled at him, cupping his cheeks. "Come on. Let's have some fun." She turned to Claire. "Put some music on, my dear. Let's make this into a party."

Claire jumped up and skipped over to her old-style hi-fi. "Let's see if this still works." She fiddled with it a little, then some music came filtering through the speakers. "Woohoo!"

The songs were cheesy pop songs from years back, but Bastien didn't mind. Despite the emotional story he'd been told and his own admissions, he loved being with this amazing family. If only he could keep them as his own.

Dancing, singing, laughter and information over-load had been his best friend for the past three hours, and he was worn out. He packed everything back into his case, making sure not to leave a mess by wiping up stray powder with baby wipes—they were the secret tool of his trade. They cleaned *everything*.

He would be heading home soon because he had to work that night, but Christine, Claire and Alice wanted him to see the finished product, so to speak. He was excited. He hadn't had the chance to dress up in a long time, except for when he danced, and he wasn't sure if that was dressing up or dressing down.

The door opened, and Claire wandered in, a huge smile on her face. Similar expressions graced the other two women's faces.

"Wow, you look fantastic!" Bastien gushed.

Claire was wearing a bright red, floor-length, strap-less dress with a ruched side at the waist. Bastien had helped twist her hair up into a messy bun on top of her head. Alice flaunted a straight, emerald green, knee-length, halter-neck dress with a high ponytail. Christine wore a deep blue, ankle-length dress with a lace bodice that covered her upper arms.

"Just wow! You're going to knock everyone's socks off tonight."

"Oh, I do wish you could come with us!" Claire said.

Bastien smiled. "Maybe next time." Then he remembered something. "Oh, I do have something for each of you, but you don't have to accept it if you don't like it. It's absolutely fine."

Blushing, he reached for the box from his case and rested it on the bed, sitting beside it. Taking a deep breath, he opened the chest and drew out three necklaces, draping them on the bedspread in front of the women.

"Oh my god! They're gorgeous!" Alice said, leaning forward to run a hand over one of them. "Did you make these?"

Bastien felt his cheeks heat again when he nodded.

"This is…" Christine came forward. "We would love to wear these. How much are they?"

"No!" He waved his hands. "They're a gift."

"No, no, no. I won't accept these unless you allow us to pay for them. I can guarantee that you will have more business than you could want when people see us in these tonight. But I can't in all conscience recommend you when I've not paid for them."

Bastien could see the same resolute look on each of

the women's faces, and he sighed. Choosing a price lower than what he would've put them online for, he told them the prices. Christine narrowed her eyes at him.

"That's my price," he said, clenching his jaw to stop himself from upping it to make her happy. He'd still make a profit on the jewellery, but not much.

She nodded once. "I will get William to transfer it before we leave…if you could give me your bank details?"

"Sure."

That settled, he helped put them on and admired how well the diamond designs looked with their dresses. He'd purposefully chosen stones that were colourless because he hadn't known what colour they were going to wear.

"Thank you," he said when he'd finishing clasping Christine's necklace together.

She turned to him. "You're welcome. Now, do you have any business cards?"

Bastien chuckled. She was like a dog with a bone. "Yes, Christine. I have some."

"Good. We're going to need plenty." She smiled with a little shrug.

Bastien couldn't help but laugh again. There was something about this family that pulled him in. He couldn't help but love them.

But where did that leave him when things with Logan didn't work out?

He finished packing his case and called for a taxi. It was an expense he couldn't afford, but with the extra money coming from Christine, it was one he could deal with. As he headed out to the driveway to wait, he heard Logan call his name. He paused but didn't turn around.

"I'm sorry, Bastien."

Logan came to stand in front of him, and Bastien lifted his gaze and withheld a gasp. He wore a black tuxedo with a pristine white shirt and black bow tie. His hair was still in his usual just got out of bed look, which Bastien agreed looked best on him. He looked gorgeous, though his forehead was furrowed.

"I am so sorry for what I said. No, that's not right. I'm not sorry for what I said, but how I said it. Please don't think I only want to save you. I do want to help you out, but it's because I care for you that I want to do that. I don't do subtle as you well know, and sometimes, it comes out wrong."

"No shit." Bastien crossed his arms and stared at the man as if he couldn't get enough of him.

"I am sorry. Even though I would like you to move in to make you feel safer, it's your choice, and I can't make the choice for you no matter how much I want to."

"And if I moved in? What then? You'd flaunt every

hook-up in front of me?" He lifted his chin, not backing down from the eye contact.

"Why would I do that? I haven't had a hook-up for months. I don't have hook-ups very often, and I certainly wouldn't be hooking up if we…" Logan trailed off and fidgeted with the sleeves of his jacket, his eyes lowered.

The taxi he'd ordered drove up the driveway, and Bastien picked up his bag and case, ignoring what Logan had almost said.

"What happened at The Bone Yard the other day?" Logan asked suddenly.

Bastien raised his eyebrows, then rolled his eyes. Of course, Logan knew about that. He'd probably been keeping an eye on him when Bastien didn't realise it, which should've been creepier than it was.

"I don't know what you mean," he answered, fighting to keep his face straight.

"Well, Cassidy stormed out of the place after some sort of altercation backstage and a trip to the owner's office. That doesn't sound like nothing." Logan slid his hands into his trouser pockets, appearing casual, but Bastien knew he was anything but.

"Cassidy shouldn't have tried to overthrow the queen bee." Bastien cocked his head, crossing his arms over his chest once more.

Logan's mouth twitched, but a smile never came,

much to Bastien's disappointment. "I see. I assume you taught him a lesson."

"You know what they say about assuming," Bastien said as he headed to the taxi. "Have a good evening, Logan."

He climbed in and settled himself for the journey home. Staring out of the window at the buildings that passed by, he thought back to Cassidy's words the night before and then what Logan had said about not having hooked up for a while. What did he call what they did then? Bastien had assumed it was a hook-up, but maybe it meant more to Logan. He inferred with his words that he hadn't slept with Cassidy—although he hadn't known that was what Bastien had inadvertently asked. Why would Cassidy say they had?

Bastien closed his eyes, shook his head and huffed a laugh. To piss him off. Shame it backfired on Cassidy, though.

When the taxi pulled up to his apartment building, Bastien leaned forward to pay, but the driver waved him off.

"It's already been paid for. Have a good day."

Bastien hesitated for a second, then climbed out, dragging his case and bag with him. Logan must've paid for it, the sneaky bastard.

He grabbed something quick to eat and changed clothes before walking to work. With the extra shifts he'd been picking up and the fact Rafferty was such a good guy and was not taking money off him, Bastien had been able to get enough food in for a couple of meals a day and still afford his bills. He needed to find somewhere else to live. This apartment was vastly overpriced for what it was, but Bastien had been turned away by all other places when he first started searching.

Maybe he should consider Logan's offer.

It was something to think about now he knew *why* Logan had offered, although he refused to listen to Logan's voice saying he cared about Bastien. That way lay trouble.

Entering The Bone Yard, he strolled to the dressing room, stopping when someone called his name.

"Oh, hey, Miles. How are you?"

"I'm good, thanks, Black. Um, I have a mix-up of some songs that I thought you might want to try some new dances on. You don't have to, but I had thought about the new routines you've done lately and wondered if some different music specifically for you would be good. It's okay if you don't want it—"

Bastien interrupted him before he talked himself into yet another circle. He placed a hand on Miles's arm. "I would love to listen, even if I don't use them. Thank you for taking the time to do it."

Miles's cheeks flushed, and he glanced at the floor. Bastien leaned in for a one-armed hug, then took the proffered music and waved before heading to the dressing room. He was the first one there;

therefore, he took his time getting ready, grateful to have the time to himself. While he was always alone when he was at home, he never felt lonely when he was the only one at work. He had no idea why. Maybe it was because he knew other people were in the building.

"Hey, B. How are you?" Cody's voice startled him out of his musings, and he chuckled to mask his surprise.

"Hey, Cody. I'm good. I didn't realise you were working tonight." He picked up his lip gloss and painted his mouth.

"I swapped with Ash. I have a parent thing tomorrow. They threatened to disown me if I didn't attend."

Bastien's heart thumped hard at the implication, but he breathed his way through it. He knew it was a throwaway comment, but it still hurt to think of his parents.

"It just means you get to spend the evening with me." Bastien preened.

Cody laughed. "Definitely a better choice than Cassidy."

Bastien glanced at Cody with a small frown. "I don't know if that's a compliment or not."

They both laughed, then carried on getting ready for their first dance. Bastien was up first, and it gave him a little thrill knowing that some of the customers were here to see him and only him. It was a shame that

Logan wouldn't be there that night. Bastien had a feeling it was going to be a memorable one.

Bastien collected the tips he'd received from his locker and counted them out. He'd been right. That night, he'd made more than he had the whole week prior, and it meant he could put it aside for his rent for the following month and not have to worry about scrimping and saving. He would be able to afford to get some of the jewels he'd wanted for another necklace.

Giddy with relief at his change in circumstance, he tucked everything inside his bag, wrapped a coat around him and waved to everyone before leaving the almost empty club. He had never been bothered about walking alone at night. He'd seen worse things in his time on the street before he'd managed to find a place to call home. Dark corners and shadowy alleys were not bothersome to him.

But it felt like someone was following him. Bastien had always tried to trust his instincts—not his heart, his instincts—and it was telling him that whoever was behind him with their heavy steps did not mean well.

Slipping his hand into his coat pocket, he brought out his phone and pretended to message someone while keeping his ears out for a change in the pace of the person behind him. He didn't want to chance trying to take a selfie, but he did lift the phone a little higher, hoping to see who it was and that the person behind couldn't see what he was doing. It didn't make any difference, though. It was too dimly lit to be any good.

Continuing at the pace he'd been walking, he crossed over the road. He had no idea how long he'd been being followed, and he refused to change his routine in case the person figured out that Bastien knew he was behind him. It was in his own best interests to pretend everything was normal. With a thundering heart, he trudged home, letting himself into the building, then his apartment as if nothing was amiss.

As soon as his door was closed, he dropped his bag to the floor and peered through the peephole. No one walked past, so he breathed out a sigh of relief. He needed to make sure he was aware of everything around him from now on. Being a stripper had its perks, but it also had its downsides. One of those was that some customers believed being a stripper meant he was always up for a good time.

Bastien shook his head and headed for his bed. He grabbed the jar that he kept his tip money in from its hiding place, emptied all but a couple of notes from his bag, then hid it again, enclosing it away from sight.

Changing into his joggers and a hoodie, he added

fluffy socks to the mix and traipsed to his kitchen area to grab something small to tide him over until the next day. Although he had more money, he wasn't going to waste it.

He filled a glass of tap water and carried it to the table, scanning over what he had to get done. He hadn't had any orders for a while, which meant he needed to get some new pieces up on the site as soon as possible to gain some people's interest. Hopefully, Christine was right, and some of her friends would be interested in his custom pieces. That would be a nice bonus.

Pulling out his tools, he began placing the jewel in the position he needed it to be, then sealed it in place. His movements focused him completely, and it wasn't until his back began to ache that he realised he'd been working for over an hour. He stretched his arms above his head and moved from side to side to manoeuvre his spine. The action reminded him of Miles's music, and he stood to fetch it from his bag. He'd give the first one a listen to and see what he thought while he was getting ready for bed.

He put the CD in the player he'd bought when he first moved in. He often found older CDs in the charity shop to help give him ideas for dances. As the low bass beat began, he paused and closed his eyes, letting his body feel it. That main beat was enticing for sure. When the sound of other instruments was added, he wasn't as sure, but that low beat still held him entranced.

His body followed the beat, and he danced for no other reason than he wanted to because the music called to him. When it stopped, he was breathing heavily but excited. He'd speak to Miles about it tomorrow because if he could strip some of the additional sounds, it would work brilliantly as a deep, sensual routine.

Smiling to himself, he switched it off, then flicked off the living area light before heading to his bedroom. He stripped off and slid, naked, under the covers.

As tired as he was, especially after that unexpected dance, he was too wired to sleep. He lay on his back and stared at the lights flickering across the ceiling as cars drove past. The noise from his neighbours was more apparent now that his apartment had gone quiet, and voices rose in argument from above him and in sounds of pleasure from next to him. He rolled his eyes. They were always at it, didn't matter the time of day or night.

The thought made him think of Logan. He wondered whether they'd all had a good night at the charity event. He glanced over at his bedside table, then flicked the sheets back, stumbling to his bag to retrieve his phone. Plugging it in to charge, he slid under the covers once more. He checked the screen and saw he had five messages.

Frowning, he opened it, then smiled when he saw pictures from Logan. The first two were of his sisters and mother, the third one was of his brothers and father, the fourth one was of Logan and his parents, and the fifth was of Logan by himself.

Bastien stared at him, seeing the twinkle in Logan's eye and the slight smile he always wore when he thought about something funny. He zoomed in on the man's face, wishing there could be more for them than just friends, but he didn't know how. They were too different. If their relationship ever became public knowledge, Logan would be laughed out of the police force—a police officer with a stripper!

Bastien sighed and turned off the phone, putting it back on the table. He would've loved to try, but he didn't understand how they could work, especially with Logan being as protective as he was. Bastien would no doubt be put under lock and key, and there was no way he'd put up with that. They'd be arguing before day one was over.

The thought of the place to live, though. That kept circling in his head. It would be nice not to have to worry about certain things, and Logan's house was so quiet, he'd be able to get his work done without interruptions.

He sighed again and rolled over to the opposite side, plumping the pillow beneath him. How could he even think he'd be able to have a relationship with the man?

He wasn't worthy of Logan's love. Bastien's own parents had told him, and he was inclined to believe them. All he had to do was look at where he lived.

CHAPTER ELEVEN

LOGAN

His phone woke him in the early hours of the morning, and Logan reached for the bedside table where he kept it. It went silent, then began ringing again. Rising to his elbows, he pulled the phone to his ear.

"Hello," he croaked.

"Logan. Get your ass up. There's a been another murder."

His chief's voice woke him immediately, and he scrambled up before it had even registered. "Who?"

There was silence on the other end of the line, then Bryan said, "The woman who came in to report the stalker a couple of weeks ago."

"Fucking hell!" Logan wanted to throw his phone across the room but refrained. Instead, he tugged on his clothes while keeping the phone between his ear and shoulder. "Any other information?"

"Not yet. I called you first. I'll call Ava in as well and get her to meet you at the woman's address."

"Sure thing."

He ended the call as he ran down the stairs, shoved his feet into his shoes and left the house, slamming the door behind him. As he started the car, he repeatedly swallowed at the thought that he'd done nothing that could've helped her. He'd tried. Of course, he had, but it hadn't been enough.

Parking his car on the street outside the woman's house, he climbed out, clipping his badge to his belt hoop as he'd not put a belt on in his rush. He identified himself to the police officers on the scene, then stepped into the property after putting on some shoe covers. Keeping his hands loosely by his sides, he moved closer to the victim. The image of the two dead women would haunt him for years to come, and all because he couldn't do his fucking job.

Logan heard Ava at the door and waited for her to join him. He began scanning the room as he did every time he entered a crime scene, trying to see if there was anything out of place. It was difficult to tell sometimes because he wasn't familiar with the room, but like with the previous victim and the knife that was unexpectedly on the mantelpiece, there might be something similar.

"See anything?" he asked Ava.

"No, nothing."

"Me neither. Let's have a look around." He headed down the hallway to the kitchen and felt like he'd stepped back in time. "Wow."

Staring around the room, it was like he'd been transported to the 1970s. The cupboards were lime green with cream counters and gaudy black and white patterned tiles on the backsplash. It hurt his eyes just looking at it. It also reminded him of something.

"Both victims were women in their late twenties, both filed a complaint about a stalker, and both have retro-designed homes, be it on purpose or by inheritance, and both have antiques throughout their houses. This connects them in my book," Logan stated, pushing back the need to rage at himself for his incompetence.

"Same here. That's three similarities. I wonder if there are more," Ava said.

"We need to get photographs of both women's houses and see if there is a connection with something going on in Cambridge or the surrounding areas. Maybe a convention or a big event or something similar."

"Wasn't there something in the paper about an antique fair this month?"

Logan shook his head. "I've no idea. I don't look at the paper."

"How do you find out what people are saying about your cases if you don't read the newspaper?" Ava asked with a small smile.

"I ask you."

They continued through the house, making notes about anything of significance, then returned to the main room, where the forensic pathologist was still examining the scene.

"Anything to give us?" Logan asked her.

She shook her head. "No. There doesn't seem to be anything out of place on her body, except for the broken neck as with the other victim. There are no other contusions visible at the moment, but whether any show up back at the examination room…" She shrugged. "I'll keep you posted as always."

"Thanks, Kat."

They headed back out into the fresh air, and Logan realised how musty it smelt in the house. He made a note of that, too, in case it was relevant.

"I suppose this is going to be a long night and day for us," Ava asked, shielding a yawn.

"Yep." Logan grimaced and scratched at his cheek. "How can this happen? There was no evidence to assume she was in trouble, and even taking her at her word, we found nothing. It doesn't make sense."

"I'll get started checking out the antique fair and that area. I'll let you know what I find."

"Sure. Thanks, Ava. I'll see you at the station in a bit."

When he was back in his car, he pointed it towards the station but pulled over after several streets, clenching the steering wheel and breathing deeply to stop the wave of nausea. His stomach churned with the thought that he was losing his touch, and people were suffering for it. He allowed himself several minutes to get himself back under control and continued to the station.

He strode directly to his desk, dropping down into his seat and pulling up the screen he needed on the computer. Inputting the details he had onto the database, he decided to check over known associates for both cases and compare them. There may be something they'd missed previously.

Several hours later, and too many wrong turns for his liking, he stared at the photographs of the victims, swallowing hard when their faces morphed into Casey's. He blinked repeatedly, trying to wipe away the vision. He hadn't even been able to save his brother. How could he save these women?

"I've nothing left, Ava. I've turned over everything, and there's no common ground between them other than what we said earlier."

"Well, look here. Where's your mojo now, Taylor?"

Logan rolled his eyes at Ava, then sighed and

twisted in his chair to see Henry. "To what do I owe the pleasure, Henry?"

"No reason. I just wanted to see what it looked like to fall from grace." The man appeared positively gleeful at the idea.

"Have you been looking in the mirror again, Henry? I keep telling you not to scare yourself like that."

Logan's words gained a few chuckles from their surrounding audience. Usually, he wouldn't entertain him, but Logan was tired and fed up, and it had loosened his tongue.

Henry pursed his lips and tilted his head. "It's a shame you can't find any clues, Detective. Enjoy your walk of shame. Oh, by the way, Chief wants to see you."

Logan shook his head, knowing Henry had only come over to give him the summons but had made it into something more. "Finish your coffee. I don't know if it's just me he wants to see, but I'll go, and if he wants you as well, I'll come back for you."

"All right."

He headed down the corridor to Bryan's office, wondering what news he would be receiving. Knocking on the door, he waited until the man called for him, then poked his head in and asked if Ava was needed, too. When Bryan shook his head, Logan's stomach dropped. It was never good if he wanted to see him on his own.

"Sit down, Logan."

Logan sat, exhaling heavily. "What have I done now?"

"Nothing. I wanted to check in with you. I've noticed you seem more stressed than usual. After everything that happened with your brother, you need to speak to the psychologist." He held up his hand to forestall Logan's words. "I know you don't think you need to. I'm making it mandatory."

Logan shifted his attention to the ceiling, trying to calm his heart rate. Refocusing on his boss, he said, "I really don't think it will do anything. I'm fine, Chief."

"Maybe so. If you are, then the sessions will be a breeze, and you'll be done before you know it."

Logan knew he'd been backed into a corner, and he wasn't happy about it. "Can I at least finish these cases first? They are homicides, after all."

Bryan narrowed his gaze on Logan. "I will give you three weeks maximum. If nothing has come from your investigation after that, you start the sessions regardless."

"Yes, sir." He clenched his hands in his lap, trying not to fidget under the intense gaze of his boss. It was almost as bad as his mother's.

"For now, I want you to go home. You and Ava.

Nothing will happen until forensics come back with their results. Get some rest."

Logan's chest tightened at the thought of leaving the case behind while he went on his merry way. The victims couldn't, so why should he be allowed to? Unfortunately, he had no choice. After bidding good-bye, he retraced his steps to his desk but didn't sit down. Leaning down, he switched his computer off.

"Ava, we're heading home. Chief has spoken."

She raised her eyebrows. "Can I ask why?"

"He wants us rested for when forensics come back."

She opened her mouth as if to speak, then closed it again and nodded. "Okay."

Logan walked Ava out to her car, his protective instincts proving too much for him to allow her to walk herself, even though she was as capable as he was, maybe more so.

"Sorry," he said when they arrived.

"Don't be. This case has us all jittery. I appreciate it."

He watched as she climbed in and left the car park with a wave, then strode to his car. Clenching his jaw, he closed his eyes, but the women's faces swam in front of him, interspersed with Casey's. Flicking open his eyes quickly, he blew out a breath and started the engine. He directed the car towards home and tried to think about something different, namely Bastien. Logan had not seen the man properly since the charity event, but he had popped into The Bone Yard a couple of times to check on him. There had been a lightness to Bastien that Logan had not seen before—he'd seen it when Bastien danced, but not during his downtime.

His mouth quirked at the idea of Bastien as queen bee as he put it. It fit him like the outfits he wore for his routines. Perfectly.

When Logan stopped the car, he paused with the engine running. He wasn't at home; he was at his parents' house. It was barely six in the morning, and he didn't want to wake his parents, but for some reason, he couldn't leave either. He rubbed his palm over his forehead and felt his throat closing up, but everything was shut up behind this door he rarely opened. The door he needed for him to be able to do the job he did. The door that was beginning to fragment.

His car door opened, and he startled, his hands curling into fists. When he saw his father, tears over-flowed. His dad switched off his car and pulled the keys from the ignition, then manhandled Logan from the car to the house. As soon as he was sitting on the sofa, his mother sat next to him, wrapping her arms around him.

That was the moment he broke.

He hadn't known how to let all his feelings out after bottling them up for so long, but he needn't have worried. Once the door was open, there was no stopping the flood. He covered his face with his hands and sobbed in his mother's arms, feeling like a little kid again.

He had no idea how much time had passed. All he knew was that his throat was raw, his nose was running, and his eyes wouldn't stop leaking despite the soreness. When he finally pulled away, his back complained about the position he'd been in, but he didn't care. He glanced across at his mother and saw her eyes were red, too.

"Thank you," he croaked.

"You don't need to thank me," she said with a smile. "You're my son. This should be a normal occurrence for us. Unfortunately, it's taken you a lot longer to cave than the others."

Logan snorted. "I bet Liam or Claire hasn't."

"You'd lose that bet."

He checked her expression and raised his eyebrows. "Wow. I'm a stubborn asshole, aren't I?"

She cocked her head. "Sometimes."

Logan chuckled. His dad came into the room with a glass of water and a cup of tea. "Here. Get some fluids back into you, then you can tell us what's going on."

Over the next hour, he explained what he could about the cases and how useless he felt when he wasn't good enough to find their stalker before they were murdered. He was just finishing his story when Casey burst into the room and threw himself into Logan's arms.

Logan instinctively tightened his embrace. "What's wrong?" Panic flooded him.

"I love you, you asshole. Stop beating yourself up about what happened to me."

"I'm no—"

"And if you say you're not, I'm going to hit you. Hard. Luke's been training me, you know." Casey pulled back, his eyes pained. "It wasn't your fault, Logan. All the blame goes on the fucker who did it. Except for one tiny piece that goes on me because I should've told you."

"No! If you say I can't blame myself, then you can't blame yourself."

Casey took a seat next to him but kept hold of his hand. "We need to talk this out. Get it over and done with once and for all."

"How did you know I was here anyway?"

"Dad called earlier, said you needed me."

For once, Logan let himself fall, knowing his family would catch him. He rested his head on Casey's shoulder, his tears overflowing once more. Then he took a deep breath and let everything out. Everything he'd been feeling. He didn't hold anything back. When he was done, he felt lighter. His mind seemed clearer.

Once everything was out in the open, their mother

made breakfast, and the four of them spent the day together after Logan had taken a nap. He was expecting to be called back into work when the forensics report had been finished, but by the time evening came, he still hadn't heard anything. He decided, for once, to not ring and find out. They'd call him if they needed him.

He stayed in his old bedroom, enjoying the feeling of being close to his parents.

The following morning, he woke, feeling rested for the first time in a long time. He lay, staring at the ceiling, then messaged Bastien, knowing he wouldn't get the messages straight away because he'd hopefully be sleeping off his shift.

Next time you dance for me, you need to wear the purple suit and top hat combo you wore the other day. It's hot. L x

He chuckled to himself, knowing Bastien would probably tense up at the idea of being told what to do by Logan, but that outfit had been fiery. He'd love to know how Bastien had kept the hat on his head when he'd been upside down on the pole. Tricks of the trade, obviously.

Washing away his troubles, he dressed in clothes that were way too small for him and headed downstairs to the scent of bacon and the sounds of conversation.

"Good morning, sweetheart. Did you sleep well?" his mother asked.

"Yes, thanks, Mama. Think I need to bring some clothes here, though." He held out his hands at the too-small clothes, and they all laughed.

"I can't believe how much you've all grown. It seems like yesterday when you were knee-high and pulling at my skirts."

Logan chuckled, sitting down to eat the plate that had been placed in front of him. He managed to get halfway through when his phone chimed. He ignored it until he finished his food, relaxing a little when no other messages came through. Unless he received a flurry of messages one after the other, he knew it wasn't urgent.

When they'd finished breakfast, and he'd helped clean up, he pulled his phone out and checked the messages. Clenching his jaw, he said goodbye to his parents and climbed into his car.

"We gonna get you, asshole. I can feel it," Logan muttered to himself as he drove towards the station. "Dial Ava."

"Logan?"

"Hey, Ava. Did you get the message about the report?"

"Yeah, I'm just on my way into the station now."

He smiled, knowing she was a huge asset to the detectives, despite what some officers thought. "Great.

I'll see you there in a few. I just need to nip home and grab a change of clothes."

"Okay."

He hung up and concentrated on the road ahead of him. The message hadn't detailed anything about what was inside the report, only that the report had been finished and was available for them to look at. He hoped there was something in there they could use.

After changing, he parked up at the station, nodding at several members of staff he knew as he weaved his way down the corridors and up the stairs to his desk. Ava was already there, and a coffee was waiting for him.

"Thanks." He dropped into his seat. "Have you read it yet?" he asked as he sipped his drink, wincing at the bitter taste.

Ava shook her head. "I thought it would be better to check it at the same time, then we can compare notes. Unless you want to go through it together?"

"No, individually would be better. You might see something in a different light from how I read it. Let's go for it and hope there is something we can work with."

Ava's grim expression reflected his feelings on the subject.

As Logan worked his way through the forensic pathologist's findings, his mood grew bleaker and bleaker, and the noise around him seemed to increase, irritating him. The cause of death was a broken neck, but there were no lacerations or bruising around the area to show what did it. There were no other signs of trauma or injuries, and the drug screen was clear. All in all, they were no nearer to obtaining anything of value. No unexplained fingerprints were found, no stray fibres. It was as if the murderer was a ghost.

Logan pushed the file away with a huff and leaned back in his chair, staring at the ceiling, his heart racing. There had to be something they'd missed. There couldn't be two murders of similar methods and no evidence. They were still waiting on the DNA results, and he had to hold out hope those would highlight something.

"Nothing." Ava's voice was strained, as was her expression when he glanced at her.

"We're missing something. We have to be." He ran through the information in his head before straightening. "I've had enough of sitting around. I think we should go and visit the people we've visited already and double-check their stories. I can't just sit here."

"All right. Where are we starting?"

"At the beginning. Winona Conrad. If we take the files with us, we can check out the information as we go." He stood, gathering the paperwork. Some officers used laptops to work from, but Logan was old-school. He liked using paper copies where he could write his thoughts directly onto the sheets. He typed them up afterwards, but while the investigation was in progress, he used pen and paper.

"Your car or mine?" Ava asked.

"Would you mind driving today?"

She raised her eyebrows. "Not at all."

They trudged their way to the car and set off in the direction of the first person they needed to speak to, Winona's neighbour.

"Mrs Graham has been her neighbour for about a year." Logan skimmed through the statement the woman had given when they first spoke with her. "She had only noticed that one person hanging around Miss Conrad's house but was never told that Miss Conrad was seeing anyone. They weren't joined at the hip, so that doesn't mean Miss Conrad hadn't been seeing anyone; it just wasn't when Mrs Graham was around."

"Isn't that a bit strange?"

"What?" Logan turned to Ava, seeing her creased forehead and frown.

"If they had been jogging friends for over a year, surely some personal information would have been exchanged, even if it was to know the other person wasn't a serial killer."

Logan snorted at that. "That's true. A year is a long time to keep a polite distance when they had a standing appointment." He marked it down on the statement to ask the question. "Did you find out any more about the antique fair or whatever it was?"

"Not really. I know when it was, and it overlapped the first victim by two days, but it would've been finished before Miss Jarrod was killed."

"People loitering behind afterwards maybe?"

"Could be. I'm still checking out whether there are any other antique events or shops that might have had contact with either victim."

They pulled up outside the house and saw Mrs Graham in her garden. "She looks mighty content for someone whose neighbour has been killed," Logan murmured.

"Everyone grieves in different ways."

Logan raised his eyebrows in Ava's direction, and her mouth twitched. He climbed out of the car, heading over to the older woman, calling her name softly because he didn't frighten her by appearing from nowhere.

"Oh, hello. Have you any more news?" Her voice was concerned, and Logan wanted to dismiss his earlier thoughts of her hiding something, but he couldn't do it yet. He knew to trust his instincts, even if they were a little out of sync lately.

"Good morning, Mrs Graham. Sorry to disturb you again, but we wondered if we could have another chat if you have time?" Ava said.

"Of course, of course. Come on in. I was about ready for a cup of tea anyway." She shuffled up her steps and into the house, leaving the door open, allowing them to follow.

When they were situated with drinks, they all sat in the comfortable living room. "Would you mind walking us through that day again, Mrs Graham? I know it's difficult to think about, and I apologise, but we really need to go through it once more."

Ava's tone was soft and gentle, but there was a steel thread behind it that brooked no argument.

"Of course. If it will help, I'll go through it as many times as you need me to."

"A quick question before we start. Are you still jogging?" Logan asked.

A flash of something crossed Mrs Graham's face before she smiled. "I have been a couple of times, but it's difficult to get up the energy after what happened. It feels…empty without her with me."

Logan bobbed his head and glanced at Ava, who took control of the conversation. He wrote down a note about her responses as he examined his surroundings. There was something in the back of his mind that wasn't fitting, and he couldn't figure out what it was.

Then his gaze snagged on something encased in a tall glass cabinet next to the fireplace.

"Do you have a key to Miss Conrad's home?"

Mrs Graham startled at the interruption and stared at Logan. "No." She appeared confused.

Logan stood and crossed to the cabinet. "Then why do you have a figurine of hers?" He pointed.

"She told me I could have that weeks ago."

Logan pivoted and stared at the woman. "So, if I go next door, there won't be a space where that figurine stood when Miss Conrad was first found?"

Mrs Graham paled.

CHAPTER TWELVE

BASTIEN

Bastien knew he was a strong person for the most part but knowing someone was following him around was unnerving. If it had been only once or twice, he could've dealt with it, but it had been happening every time he set foot outside his door for the last two weeks.

He never saw anyone, either before, during or after, but his instincts were screaming at him, and Bastien decided to go to Logan for help; he was a police officer, after all.

It was why he found himself being dropped off outside the man's house late on a Saturday night, having ordered a taxi to take him straight from work. There were no lights on that he could see, which was why he asked the taxi to wait until he knew there was someone there.

Climbing the front steps, he knocked tentatively, biting his lip and wrapping his arms around himself. After a few seconds, he knocked louder and glanced over his shoulder to make sure the taxi was still there. His gaze whipped back when the front door was yanked open, startling him.

"Bastien? What are you doing here?" Logan's confused expression gave way to a small smile as he opened the door wider. "Not that I don't mind impromptu visits."

Bastien twisted to the side and waved the taxi away, then entered the house, his shoulders relaxing some when the door closed behind him.

"Would you like a drink?"

"Anything you have, thanks."

Logan strode down the hallway, and Bastien followed, glancing around, trying to catch more details as he went. He hadn't seen much the last time he had been there. He stopped at the photographs in the hall-way, seeing Logan's whole family standing in their back garden on a beautiful sunny day. Logan looked much younger, but every single one of them had a smile on their faces. He wished he could remember a time like that. Even before he'd come out to his parents, he had never experienced that. His family had treated him as something that could be brought out when he was needed as a show and tell piece. When he wasn't needed, he was with the nanny.

"Bastien?"

Logan's voice brought him out of his musings, and he focused on the man. "Yes?"

"Your drink is ready."

Bastien could see the concern in Logan's eyes—he had yet to explain why he was there, and he knew the concern would linger once Bastien explained what was happening. Stepping into the kitchen, he slipped into a chair and wrapped his hands around the mug of tea.

"Sorry for visiting so late."

"It's not a problem. You're more than welcome to visit whenever you like." Logan sipped his drink, his eyes remaining focused on Bastien.

"I saw the pictures you sent of the charity event. You looked like you were all having a great time."

"Surprisingly, yes. It was good fun. I think Mum had the best time ever, though. She's talked so much about it since that it's going to become one of our annual events."

Bastien grinned at Logan's expression, knowing he hadn't wanted to go in the first place but went because his mother asked him to. "It won't be too bad for you. You'll only have to dress like a monkey once a year."

"Yeah, but once a year is once a year too many."

"Ah, don't be like that. You just said you had fun." Bastien chuckled, his mood lifting at the playful banter.

Logan hid a yawn behind his hand. "Yeah, all right. Maybe once a year wouldn't be too bad."

Bastien studied the man, seeing the dark circles under his eyes. "I'm sorry, I came too late. I'll just go."

"What's wrong, Bastien?"

Bastien's gaze remained on his mug, but he pursed his lips. "I think I'm being followed."

Logan was silent for so long, Bastien glanced up at him. His eyes widened at the paleness of Logan's features, and he scrambled from his seat and dropped to his knees in front of the man.

"Logan! What's the matter?" Bastien removed Logan's grip from his mug, pushing it further onto the table out of reach. Taking Logan's hands in his, he squeezed and stared at him. "Logan? Shit! You're scaring me. What the fuck is wrong?"

Logan's throat worked as if he was trying to say something, but nothing came out. When tears began streaming down his cheeks, Bastien began to panic. He fumbled for his phone, having to type in his password several times before it unlocked for him, then brought up the contact details for Christine.

The time it took for her to answer seemed interminably long, but it was likely only seconds.

"Bastien! How lovely to—"

"I'm sorry for interrupting, Christine. I'm with Logan. He's gone completely pale and started crying! I don't know what to do!" His voice rose with each word, and his heart joined in, pounding a staccato beat that had him feeling light-headed.

"Calm down, Bastien. Listen to me. We're on our way. Now, tell me what happened?"

Christine's calm voice had Bastien relaxing a little, though one of his hands still held Logan's. The silent crying hadn't stopped, but Logan had closed his eyes and lowered his head, the tears dripping onto his chest.

"I came to him because he's a police officer, and I felt comfortable talking to him. I told him that I was being followed, and that's when he started…" Bastien's throat closed up as his tears threatened. He hated seeing Logan looking so lost.

"Oh, dear. Okay, Bastien. What I need you to do is stay there with him. Hold him if he'll let you but try not to let him leave if you can. Don't hurt yourself trying, but only if you can. I'll explain more when we get there, but Logan has been through a really tough time over the past few days, and this may have been a bit more than he could handle."

"Oh, shit. I'm so sorry, Christine. I shouldn't have come to him with my problems." He stood, dragging his chair as close to Logan as Bastien could then sat, wrapping his arm around Logan's shoulders and tucking his head into Bastien's neck. He held him as tightly as he could.

"Now listen here, Bastien. You *should* go to him with your problems. You two are two peas in a pod, neither wanting to ask for help but both needing it. I'm glad you reached out. Don't ever think you shouldn't do it because you can do it whenever you like. We will be there in a few minutes, and everything will be clearer. There will be several of us coming, but we have a key and can let ourselves in."

"Okay." He sniffed, squeezing Logan's hand again. He wanted to cuddle up onto his knee, but he didn't want to do anything that might spook Logan. The man seemed completely gone from this reality, completely inside his head.

"Right, I'm going to hang up now because I need to call some of the others, but be confident like I know you can be, Bastien. You can do this. If you can't do it for yourself, do it for Logan. I will explain when I get there."

"Okay," he whispered, barely getting the word out.

"Hold tight."

The phone beeped in his ear, indicating the call had ended. Not wanting to move too much and cause Logan any more emotional pain—the expression on Logan's face told Bastien that much—he gently slid the phone onto the table. There was no movement from Logan, and Bastien listened intently for any sound of cars driving up or the front door opening.

Unable to take much more, he gently rested his head on Logan's and waited.

He had no idea how long it had been until he heard the first set of wheels on the driveway. All he knew was he was stiff from sitting in the same position, which meant it had to have been a while. He heard the front door open but no voices and assumed they were being quiet so as not to startle Logan.

When Christine rounded the doorframe, Bastien felt his eyes fill, but he stayed in position. He had no idea what the hell had been going on, but it felt like Logan was having some sort of breakdown.

Christine crouched down beside her son and rested her hand on his forearm. "Logan, sweetheart. How are you feeling?" She rubbed her hand up and down. "Logan? Come back to me, sweetie. Come on. There you are. Come on, sweetheart. Mama's here now."

Bastien felt Logan tense, then relax again, and he lifted his head, giving Logan a bit more room in case he wanted to move.

"Mama?"

Logan's voice was childlike and small, and it brought tears to Bastien's eyes.

"Yes, darling. I'm here. Let's get you a nice cup of tea."

Bastien had been concentrating so much on Christine, he hadn't noticed anyone else in the room. William brought over two steaming mugs of tea and handed one to Christine before passing one to Bastien. To accept, he had to let go of Logan, and he wasn't sure if he was ready for that. He was shaken to the core about what happened, and he didn't even *know* what happened.

William must've seen his indecision and placed it on the table in front of him. The older man squeezed his shoulder then stepped away.

"There you go. Nice and easy. Not too much, sweetheart."

Christine's motherly coddling made Bastien even more teary, knowing he had no one to do this for him.

Suddenly, Logan stood and turned to Bastien, pulling him to his feet. "We need to keep you safe. You need to be safe. You'll have to stay here. I can protect you if you're not out there."

"What—?" Bastien stared wide-eyed at Logan, not understanding anything. "What's going on?"

"Logan, sweetheart. Let Bastien go, and we can have a drink in the living room. There are plenty of us here to keep Bastien safe now." Other people stepped inside the kitchen, making their presence known. "Look, we have you, me, Dad, Casey, Claire, Ava and Luke. The others are on the way. We can take good care of Bastien. No one will take him from you."

Christine moved closer and gently disentangled Bastien from Logan's arms, even though she had to pry him off. When Logan finally released him, Bastien found he didn't want to be and grabbed hold of Logan's hand and held it tightly.

"I'm safe here, Logan," he whispered.

Logan stared at him, the frantic look in his eyes

calming a little. His shoulders lowered, and he hung his head. "Sorry."

"Don't be sorry, my boy. Bastien will be fine. We'll see to it."

Bastien glanced at Logan's dad, frowning. He wished someone would explain what was going on. His heart was still racing.

"Let's go and sit down somewhere comfortable," Christine said, gesturing to the doorway.

They silently headed to the living room; some people sat on the floor or remained standing. Logan sank onto the sofa and pulled Bastien with him, wrapping his arm around Bastien's shoulders.

"All right. Logan, we're going to have to explain a few things to Bastien. You gave him quite a scare."

Logan tightened his grip, then lessened it again. "Sorry, Bastien. I didn't mean—"

"Don't worry about it. I'd just like to know what happened." Bastien cupped Logan's jaw. "Are you feeling okay now?"

"Better than I was, thanks. It was a bit of a shock."

That was what Bastien didn't understand. "But why? I only told you I thought I was being followed."

Logan's jaw clenched, and he moved his gaze away from Bastien.

"Have you heard about the recent murders?" Christine asked.

Bastien nodded. "Yeah. It was why I thought I'd

better check in with Logan about my situation. I didn't want to be another statistic." After saying the words, he knew he would have some explaining to do. "When we said I was a dancer…I'm actually a stripper." He stared at his hands, not wanting to see the disappointment or disgust on their faces.

"Oh, wow. Can you show me how to pole dance?" Claire asked.

Bastien's gaze flicked to hers, seeing excitement all over her face. He chanced a glance at the others, and they all showed differing expressions, but none that he would call negative. "Sure," he said hesitantly.

"Awesome."

"Well, going back to the cases, Logan is the lead detective on them. Both victims were stalked before they were killed. Logan, bless him, has taken it to heart and has struggled to distance himself from it, especially with what happened last year."

Bastien examined Casey, seeing his hands and jaw clenching and his nostrils flaring, but the tightening around his eyes gave away his pain. "I was kept for ten hours—"

"Eleven," croaked Logan, tears pooling again.

Casey cleared his throat. "Eleven hours, but Logan found me before the man could do anything serious." Logan scoffed at that but didn't say anything. "He believes it was his fault, but it wasn't."

"You're worried it's the same person stalking me that killed those women?" he asked Logan.

Logan's nod was almost imperceptible. "You've come to mean a lot to me, Bastien. I don't want anything to happen to you," Logan whispered against the side of his head.

Bastien slid his arms around Logan's waist and hugged him tightly. He couldn't voice his feelings yet, but he knew he felt something more than he'd felt for many people he'd met. They needed to get through this before he said anything. He knew better than anyone that throwing on some petrol would make a fire. He wasn't ready to pin all his hopes and dreams on someone when no one could know the outcome of this. It wasn't fair on either of them.

"Will you stay here? Will you move in? Even if for a while?" Logan asked.

"Logan—" Christine started.

"It's okay. He'd asked me before, and it was a resounding no at the time, but I think it might be a good idea." He wasn't at all sure it was a good idea, but he couldn't let Logan go through whatever he'd been through again because he didn't know where Bastien was. So, he'd move in. It would help him save some money, too.

"If you're sure." Christine frowned but didn't say anything further. "I'm going to go and make us all some food. I trust you have something in the fridge worthy of eating?" Her eyes twinkled at her son.

A small spark came back into Logan's demeanour, and his mouth twitched. "There is something in there. Not sure how edible it will be."

"Lord, save me from my children." Christine raised her hands to the ceiling and headed out of the room.

"There's plenty of food," he whispered to Bastien, causing a smile to curve his lips.

"Are you okay?" he said to Logan, trying to keep his voice low, so the others didn't hear. They had begun chatting between themselves now that the tension had somewhat dispersed.

Logan inhaled through his nose and out through his mouth before answering, "I will be. I'm sorry for going off like that. I have no right to make you move in, but…I don't know what else to do."

"It's okay. It's fine. Honestly. As you stated before, it'll make things easier for me if I did. Just don't throw me out before I find a new place to live, okay?" he half-joked.

"No way. If I did, Mum would adopt you."

"Bastien!"

"Speak of the devil."

Bastien rose from the sofa after a brief tightening of his arms around Logan and shuffled into the kitchen to Christine.

"I'm sorry, Christine. I didn't mean to make all this

happen. I didn't realise he was the officer dealing with it all; otherwise, I wouldn't have bothered him."

"No, no. Don't say that. You *should* bother him, definitely. He's a police officer for a reason. It's his calling. He needs to do the job." She paused her actions of breaking eggs into a bowl and wiped off her hands. "I wanted to make sure you were okay. You told us something you didn't really want us to know, and I wanted to check to make sure you were feeling all right about it."

Bastien let out a breath. "I'm fine with it. I only hold it back because it makes people look at me differently, as if I'm dirty or something. I don't mind people knowing usually, but you mean..." He trailed off, not wanting to let his feelings known.

"Do you have any family around?" she asked, changing the subject. Bastien was initially thankful until he realised he had more to explain.

"No, I don't," he muttered. "No one worthy of my time anyway." Christine glanced at him, inviting him to talk. "My parents come from old money. The moment they found out I was gay and didn't fit into the nice little box they had arranged for me, they kicked me out. I've been on my own since I was fourteen."

The bare bones of his story still made him angry, and by the looks of Christine's reaction, she felt the same.

"Those good-for-nothing asswipes. If I ever cross paths with those people, they will know my wrath."

Bastien raised his eyebrows, biting his lips to stop his laughter. He had never seen someone get so angry at someone else's story. "It's all right. I'm away from them now."

"Yes, you are. And now you have us. I officially adopt you into this family. There is no escaping from us now, my dear."

"Why do I feel like you're a wolf, and I'm the prey?" Bastien joked, trying not to think about Logan as being his brother. It was too weird, especially with what they had done a few weeks ago.

Christine chuckled. "You're already caught, my dear. You've no choice." Bastien snorted. "Are you sure you're okay with moving in with Logan? You don't have to."

"To be honest, I'm a little wary, but only because I don't know where I will be once this is all over and I need to move out again. But as for staying, I'm happy to be here. I love how quiet it is."

"I wouldn't worry about moving out just yet. Cross that bridge when you come to it but know there will always be a place in our house for you, even if you no longer have ties with anyone else."

Bastien's eyes filled, and he blinked rapidly, trying to withhold the overflow. "Thank you."

"I don't think you have anything to worry about, though," she said, winking.

"Logan seems to have settled down a little more." Casey walked into the kitchen, bringing empty mugs with him. "There's no guarantee that it won't happen again, but he seems calmer. I was thinking…Can you manage with the clothes you have until later? If you can, Logan or one of us will take you back to your place to grab all your stuff."

"I'll be fine. You don't need—"

"I know we don't. Unfortunately, Logan will have someone with you at all times at the moment until the stalker is found. It's going to feel mighty claustrophobic for you, Bastien." Casey's tone was concerned but also firm.

"I can imagine." He sighed. "Yes, it's fine. Whatever needs to happen can happen. Not sure how it will work out with being at the club, but I can speak to Rafferty."

"You'll need to sit down with Logan and Ava and talk them through what you've been feeling and seeing. It's not the nicest thing to go through, and although I haven't been through the same thing, I can sit with you if you'd like me to."

Bastien bit his lip. "Yes, please. If you don't mind."

Casey shook his head. "Not at all."

"Well, before any more questions are answered,

let's get some scrambled eggs and toast inside us. We need our energy to last the day."

Bastien had no idea how long this whole situation had gone on, and when he looked at the clock, he was astounded to find it was nearly five in the morning. "Oh my god! I didn't even think about the time when I called you. I'm sorry!"

Christine waved her hand. "Don't worry about it. Family comes first. But food comes a close second, especially with my kids." She pointed a finger at Bastien. "And that means you, too."

Bastien's cheeks heated when Casey laughed. "You've been collared! Hey, Logan! Bastien is our new brother!"

Bastien heard Logan's splutter from where Bastien had parked himself on a chair at the table, and he dropped his head into his hands, mortified. That was all he needed. To be thinking about Logan as his brother, but that was no doubt, precisely why Casey had done it.

The amount of eggs and toast Christine had made was staggering, but every bit of it was devoured by the eight of them within minutes. Christine and William decided to head home and get a few things organised, saying they would return at a more convenient time with plenty more supplies. Casey and Luke took Ava and Claire home, leaving Logan and Bastien to figure out what they were doing.

"Will you sleep in my bed?" Logan asked hesitantly. "Not for anything other than for me to hold you."

Bastien swallowed hard and nodded. He wanted nothing more than to stay safe and sound in Logan's embrace and forget all their worries for a few hours.

Logan held out his hand and threaded their fingers together when Bastien took it. They climbed the stairs and trailed to Logan's room, not saying a word. They separated, and Bastien glanced nervously at Logan before beginning to strip off his clothes. Logan stepped to the drawers, rifling through them before holding out a large t-shirt.

"You can sleep in that if you want to."

"Thanks."

Bastien pulled the cool fabric over his head, inhaling the scent of detergent and Logan before settling it into place and removing his trousers.

"Do you want some briefs or shorts or something?"

Bastien shook his head, his mouth curving. "I think this t-shirt buries me enough to cover what needs to be covered."

Logan glanced at him and chuckled. The t-shirt reached Bastien's knees, and the neckline slipped off one shoulder.

"There are spare toiletries in the bathroom. Use whatever you need."

Bastien did that, then returned, sliding under the covers while Logan went to use the bathroom. When

Logan came back, he climbed into bed, switching off the bedside lights and rolling towards Bastien.

"Can I hold you?" Logan whispered.

Bastien's heart broke at the wrecked tone of his voice. He slid as close as he could get, entwining their legs and tucking his head underneath Logan's chin. And there he stayed, despite being unable to sleep.

Too many thoughts were running around his head, but the main one was that Logan was steadily becoming more important to him than anyone else had ever been. And wasn't that a shock for someone who was adamant that he would be fine by himself and didn't need anyone?

CHAPTER THIRTEEN

LOGAN

The panic that overwhelmed him when Bastien had said those dreaded words had dampened to a simmering worry. As he lay with his arms wrapped around the man who was so much more than a hookup, he tried to figure out the best way forward. Bastien would hate having someone with him all hours of the day, but Logan wouldn't rest if Bastien was on his own. When Bastien went into work the following night, he would be going with him and speaking with Rafferty about the situation. He didn't care what the man said —someone would be watching over Bastien all day, every day until the fucker was caught.

Bastien's body relaxed, and Logan knew he was finally asleep. Despite not having slept at all that night, Logan was still too wired to sleep, but with Bastien in his arms, he could at least stay calm and think clearly.

While Bastien had been in the kitchen with his mother, Logan had discussed a couple of scenarios with the others. His dad had agreed to let Bastien stay with them when Logan had to work, and Casey had offered the same when he wasn't working his shifts. Luke had offered to train Bastien, and Logan made a note to ask him about it after he'd had some sleep.

Logan and Ava knew they needed to go through everything all over again with a fine-toothed comb, but until he knew Bastien was safe when Logan wasn't around, he couldn't do it. Therefore, Ava offered to go straight to the station to start looking for anything they might have missed, and Logan told her he'd join her the following day.

When Logan made it into the station the day after —while Bastien was staying with Casey and Luke—he was called into the chief's office.

"Mandatory counselling. She's waiting in the spare office at the end of the hall. No arguments, or you're on leave."

Logan clenched his jaw, but he could see from Bryan's face that he was worried about him. Ava must've mentioned something. He nodded. When he entered the office, he was met by a slightly overweight woman with glasses and a friendly demeanour.

"Logan?"

"Yes, ma'am." He shut the door and sat on the seat opposite her.

"This is not the optimal conditions for a meeting, but I was told you were coming in today and needed to be seen as soon as possible. Hence, I'm here."

"I wasn't expecting to see you today either," he mumbled.

"My name is Amanda, and although counselling sessions are usually less direct, I'd like to talk to you about your brother Casey."

Logan stared at his fingers and swallowed hard. "Okay."

"How did you feel when you found out about the sexual harassment?"

Logan huffed a laugh. "How do you think I felt? Useless. Stupid. Careless. Shocked. To name a few."

"Why did you feel useless?"

He fidgeted in his seat, unable to look her in the eye. He felt idiotic doing this, but he knew he wouldn't get away with giving half-answers. Being honest was the only way he was going to be able to keep doing his job.

"I'm supposed to be a police officer. Someone who serves and protects. How can I not feel useless when I can't protect my brother?"

"But how can you be expected to protect him when you didn't know it was happening?"

"I should've known! He's my brother!" Logan dropped his head back and stared at the ceiling before bringing his gaze back to Amanda's.

"Your job description does not expect you to be a police officer above all else. If you didn't see the signs, it could be that they weren't there or that they were being hidden."

"I still should've known."

Amanda shook her head. "No, Logan. You are not invincible. You cannot take the whole world's problems on your shoulders. Or even your whole family's problems. You are one person. You need to remember that Casey made his own choices, and he was allowed to do that. Were they the best choices? That's not up to anyone but him to decide. All you can do is deal with the aftermath."

Logan swallowed repeatedly, trying to stem the tears. "But he's my brother," he croaked.

"And he always will be. You are more than capable of doing this job, Logan, but you need to lean on others, too."

Several days later, Logan was still on alert, and he hadn't believed he would be able to sleep, but every morning he woke with his body covered by a smaller one, and he couldn't help but smile.

He cleared his throat gently. "Are you quite

comfortable there, Bastien?" he whispered, nuzzling at his head.

"Yes, thanks. You're so warm." Bastien snuggled in closer if that was possible.

"Glad I could be of help." Logan chuckled.

Bastien yawned. "What time is it? I'm too worn out to move my head anymore."

Logan twisted his head to where the clock sat on the bedside table and squinted. "It's just after nine o'clock."

Bastien grumbled but didn't say anything else. Logan thought he'd fallen back asleep when a small rumble sounded.

"Was that your stomach making its presence known," Logan asked.

"Maybe."

"Let me up. I'll grab you something to eat."

"Nah, I'm all right."

Bastien rubbed his face against Logan's bare chest. Logan hadn't thought anything of it, but his eyes shot open when a tentative lick swept over his nipple.

"Hmm, is someone feeling a little frisky this morning?"

Logan slid the hand that had been resting on Bastien's back down his spine until it reached his ass, giving it a squeeze before using his fingers to pull at the fabric until the hem was within reach. Once it was out of the way, his palm covered Bastien's ass cheek, his other hand coming to join in the fun.

Not going any further, Logan plied and moulded the globes until Bastien was grinding against him. Logan held him tighter to him, giving Bastien more friction and allowing him to reach for what he wanted.

"Wait!"

Logan immediately let go, and Bastien scrambled to his knees, straddling Logan's waist and shuffling down to his thighs to align their cocks. Bastien encircled both dicks but frowned when his small hand barely went around half of them.

"Let me," Logan said gruffly, taking hold of both and stroking firmly. Bastien arched his back and let out a little whimper of need as Logan pleasured him —them.

Logan watched as Bastien dropped his head back and groaned, then rested his hands on Logan's knees, spreading himself open. As Logan's hand did the work, their balls rubbed together. Bastien's hips began thrusting in time with Logan's actions until he was panting. He sat upright again and lowered himself down to flick his tongue over Logan's nipples. Logan's free hand clamped down on Bastien's ass, encouraging him to keep up the movement.

Logan could feel the tingle beginning at the base of his spine and tunnelling into his groin. He knew he didn't have long. His hand left Bastien's ass and travelled to the man's nipples, tweaking and flicking as Bastien cried out, his muscles tensing as his release coated Logan's hand, closely followed by his own.

Bastien collapsed on top of Logan, his hot breaths fanning across Logan's sweat-beaded skin. "Fuck," Bastien breathed.

"Maybe later." Bastien snorted. "Shower first." Logan lifted Bastien's head and sealed their lips in a chaste but sweet kiss, sipping gently at the mounds.

Logan helped Bastien to his feet, grimacing at the stickiness coating his stomach—both their stomachs. They trudged to the bathroom, and Logan switched on the shower, coaxing Bastien underneath the spray when the water was warm enough.

He heard his phone chime. He waited for a second to see if another notification came through and, when it didn't, followed Bastien under the warm water. Wrapping his arms around Bastien, he stayed with him until their releases became itchy.

"Let's get washed off, then we can snuggle on the sofa. I don't have anywhere I need to be yet." He hoped. The message might've been a simple update from Ava, but he might need to nip into the station if she had found anything.

After drying off and grabbing some more clothes for Bastien, Logan dressed and picked up his phone.

Might have found something, but it's not urgent. I've spoken with the chief, and we're waiting on a warrant before you need to come in. I'll call you later.

Logan raised his eyebrows. It must've been something big if they needed a warrant. Curiosity warred with staying in their little bubble for a while longer; the silence and Bastien's company won. He didn't say anything to Bastien, and they made do with some cereal, yoghurt and fruit for breakfast before taking their choices to the sofa. Logan passed the remote to Bastien, who chose a comedy film for them.

Once their food was devoured, they cuddled, small comments drifting back and forth for the duration of the film. The credits had begun rolling when Logan's phone rang. He snatched it up and answered.

"The warrant should be here within the hour," Ava stated.

"Okay. I'll call Mum and Dad. I'll be there soon."

He turned to Bastien once the call ended, explaining that he needed to head into work for a short time. "Are you all right going to my parents for a few hours?" He waited for Bastien's nod and put a call into his parents.

Bastien dressed in the clothes they had picked up from his house a couple of days before, and Logan drove him to his childhood home. His mother welcomed Bastien as if he was one of her own—and he practically was now. Logan left him with a sweet kiss and a promise to be careful, then he climbed into his car and headed to the station.

The minute he was within talking distance of Ava, he asked what she'd found.

"Barry Jamieson, the guy from the antique shop, had mentioned hiring a man for the two weeks of the antique fair. When he made his statement, the man was still working for him as Mr Jamieson had planned on taking a week-long holiday as well. I went back over his statement. Apparently, the man is a martial arts expert who often detailed how antique weapons were used. Now, on its own, it's not much to go on, but when we asked Mr Jamieson what else he knew about the guy, he said he liked hunting for antiques more than Mr Jamieson did, often finding trinkets and persuading their owners to part with them for a fraction of the price. Mr Jamieson was happy with this, for obvious reasons." Ava took a deep breath. "I contacted Mr Jamieson this morning because I couldn't remember the name of the item he said he'd been trying to locate for years. Something about it was in the back of my mind, and it was bugging me."

"What was it?"

"The figurine."

Logan frowned, then raised his eyebrows. "The one Mrs Graham took?"

"The exact one. From what I could gather, that

figurine is worth over ten grand to the right person, and Miss Conrad had been given it as an inheritance. She had agreed to sell the figurine to…" Ava paused.

"Miss Jarrod?"

"Yes, but Mrs Graham took it."

"Why didn't the guy take it if he killed Miss Conrad?"

Ava shrugged. "I'm not entirely sure, but maybe he believed there would be a check of all the items or something. I'm assuming, when he couldn't find it, he went after Miss Jarrod."

"And we know where he is?"

Ava grinned. "We do. Mr Jamieson agreed to keep the guy on for several more weeks to see what else he could manage to find."

Logan clenched his jaw. "Typical. It's all about the money as usual."

"Taylor! Walker! Warrant's here!"

They scrambled to their feet and strode to the chief's office. "Thanks, Chief."

"Get this asshole. You have a team of four coming shortly behind you to undertake the warrant."

They hustled out of the office, and Logan shook his head. "I still can't believe you told him."

"You know what he's like when he smells a bone. He started questioning me about why I was there, and you weren't. It was easier to tell him some of the truth, so he knew if you became frantic from news about Bastien."

"Hmm," he grumbled.

"Quit whining."

Logan snorted. "You're getting too big for your underwear, Detective Walker."

"You could do with loosening yours a little, Detective Taylor."

They climbed into Logan's car and screeched out of the car park towards the employee's home address. The antique shop owner had told them that today was the man's day off. Logan pulled over a few houses down from the address they needed, and they sat there observing it for a few minutes.

"See any movement?"

"Nope."

"Come on then." Logan climbed out and drifted up the street to the house. It was a little house that people rented for short-term leases in the city. There were several of them on this particular street as well as several other areas throughout the city. It was often used for people who had come from abroad on exchange or loan from what Logan had gathered.

He knocked on the front door, hearing a muffled sound from inside before the door opened. A tall man with an athletic build stood before him. His age was difficult to determine because he was losing the hair from the top of his head. He only had hair at the back and sides, but his face looked fairly youthful. Mr Jamieson had not given them any details as to the man's age.

"Can I help you?"

"Mr Brooke? I'm Detective Sergeant Taylor. This is Detective Constable Walker. Could we talk to you for a moment?"

"Of course, come on in."

The man opened the door further, and they entered, Logan's eyes widening at the sight of several boxes, opened and unopened, within the small house. He hadn't thought so many could fit in such a tiny place.

"What can I do for you, Detectives?"

"We'd like to ask for your whereabouts on the nights of March 14 and June 2."

Logan watched as the man's eyes tightened a fraction before resuming their gentle stare. "Let me grab my diary." Robert Brooker headed over to a table where a large tomb-like book lay. He flicked through a few pages, then said, "I was bowling on March 14 and," he flicked another few pages, "here alone on June 2. A new film had come out, and I'd marked it to watch." He stood upright again. "Can I ask…oh, is this about the murders? You think it's me?" He chuckled.

"You think that's funny?" Logan could feel his

temper rising at the blatant disregard for the women's lives.

"I think it's funny that you think I did it."

Logan wasn't so sure. "I would like for you to accompany us down to the station for questioning. We also have a warrant to check the premises." Logan pulled the paperwork from his pocket, passing it to the man.

Mr Brooke checked it over, and Logan once more witnessed the minute tensing of his muscles. He was hiding something.

"Okay, not a problem." Mr Brooke handed the warrant back when there was a knock at the door.

Logan indicated for Ava to answer it. "That should be the team to oversee the warrant." Ava came back with three men and one woman. "If you will come with us, please, Mr Brooke, we will take your statement down at the station and get you back home as soon as we can." Or maybe not.

Logan's instincts were screaming at him that the man was hiding something. He just had to hope it came out in the questioning.

They drove Mr Brooke to the station and signed him in for the interview process. Once he was seated within an interview room with a coffee, Logan and Ava retreated to gather themselves and decide how to approach him before actually doing it. Once it was settled that Ava would take point with Logan as a backup, they entered the room and sat down.

"Mr Brooke, can you give us an idea of what your job entails with Mr Jamieson?" Ava asked, staring at her paperwork as if it held her questions.

"Initially, I was there to cover for the antique fair that lasted over two weeks, then Mr Jamieson wanted to take a week holiday, so I offered to stay longer. When we realised how well we worked together, he asked me to stay a little longer and help him source some antiques. I'm very persuasive when I want to be."

Logan didn't like the way he said that and shifted in his chair, wanting to ask questions but leaving Ava to do it instead.

"In what way?"

"I know how to talk to people. Among other things, money always talks when it comes to antiques." Mr Brooke leered.

Ava leaned forward, resting her elbows on the table and tilted her head. "What else talks?" she asked.

Brooke's forehead creased, but Logan could see the calculation in his eyes. "What do you mean?"

"You said, 'Among other things.' What other things talk?"

"It was a figure of speech, that's all."

"Really?" Logan said, crossing his legs. He held a notepad and pen and crossed his wrist on top of the other, feigning relaxation.

"Money always talks."

"I can imagine it does. What about blackmail? Or threats? Or intimidation? Do they work too?" Ava asked.

"I wouldn't know. I've never used them, though I know of some people in the business who do."

"I can imagine you meet a lot of people within the antique business. Are there a lot of younger people involved, or are they mainly older people?"

Brooke cocked his head. "It's a variety really, although the younger generations appear to want to sell what they have received through inheritance rather than buying them because they like them. The older generations are a mixture."

Logan's phone buzzed in his pocket, and he pulled it out, standing when he saw who it was. "We'll be back in a few moments." He indicated for Ava to come with him and hit answer and lifted it to his ear. "Taylor."

"Hey, Logan. It's Marie at Mr Brooke's house. We've found something I think might be better seeing for yourself."

Logan couldn't tell from the tone of her voice how to take her words, but he felt a thrill of excitement that something might be able to nail this asshole to the wall. "We'll be there soon."

Starting towards Bryan's office, he filled Ava in, then knocked on his chief's door. "Chief, we've had a call from the team at Mr Brooke's house. They want us to go check something out. We've left Brooke in the interview room. Can you get someone to keep an eye on him?"

Bryan waved them away. "Sure, I'll send someone. Go."

They hustled out of the station and were at the property shortly after. Marie came to meet them.

"It's freaky," she stated, climbing the stairs. "We checked most of the downstairs, and there was nothing to report, except that the place is exceptionally clean. When we started up here, things are still clean, but there was a discrepancy between the look of the ottoman and the actual inner size. See for yourself."

They entered a bedroom, and Marie headed to the base of the bed, where a large ornate ottoman stood. Marie lifted the lid, and Logan and Ava peered in. Logan glanced at the front of the piece of furniture and tried to gauge how much difference there would be.

"There's about a foot difference, isn't there?"

"Yes, roughly. Here's what we found." Marie felt around the inner edge at each side and lifted a base from the ottoman.

When the underneath was revealed, Logan's eyes widened. "What the hell?"

"It's human hair."

Logan pulled on a pair of gloves that Marie passed over and pulled out one clear plastic bag filled with blonde strands around four inches in length. He picked out another bag, this time with black hair and around two inches in length. "He collects hair?"

"I believe this hair comes from his victims."

"What makes you think that?" Ava asked.

Marie reached in and lifted a small notebook. "The codes in here match the codes on the bags. I believe the code is the initials of the person, the date and some other numbers after it. I haven't quite figured that out yet, but I've sent pictures to the tech guys to see if they can come up with something."

"If that's right, there should be a code for Winona Conrad and Rebecca Jarrod." Logan took the notebook and flicked through the pages. He came across a WC1432131132. "The first part of these looks right, but the last part is confusing."

"I have Miss Jarrod's, potentially. RJ262131132. The latter part is identical. A reference to the item, maybe?" Ava frowned.

"Maybe. Thanks, Marie. I'll take these two with me, but if you can get the rest in the database, we might be able to find some correlation between them."

"Sure thing."

"Oh, and can you get a tech to give me a ring as soon as they have any information. I would love to be able to throw something at him. He's far too smug for my liking."

Marie's lips tightened. "Yeah, I didn't like the look

of him." She passed over the form Logan had to sign to say what he'd taken with him.

"I think it's safe to say we can arrest him and keep him for at least a couple of days while we check the house inside and out." He nodded at Marie. "Thanks."

"No problem."

When they arrived back at the station, they followed protocol and signed the evidence in, also signing to say they were keeping it with them while they interviewed Mr Brooke. Before heading to the suspect, they hustled to the chief's office to keep him in the loop.

"Did forensics not notice any missing hair?" Bryan asked.

"Nothing was noted on the report, but if he cut a length off the whole of their hair, it wouldn't be obvious. It would only be telling if there was a small section missing."

"There's definitely enough in the bag for a trim," Ava stated. "I doubt it was obvious, and even if someone had noticed, the victim could've had a haircut the day they died."

"Good point."

Logan marked it down to check out both victims to see if they had been to any hairdressers or anything on the day or a few days before they died. Choosing to continue questioning Mr Brooke straight away, they entered the room to find the man pacing behind the table, holding a cup of what smelled like coffee.

"If you could take a seat, please, Mr Brooke. We have a few more questions for you."

The man sat, wrapping his hands around the cup.

Ava sat forward again, though the man's eyes remained on Logan's face. "Mr Brooke, can you remind us again where you said you were on March 14?"

"If I remember right from checking my diary while we were at my house, I said I was bowling."

"And who did you go bowling with?"

"I would assume it was the usual people at the bowling club. I don't have someone I go with, but once a month, there is a group of people who get together to play. Kind of a singles night, if you like."

"How did you know about that if you'd only recently arrived in Cambridge? Didn't you start working for Mr Jamieson on February 22?"

Logan was pleased with the direction Ava was going. She was ready for her promotion. He never introduced her as Trainee Detective anymore; he didn't see the point.

"I did start that date, yes. I knew about it because I mentioned to Mr Jamieson about being single, and he told me about that because his son had been to one a few times."

Ava nodded slowly. "And again, where were you on June 2?"

"I was at home watching the new film that had come out."

"Alone?"

"Yes."

"Can anyone verify that?"

"Only from what I told them. I'd been telling Mr Jamieson that had been my plan for as long as I had known the film was premiering that night."

"Have you ever visited The Bone Yard?"

Ava's question caught Logan off guard, but he understood why she asked. He studied the man.

He bit his lip, then firmed his jaw. "I have visited a few times, yes."

"Can I ask why?"

"I'm…curious, or at least, I have been lately."

Logan could see no lie in those words, but it seemed to confirm his suspicion.

Ava glanced at Logan, and he nodded imperceptibly. "Mr Brooke, can you tell me what these are?" Ava pulled out the two bags of hair and deposited them in front of the man.

Logan watched carefully, noticing the man's face paling and his eyes widening. He waited, but the man said nothing, just swallowed repeatedly.

"Mr Brooke?" he said. "Can you answer the question, please?"

"I'd like a lawyer."

Logan gathered up the bags. "One will be here shortly. But I would like you to know that you are under arrest for the murders of Winona Conrad and Rebecca Jarrod. Anything you say may be used against you in a court of law. Do you understand?"

The man nodded, and they exited the room, calling a guard over to stay in front of the door.

Once more, the duo headed the chief's office. "He didn't cave, but as soon as we showed him the hair, he asked for a lawyer. I've arrested him."

"Fantastic. Well done, the pair of you."

"Put this one on Ava. If not for her finding that clue, we would still be sitting on our asses."

Bryan glanced at Ava with an approving look. "Yes, she is becoming quite the detective." He focused back on Logan, giving a small nod of understanding.

After they went back to their desks, Logan congratulated her again. "I know you don't like being the centre of attention, but you do deserve this. You're going to be awesome."

"I haven't finished my training yet."

"I don't think you have too much to worry about." Logan picked up the things he needed. "Anyway, I'm heading back to give Bastien the good news. We caught the bastard."

Logan jogged to his car, ringing Bastien's phone to find out where he was. It turned out his dad had just dropped him off at the club, so Logan headed there.

When he entered, he was surrounded by loud music, even louder than before, but the spectacle on stage was astounding. Three dancers on each part of the stage were dancing in time with the beat wearing police outfits. Logan chuckled and sat on a stool at the bar.

"What do you think? Do you like my idea?"

Logan turned and saw Bastien standing next to him with a cheeky grin.

"It's…enlightening. Is this how you think of me?"

Bastien chuckled. "No, but it wouldn't hurt. Couldn't you wear a uniform every now and then?"

Logan slid his arms around his waist and pulled him closer. "I might be enticed, just for you." He leaned closer, whispering in his ear, "We arrested the stalker."

Bastien pulled back, his heart racing. "Really?" Logan nodded, and Bastien threw his arms around his neck. "I think this deserves a lap dance."

"If you insist."

Bastien eyed Logan as he stepped back, cocking his hip. "Nolan, I'm busy if anyone asks." Nolan chuckled and waved him away. "Follow me, handsome." He turned, eager to get away from prying eyes.

"Don't do anything I wouldn't do," a voice called,

and Bastien twisted, seeing Cassidy leaning over a customer, though his eyes were on him.

"Doesn't give me much to keep to myself," Bastien replied.

"I'm here for when he can't perform," Cassidy purred at Logan.

"I don't have any concerns about that, but thank you for the offer," Logan replied, stepping past Bastien and behind the curtain.

Bastien grinned at Cassidy, then sashayed away. Logan was waiting outside a room for him. "Our usual?"

"Why not?" Bastien said, entering the small room and heading straight over to the music. He felt a warmth at his back as he pressed buttons to get to the right song. Hands slid along his sides and around to his stomach as his hips began moving to the beat.

Bastien lifted his hands above his head and linked them behind Logan's head. "This is supposed to be a lap dance, not a couple's dance," he murmured.

"Can't it be what we want it to be?"

"I could get fired for this."

"But you won't." Logan knew as well as Bastien did that it was unlikely for Rafferty to fire him unless he was seriously over the line.

"Hmm." Bastien twisted in Logan's embrace, returning his hands to Logan's neck and moulding their bodies together. Logan's hard cock was pressed against Bastien's stomach, and Bastien knew there was no stopping this from happening. Not when they had so much to celebrate.

Logan's lips caressed Bastien's with soft strokes until Bastien could take no more, and he opened his mouth, pressing his tongue against Logan's, seeking entry. The kiss set fire to their passion. Bastien held tightly around Logan's neck, lifting to his tiptoes to reach higher still. Logan slid his hands to the back of Bastien's thighs, putting pressure on them until he took Bastien's weight, and Bastien wrapped his legs around Logan's waist. Their kiss went on, their breathing heavy and loud despite the music.

Logan pivoted away from the sound system and knelt on the sofa, gently laying Bastien down beneath him. Bastien pulled his mouth away, panting hard and trying to recover. Logan continued kissing down the column of his neck to the collar of his shirt, gently teasing it to one side to reach more skin. Bastien couldn't take it. He pushed Logan away slightly and tore the shirt off, leaving his soft, smooth skin on display.

"Fuck, you're gorgeous," Logan breathed.

"Says the police officer with ample muscles for everyone to sink their teeth into," Bastien replied, lifting his head and licking at Logan's collarbone.

"I'm not concerned about anyone but you."

Bastien's heart raced at the words, and he let a tiny

bit of hope flicker within his soul. He gripped the side of Logan's head and pulled him in for another kiss, licking and exploring and tasting his mouth. He couldn't get enough of him. Their background music had taken on a deeper, more sensual beat, and Bastien found himself grinding against Logan's stomach in time with the sound.

Logan's hands were busy sliding down Bastien's sides and to his legs, dragging them further up until they were bracketing Logan's hips. He pressed their arousals together, his hips grinding in small circles and making Bastien's head whirl.

"Oh, fuck! We shouldn't be doing this here!" Bastien muttered, breaking away from the kiss again.

"No one has to know."

"You're supposed to be an upstanding, law-abiding police officer. How can you say that?" Bastien's chuckle tapered off into a moan when Logan's hand cupped his dick.

"I can say that because I'm not a police officer right now. I'm a horny man who needs his boyfriend to get off."

The word 'boyfriend' had Bastien about to tense before Logan licked at his nipple, setting a fire deep in his groin. The word floated away on a whimper of need.

"Please, Logan. Fuck me, please!" Bastien whispered.

"My pleasure…and yours."

Logan pulled at Bastien's boy shorts, sliding them down his legs and struggling to get them over the heels he was wearing.

"Take them off," Bastien muttered.

"Nope. I'm fucking you with these beauties on." Logan grinned at him. "I want to feel the heels pressing into my ass as my cock drives into you."

Bastien's eyes rolled back in his head, and he pressed a hand to his dick, the gravelly spoken words having him close to coming. When he had regained some composure, he focused on getting Logan's jeans unfastened. He was under no illusions that this would be anything except a quick, hard fuck, and he was fine with that. If anyone came down the hall while they were doing this, there was a chance they would be heard. And didn't that make Bastien's cock perk up?

Logan resituated himself over Bastien, his cock hard and hot between their bodies while he reached for his back pocket, pulling two packets free. He put one in his mouth, and the other he offered to Bastien, who took it and ripped the condom from it. Sliding it down Logan's shaft, he felt the heaviness of his need, the tight restraint he had on his movements. Logan tore the second wrapper, squirting some lube onto his fingers and pressing against Bastien's entrance. Bastien bore down, wanting Logan inside him as quickly as he could get him. The slight burn didn't bother Bastien, and he encouraged Logan to go faster.

When Bastien was taking three fingers, he'd reached his arousal limit and pushed Logan's hands away, grabbing Logan's dick and pressing it to his hole.

"Fuck me! Now!"

"All right, Queen Bee. Take it easy."

Bastien almost laughed at the name, but he was too far gone to care what he was called. All he wanted was to feel Logan inside him, sliding deep. He got his wish. Logan pressed forward, not stopping until he was fully seated, where he waited for Bastien to accommodate the intrusion.

Nothing would ever prepare him for the feel of Logan. The length reached further inside him than anyone else ever had, and it was a wonderful feeling. He slid his hands around Logan's neck, pulling him in for another kiss, slightly less frantic now they were entwined.

Logan began moving, slowly at first, then faster, rising to brace his hands beside Bastien's abdomen as he thrust repeatedly.

"Let me feel you, Bastien," Logan growled, and Bastien knew what he meant.

He lifted his feet, bending his legs around Logan's waist and pressing the heels of his shoes into Logan's skin. He had no idea where they landed, but they must've been in the right place because Logan groaned and sped up his movements. Bastien wrapped a hand around his cock, tightening his grip as much as he could and stroking in time with Logan's thrusts.

He felt the tell-tale tingling travelling down his spine and into his groin before he moaned a warning and came, spilling his seed all over his stomach. His free hand reached behind him while his body arched closer to Logan as his ass contracted rhythmically on Logan's cock. Distantly, he heard Logan's muted growl, and then his body was covering Bastien's, though not smothering him.

They lay that way for a short time before the music changed to something quicker. Bastien slid his hand up and down Logan's spine, enticing a shiver from the man before Logan lifted his head and pressed a kiss to Bastien's lips.

Bastien dropped his legs, one to the floor and one to the sofa cushions, allowing Logan room to move off him. The man did, and Bastien chuckled at the sight of his t-shirt, slick with come and sweat.

"We should've taken that off you. You're showing evidence as clear as an admission of guilt."

Logan grinned. "And I'll wear it with pride, although I'll put my coat on first and make sure only I see it."

Bastien glanced down and saw the mess he'd made of himself.

"Give me a minute, and I'll get you a towel or

something to clean up," Logan said as he removed the condom and tied it off.

"It's fine. I'll just put my shirt back on and hit the showers before my next dance." His cheeks flushed a little, but he met Logan's gaze with a smile. "Who's Queen Bee now?"

Logan laughed. "You'll always be my Queen Bee." He leaned forward and pressed a kiss to Bastien's mouth.

"Always a charmer."

They made themselves presentable, then Bastien turned off the music, and they returned to the main area, making their way over to the bar. Bastien glanced at Logan and smiled, then whirled around to the dressing room. Unable to keep the smile from his face, he didn't even care that Cassidy was in the room, especially as Cody and Ash were in there, too.

"So, the cat got the cream, did he?" Cassidy sneered. "What would the boss say?"

Bastien sauntered over to him so only Cassidy could see and hear what he said. Lifting his shirt to show the evidence, he stared at Cassidy. "He would tell you that the man is mine, so keep your hands off him. My boyfriend is off-limits, understand?" Cassidy's eyes widened, and Bastien cackled at his shocked face. "Keep doing your job, Cass. It's all you've got going for you."

Anger darkened the other man's face, and Bastien

expected him to throw a punch, but nothing came. Instead, Cassidy stalked out of the room, slamming the door shut behind him.

Bastien dropped his shirt and headed for his locker, grabbing his toiletries and realising he better be fucking quick because he had fifteen minutes until his dance.

"What was all that about?" Cody asked, staring at Bastien as if he had horns growing.

"Just a misunderstanding that I was clearing up. Cassidy knows better now."

"I wouldn't be so sure. He looked pissed. I bet he'll think of something to mess with what you've got going on."

Bastien shrugged. "Nothing I can do but do my job and do it well."

He headed for the showers, cleaning himself vigorously but unhappy at having to take Logan's scent off him. At least, he'd be going back to Logan's house that night—or would he? Now that the stalker had been caught, did Bastien need to stay there any longer?

Pushing the thought aside, he dressed and did his makeup in record time, stepping backstage just as Miles was coming to meet him.

"I wondered where you were. Which song is it?"

"The one you created without the backing sounds, if that's all right?"

A flush graced Miles's cheeks, and he looked at the floor. "Yeah…um, yeah, okay."

He rushed away, and Bastien smiled to himself. If he gave even a little bit of happiness to that man, he was happy himself. Miles had no one as far as he could tell. His family had died when he was younger, and Rafferty had taken him in, just like Rafferty had taken care of Bastien when he needed it.

Bastien stepped on stage quietly, waiting for the beat to begin and started to dance. All his issues melted away as he focused on the music, focused on the rhythm, focused on his body. That was all that mattered. His hand met the pole, and he swung around, legs outstretched, his arms holding him strong and firm in a horizontal position. This was all that mattered.

Ten minutes later, he was energised and buzzing. He headed for the showers once more and washed himself clean, dragging on a second set of clothing for the floor work he had to do. Mixing with the customers and making small talk was as much a part of the job as dancing. Lap dances were extra money for the dancers, and tips from talking with the customers were for the club and the dancers. Rafferty was a fair boss.

He spent several long minutes chatting up and touching the customers before heading to the bar to get a drink for himself.

"An orange juice, please, Nolan."

"Coming right up."

Bastien slid a little closer to where Logan was sitting. "Did you enjoy the show?"

"I did." Logan's jaw tightened. "Are you coming home with me tonight?"

Bastien stared at him, unsure what the correct response was. "Um, I thought I was, although I could go—"

"Perfect. I'll wait around until you finish and take you home."

"Home?"

"My home. Your home. Our home."

"But the stalker has been found?"

"Do you not want to stay with me?"

"It's not that…" He gazed at the counter. "I didn't know if I was still supposed to stay. We never discussed what would happen when the threat was over," he admitted.

"Bas—Black. I want you there."

Bastien glanced up at him. "I want to be there."

"That's settled then."

Nolan pushed the orange towards him. "Have you two finally sorted yourselves out?"

Bastien cocked his head and curved his lips. "Whatever do you mean, Nolan?"

"I mean, have you two figured out that you're more than fuck buddies? It's taken you long enough."

For once, Bastien didn't have a snappy comeback,

and Nolan laughed at him. Logan stared at Bastien for a long few seconds, then smiled.

"It's taken too long."

Bastien focused on his drink, sipping at the sweet concoction to hide his smile.

Bastien was concerned. He'd been staying with Logan for over a week now, but his emotions were all over the place. Logan had told him the stalker had been found, but Bastien was sure that he was still being followed—if anything, more often than before. He didn't know what to think. He was scared to say something to Logan because of the response he'd received last time he did it, but he needed a sounding board.

Which was why he found himself on Logan's brother's doorstep. Why he'd chosen Casey, he had no idea, but he needed someone to talk to, and Casey was the first person he'd thought of. Well, the second actually, but he didn't think talking to Logan's parents was the way to go.

"Hey, Bastien. Everything okay?"

"Hey. Um, not really. At least, I'm not sure. I don't know. Maybe."

Casey chuckled. "Okay, let's get you inside. You're not making a lick of sense."

Bastien entered the warm house, being greeted by two dogs, one large and one small.

"Oh, these are Nessie and Samson," Casey introduced, pointing to the large and small one, respectively. "They're harmless if a little eager. Come on through."

He followed Casey to the kitchen, sinking into a chair when Casey indicated. Stroking the dogs was very therapeutic, and before he knew it, Casey was placing a steaming mug in front of him.

"It's hot chocolate if you couldn't tell. Now, what's happened? Is my brother being an asshole?"

"No!" Bastien said, startling the dogs. "No, not at all. It's..." He swallowed hard. "Logan told me the stalker had been found, so although I'm still staying with Logan," his cheeks heated at those words, "I'm back to sorting myself out if you see what I mean. I don't have anyone babysitting me."

"Okay. Is that a problem?"

"No, not at all. Except..." He exhaled heavily. "I think someone is still following me."

Casey's eyebrows raised, and he sat back in his chair. "Okay. Have you spoken to Log... Of course you haven't because of what happened the last time." Understanding dawned clearly on Casey's face. "Right, you need to tell him. He can investigate and find out what's happening."

"I don't want him to get depressed again. I hated that I did that to him."

"Woah, woah, woah. You didn't do anything to him." Casey leaned forward, resting his hand on Bastien's arm. "That wasn't what it was about. He was scared for you, Bastien. That was all. You did nothing wrong."

Bastien tried to take his words in, but he couldn't believe them.

"Do you want me to call him, and you can talk to him here? That way, I will be here, and so will Luke in case anything happens?"

"Would that be okay?"

"Of course. Let me call him, all right? You drink up."

Casey left the room, and Bastien was left to his thoughts once more. He was truly petrified that Logan would take the news badly and spiral down again, and Bastien didn't think he could handle it if he was the cause for it. There was no information he could give them; nobody came to mind when he tried to think of who or why someone would be following him. He knew he had issues with Deacon, but he'd not seen him at all since a week or so after the incident. Cassidy would always have issues with him and vice versa, but they carried on as usual and ignored each other anywhere else for the most part. He knew of no one who would do this to him.

"Luke and Logan are on their way. Have you eaten?"

"I can't eat anything at the moment. My stomach is churning."

"I know. Try to drink, at least. You need something inside you."

They spoke about Casey's job, about the dogs, who were new additions to their family, and about Logan and Casey's parents, filling the time until they heard the front door open.

"I saw this reprobate on the street and thought I'd bring him in for some company. Hope that's okay?" Luke joked as he entered the kitchen with Logan trailing behind him.

Casey stood, giving Luke a kiss before hugging his brother, whose gaze never left Bastien.

Logan stepped closer to Bastien, crouching next to his chair. "Everything okay, Queen Bee?" he whispered, and the softness of the words melted Bastien's heart.

"I'm not sure," he croaked back, burrowing his face in Logan's neck and wrapping his arms around his back.

"Bastien thinks someone is still following him."

Bastien felt Logan tense, then pull back, gazing at him. "Why didn't you tell me?"

"I was scared. I didn't want to upset you."

"Oh, Bastien." Logan lifted him, holding him

tightly as he sat in the chair Bastien had been sitting in, cradling Bastien in his arms.

No one said anything until Logan sighed and shifted Bastien around to look at him properly. Logan cupped his jaw in one hand. "I'm mostly worried that this has been going on, and you didn't tell me about it. Anything could've happened to you, and I wouldn't have known any different."

"I'm sorry," Bastien said, tears pooling in his eyes. He wiped at them while rolling his eyes and giving a self-deprecating laugh. "I'm so emotional lately. You've completely fucked me up, you know that, don't you?"

"What did I do?" Logan said with a small smile, trying to follow Bastien's lead and lighten the mood a little, although sobering quickly. "Tell me what's been happening, Queen Bee."

"Well, you know that I've gone back to my usual routine of walking to work—it's quicker from your house. I began noticing sounds of footsteps following me, but when I turned or looked in passing windows, there was no one there. I'm still not certain that I'm not imagining it, but it's freaking me out."

"All right. Here's what we're going to do. You need to give me all the times and places you remember feeling like you were being followed, and I will head to the station to get started on tracking any CCTV that I can find. It might be a dead-end, but it will be worth trying." Logan tilted his head. "Do you ever get that feeling whenever you've left work, or is it after a certain distance away from the building?"

Bastien sniffed, biting his bottom lip as he thought. "I've noticed it once that I can remember as soon as I came out of the door. That was on the first night I noticed, which was Friday."

Logan clenched his jaw, but he exhaled through his nose, and when he spoke, he was neutral in his tone, though Bastien knew he was keeping his anger under control. "Okay. I'll check that out. I will have to give the case to Kade and Joey; I won't be allowed to stay on it, but I can get the ball rolling. Do you feel safe at home? Or would you prefer to be somewhere else?"

"You can stay here if you'd prefer. Luke and I will be here all night, and then I'll be home all day tomorrow, too," Casey said. "We've got the dogs as well, although they might lick intruders to death instead of anything else."

Everyone chuckled, which broke the tension a little.

"If you're sure it's okay, I'd like to stay with someone. It's freaked me out a bit tonight."

"Did anything out of the ordinary happen tonight to make things worse?" Logan asked.

Bastien shook his head. "No, Cassidy was his usual bitchy self; everyone was behaving normally."

Logan kissed his temple. "Right. I'll head out now and get things going. I'll check in with you later. Try and get some sleep. I know it's not easy when you're worried but try anyway."

"I will."

Logan took his mouth in a tense, hard kiss, and Bastien could feel the tension in him. Pulling back, Bastien wrapped his arms around Logan's neck, inhaling his scent before standing to let him move.

"Hey." Logan waited until Bastien peered at him. "Do you want me to tuck you in?"

Bastien bit his lip. "Would you mind?"

Logan grinned. "Which room will he be in?" he asked over his shoulder.

"Furthest away."

Bastien could hear the amusement in Casey's voice when he replied, and his cheeks heated. Who knew that having others tease him would cause his inhibitions to quake in mortification? He threaded their fingers together, and they climbed the stairs, drifting down the hallway to the last room in the house. Logan opened the door and pressed a hand to Bastien's lower back. The door closed softly behind them, and Bastien could feel Logan's presence, a warmth at his back.

"Let's get you undressed," Logan growled in his ear, shivers pebbling down his spine.

He allowed Logan to remove his shirt, then his trousers, finding a spare t-shirt in the drawers of the room. Logan slid it over his head, smoothing it into place and leading him over to the bed. Pulling the covers back, he guided Bastien to climb in and settled the cover over him, crouching beside him. Logan smoothed his hand over Bastien's hair, and Bastien's eyes fluttered.

"Sleep, Queen Bee. You're safe here."

CHAPTER FIFTEEN

LOGAN

After speaking with the chief about Bastien's fears, Bryan agreed to let Kade and Joey take on the case. Logan's body released some of the tension because he knew those two men would do their jobs and not mess it up, unlike what would happen if it was given to Henry. The anger coursing through him was not as easy to release.

He'd briefly spoken to Casey after tucking Bastien into bed two nights ago, and Casey had told him to go easy on the guy. The last six months had been a roller-coaster for Logan, and everything felt fresh in his mind with the new developments.

Also, why was it that he could not seem to keep the people he cared about safe from harm? He wouldn't be able to let Bastien go without having an escort wherever he went until the problem was resolved.

Although he was unable to work on the case properly, he had taken over watching the CCTV videos of the club that Rafferty had offered up once he'd found out what was happening. Logan had visited the man, asking for help with keeping Bastien safe, and he had stepped up without question. Because Logan was familiar with the club, he'd argued that he would be the best person to check them out because he might see something out of place. It was an argument he'd been surprised to win without too much issue.

So, he'd been watching the videos for the past two days. He'd started with the Friday that Bastien had said he'd felt someone following him from when he'd left the club. Nothing had shown up that day, and thus far, nothing seemed out of the ordinary. He paused the video where it was and headed to the coffee machine, pouring the disgusting coffee into a cup for himself.

He'd barely seen Bastien the past two days because when he was working his shifts, he did his own cases, but when his shifts finished, he stayed on to watch the videos. Exhaustion clamoured at him, but he was determined to get through all of them. He only had two more days to look at, which would take him up to the day Bastien had told him about it.

Moving his head from side to side to stretch out his neck muscles, he wandered back to his desk, dropping into his chair and taking a large gulp of hot coffee. As he drank his drink, he stared at the fuzzy figures on the screen, not seeing anything.

At least, he didn't see anything…until he did.

He narrowed his eyes and leaned closer to the screen. Reaching for his mobile, he dialled.

"What can I do for you, Logan?"

"Are any of the performances at the club recorded? You know, on video?"

"No. The only recording equipment allowed is the CCTV cameras. Why?"

"Because someone is recording them," he said distractedly.

"Who?" Rafferty demanded.

"We'll be there shortly." He hung up on the man's cursing and scrambled over to Kade and Joey. "Hey, I think I've found something. Not sure if it's related to the stalking, but it's definitely not allowed."

They headed back to Logan's desk, and he pointed out the man holding a video camera, hidden slightly behind the stage curtains.

"Rafferty said no recordings are allowed, so this guy is out of order," Logan growled the words, wanting nothing more than to smash his face in, and that was without knowing whether he was the stalker or not.

"Calm down. We'll go and have a chat."

"I'm coming."

"No, Logan—"

"I'm always there anyway. It's nothing different. I'll keep out of your way. I just want to be there as an extra pair of hands, all right?"

Kade sighed and shook his head. "Fine, but stay back."

Logan printed off a couple of picture stills from the video and handed them to Kade. He couldn't wait to find out what was happening, and he'd be able to see Bastien again. Luke had taken Bastien to work that night, and Logan was supposed to be picking him up. He would stay and wait for Bastien if everything went smoothly. If not, he'd come back for him. There was no way he was walking by himself, no matter what.

Logan took his car and met Kade and Joey there. Brandy let Logan in without question, although Logan needed to call Rafferty to get the other two in without problems. No one wanted to announce who they were unless it was necessary.

Rafferty met them at the bar, shaking hands with each of them, then led the way to his office. Once the door was closed, Logan began explaining.

"How long has Miles worked for you?"

"Jesus Christ! Miles? He wouldn't hurt a fucking fly." Rafferty rubbed his hands over his face and leaned back in his chair. "Around a year or so. Maybe a little more. I can give you definitive dates if you need me to."

"Maybe later. We found this on one of your CCTV

videos." Kade passed the printed photos over to the owner, and they waited for his verdict.

Rafferty shook his head. "I never would've believed it if you hadn't shown me these, but yeah, that's definitely Miles with a video camera. You can even see it's not a bloody phone." He dropped them onto the desk. "What now?"

"We need to speak to him. Where's the best place to do that?" Kade asked.

"Probably the lap dance rooms. Choose one, and I'll get Miles back there somehow."

"Kade and Joey are taking lead on the case, so I won't be in there with him," Logan said. "But I will be at the bar. No one is getting to Bastien on my watch."

"Or mine," growled Rafferty.

They exited the office, Logan heading for a stool where he could sit with his back to the door but see the entire club. He watched as Kade and Joey headed behind the curtained area and Rafferty went backstage. Logan checked the stage and recognised Cassidy as the spotlight dancer. It meant he would be able to have a few minutes of peace and quiet. That dancer was a pain in his ass.

"Haven't seen you for a few days. Do you want your usual?" Nolan asked, grabbing a glass but pausing before filling it.

Logan shook his head. "Nah, just orange juice tonight, thanks. Need to keep a clear head."

"Fair enough." Nolan twisted around to get his drink, returning several minutes later.

"Thanks." Logan wrapped his hand around the glass but didn't take a drink straight away. He watched surreptitiously as Rafferty led Miles towards the back curtains, gesturing wildly with his hands until the men disappeared. It was a waiting game now.

The roar of the audience took his notice, and he saw the dance had finished. Watching Cassidy pick up the notes on the stage before strutting backstage had him shaking his head. Shame Cassidy's attitude wasn't more amenable. General music started up, and customers began filling up the bar area. Logan didn't move from his position, but he kept an eye on all the people who turned up, recognising most of them from his previous visits.

"So, what has you on edge tonight?" Nolan asked, resting his elbows on the counter in front of him.

"Ah, it's just work. It's like I'm on a carousel that won't stop." Logan grinned and sipped his drink, muffling his need to spit it back out. He pretended to drink, watching Nolan out of the corner of his eye. For some reason, Nolan had ignored his drink order and added alcohol to it. Or at least, Logan thought it was alcohol. It certainly wasn't only orange juice.

"I know that feeling. Sometimes, this place feels like it never stops. Best place I ever worked, though."

Logan replaced the drink on the counter, refusing

to lick his lips. "When you find somewhere you like working, definitely stay there." As if it were normal for him, he rubbed a hand over his lips and chin, wiping the access liquid away. He pulled out his phone. "Sorry, I have to reply to this. It's my brother."

"No worries." Nolan headed off down the counter, helping out with drinks where the other bartender was standing.

Logan brought up a message to Kade instead.

The bartender has given me something in my drink. I've not drunk too much because I could tell it wasn't just orange juice, but I need you to be aware in case something happens to me. No idea why. Thought he was on the up and up. Tell Rafferty.

Logan had no idea what he'd ingested, but he hoped it was just alcohol and the bartender was trying to get him drunk for some reason and nothing more serious. Time would tell.

He smiled when he saw Bastien take to the stage and settled in to watch his performance while scanning the crowd for anyone looking shifty. A minute or two into the routine, Cassidy sidled up beside him.

"Hey, handsome. Have you had enough of Black yet?" Cassidy pouted, running a finger down Logan's shirt buttons.

Logan kept his gaze on the man and saw when he

flicked his gaze to Nolan, who shook his head. He had a feeling Cassidy had a part in the charade here.

"Sorry, Cassidy. I'm not interested."

"Do you really think he doesn't fuck those customers he takes back for a lap dance?" Cassidy's eyes narrowed, his jaw clenching as his mouth pursed. If he had been a cartoon character, steam would've been coming from his ears by this point.

"I know he doesn't fuck them, Cassidy. He only fucks me. And you wish you could."

Cassidy's jaw worked, but he didn't say anything. "I'm beginning to believe you're not worth the time I've invested in you," he muttered, sashaying away into the audience.

"Definitely not," Logan agreed. He turned to Nolan and raised his eyebrows. When he was within hearing distance, he said, "Why spike the drink?"

Nolan exhaled heavily, shoulders slumping. "Cassidy asked me to."

"And do you do everything Cassidy asks you to?" Nolan rolled his lips inwards and stared at the counter. "I'll take that as a yes. Was it just alcohol?" Nolan shook his head. "Nolan," Logan berated. "What have you gotten yourself into?"

"You barely had anything, so you shouldn't be feeling any effects."

"Rohypnol?" Nolan nodded. "Why? If you like

Cassidy as much as it seems you do, why do this to me?"

"Cassidy wanted to get back at Black. This was the way he chose."

"By what? Dosing me up and raping me? Staging a scene? Taking photos? What was the end game?"

"I don't know exactly." Nolan began polishing a glass half-heartedly.

Logan shook his head, glaring at the man. "You're going to be in big trouble for this, you know that? Rohypnol is no joking matter. There's a potential ten-year prison sentence that goes along with it."

"Why can't we brush it under the carpet?" Nolan stared at him, pleading with his eyes.

"Do you even know what my job is?" Logan raised his eyebrows in question.

"I have no idea. Cassidy said you were a hotshot teacher or something."

Logan laughed. "Oh, Nolan. When I first met you, I thought you were all clued up. But I've just realised you are being led. You need to stop following other people and start doing what's right for you. Cassidy has left you in such a mess, and the only way out will be to testify against him." Logan flicked his gaze to the curtained area, seeing Kade appear, then Miles, then Joey. Rafferty pulled up the rear.

"I can't testify against him. Why would it need to go that far?"

"Because you just tried to drug a police officer, Nolan," Rafferty said, anger blazing in his eyes.

Nolan's face paled as he stared at Logan in horror. "You're a police officer?" he whispered. Logan nodded. "Fuck! Cassidy never told me that."

"Nobody knows, except Black."

Nolan dragged his hands through his hair, squeezing his head with his arms. "Holy fucking hell."

Logan turned to Kade. "Sorted?"

"Surprising information, I must say. This is bigger than just him," Kade said, indicating Miles over his shoulder.

"Who else?"

"Cassidy."

Logan sighed and shook his head, glancing at Nolan. "What the hell is going on here, Rafferty?"

"I have no fucking clue, but I'm going to get to the bottom of it because I'm not having this happening in my fucking club."

"Right, Nolan. You need to go with Detective Stirling. I will stay here and ensure that Cassidy stays on the premises until you can get back to retrieve him. I want to know what the hell is going on."

Kade stepped closer. "Miles was the one who was following Bastien. From what he's told us so far, Cassidy persuaded him that Bastien was in love with Miles but refused to say anything to him because they worked together. Cassidy told Miles that Bastien was scared that someone was trying to hurt him and suggested that Miles follow him to keep him safe. I have a feeling Cassidy only wanted to scare Bastien."

"That fits, but what does Cassidy get out of it apart from that? What's his end game?" Logan wasn't convinced that the stalking was the only thing going on here, especially with Nolan trying to drug him. Something else was happening. "Take those two in and come back for Cassidy. If we're not out here, we'll be in Rafferty's office."

Rafferty, who had gone off to sort replacements for Miles and Nolan, came back with Bastien in tow. Bastien smiled when he saw Logan, then frowned when he saw Kade holding Nolan and Joey holding Miles.

"What's happened?"

"I'll tell you in a minute," Logan said, raising his eyebrows to make his point. Bastien swallowed and pursed his lips but nodded. "Let me know when you're on your way back," he said to Kade.

"Will do. Come on, you two."

Logan watched them lead the two guys out of the club, Rafferty trailing behind, no doubt to try and stop Brandy from asking questions. The bouncer was good at his job, but he was a nosey fucker.

Logan pulled Bastien closer. "I'm going to tell you some things, but you need to keep your head; otherwise, you will ruin what we have planned. Do you understand?"

"Yes, but—"

"But nothing. Whatever I tell you now, you need to not react in any way until Kade and Joey come back."

Bastien inhaled deeply, sighing it out. "All right." Logan could tell he wasn't happy.

"Miles was your stalker. Cassidy put him up to it. On top of all that, Nolan tried to drug me because Cassidy told him to."

Logan could see the anger brewing in Bastien's eyes. The way his eyes narrowed, his lips pursed, and his forehead creased. He grabbed hold of Bastien's hands, rubbing his thumb across his knuckles to keep Bastien from blowing up like Logan knew he wanted to.

"Why?" Bastien gritted out.

"We don't know the exact reasons yet. We will be taking Cassidy in as soon as Kade and Joey come back, but until then, it's business as usual. If you can't do that, you need to tell me now."

"I can do that." Bastien smirked. "Being a bitch to him is nothing more than normal. Now, though, I have even more excuse." Bastien pulled a hand away and placed it on his hip with a small smile. "I'm Queen Bee. Cassidy has no hope of taking that particular crown."

Logan grinned. "That's my Queen Bee."

Bastien's façade faltered. "Are you okay, though?"

"Yeah. I didn't drink much because I noticed the taste was off. I have a little bit of a headache, but that could just as likely be stress as what I ingested."

"Well, take it easy. Zara, could you get Logan a sealed bottle of water, please?" he called to the other bartender.

When it came, Logan checked the seal, then uncapped it and drank greedily. When the bottle was empty, he emptied the contents of the glass into the bottle, then put the glass into an evidence bag from the supplies he carried in his pocket.

"Always prepared." Bastien grinned at him.

"Habit of the job."

Rafferty came back in and blew out a breath when he reached them. "How are you feeling?"

"I'm all right. Bit of a headache, but I'm sure it'll pass soon."

Rafferty gazed at Bastien. "I'm so sorry this is happening. I can't believe—"

Bastien placed his hand on the man's arm. "It's not your fault."

"Well, if I don't know what's happening underneath my own roof, then who the hell does?"

"You weren't to know, Rafferty. The best you can do now is maybe do some staff evaluations or something like that. Check over everyone in the business and make sure you are happy to keep them on. Don't tar everyone with the same brush as Cassidy."

"I should've trusted my instincts with that boy. And the many times you said he was an ass." Rafferty glanced at Bastien when he said it, the smirk of the man he had been before that night poking through.

"Well, now you know. I know everything." Bastien pivoted and walked away, a sway in his hips that told Logan exactly how much Rafferty would never live down that acknowledgement.

"He's never going to let me forget I said that, is he?" Rafferty mused.

Logan laughed. "Nope." He watched as Bastien slid onto the lap of a customer, surprised to find no jealousy coursing through him.

"Does that not bother you?" Rafferty asked.

Logan glanced across at him, seeing his gaze on him rather than Bastien. "To begin with, it did. Now, though," Logan paused, "no. I know he's mine, and I know he won't go too far with anyone. He's as honest as they come. And he's mine."

"If that growl is anything to go by, he's staking a claim again." Kade's voice sounded from behind him, although it didn't startle him.

Rafferty snorted and clapped hands with Kade, squeezing Logan's shoulder with his other hand. "That he was, but nothing that anyone who looked at him wouldn't guess anyway."

Logan glanced at his watch. "Are you doing it now, or are you waiting for closing?" he asked Kade.

Kade looked to Rafferty, who shrugged. "It's up to you. Cassidy doesn't have another dance to do, so it would only be his floor work he'd miss."

Music started up again, and the stage lights rose to showcase Cody, another dancer with whom Logan had several conversations before. Bastien had said they were friends, so Logan had been happy to chat.

"—take him now," Kade finished saying.

"I'll go and grab him." Rafferty turned and headed into the audience.

"Busy night," Joey said, resting his arms on the counter and grinning.

"I doubt it's all going to be tied up in a bow. Cassidy will spin some tale, I'm sure of it," Logan stated.

He watched as Rafferty led Cassidy back to their group of three.

"What's all this about?"

Kade stepped forward. "You're being taken to the station for questioning."

"What for?" Cassidy's voice rose, and Logan knew he was going to make a show of it.

"Cassidy," he said firmly, gaining the man's attention, "unless you want to be arrested in front of all these people who will never again trust you to dance for them, I would suggest you go quietly. If this is all one big misunderstanding, I'm sure your job will be here for you."

Rafferty nodded. "It will. Go with them now, Cassidy, and don't cause a fuss."

Cassidy pouted and crossed his arms. "Can I ask least get my stuff from my locker?"

"With supervision, yes," Kade agreed.

"I'll take him," Rafferty said.

"I'll go too," Joey added.

As they watched the three men head backstage, Logan sighed. "That was easier than I thought it would be."

"Well, as you said, Cassidy probably has a tale to tell."

"I wonder who he'll blame or if he'll think he's popular enough to not have any repercussions if he admits to being the brains behind the operation," Logan said.

"How are you feeling?"

Logan took stock of his body. "I'm feeling fine. I don't think I swallowed enough to do too much harm. I tasted it on my tongue before I swallowed and then basically spat it back into the glass as I took it away from my mouth." Logan indicated his pocket. "I have the glass and liquid for evidence."

"Are you going to press charges?"

Logan shrugged. "I think it depends on what comes from the interviews. I don't really want the hassle it would bring, but if it is needed to make something stick to one of those guys for what they've done to Bastien, then I will."

"Have you told him you love him yet?"

Eyes seeking out the subject of their discussion, Logan's mouth curved. "Not yet."

Kade chuckled. "Never thought I'd see the day."

"Yeah, well, right back atcha! You and Analise have been together how long now?"

Kade grinned, his face lightening at the name of his girlfriend. "Around eighteen months now."

"Longest date ever for you."

Kade shoved his shoulder, and Logan laughed. "Shut up."

They settled down again, and Logan's gaze found Bastien once more, smiling at a customer and sliding his hand across the man's shoulder. It was a strange feeling to watch his boyfriend getting cosy with other men but not feel jealous about it at all. He knew Bastien. He would never hurt someone without cause.

The thought made him contemplate Bastien's parents. How could they have let him walk away with nothing but the clothes on his back? Or rather, how could they have thrown him out with only the clothes on his back? Why not give him something to get started with? With everything Bastien told him, which granted wasn't a huge amount, they had enough money to spare some to make sure he wasn't homeless.

Anger fizzled through his veins at the idea of Bastien living on the streets. Life is hard enough when you have stuff, including a roof over your head, without not having anything. He knew it was a subject they would have to talk about sooner rather than later, but Logan was content to let it lie for the time being.

Rafferty and Joey returned with Cassidy, and after a coy look in Logan's direction, Cassidy headed off with the police officers.

The owner dropped onto a barstool and rubbed a hand over his face.

"You weren't to know."

Rafferty glanced at him, and Logan could see the tightening around his lips, emotions warring in his eyes, belying his feelings. "Doesn't feel that way. It feels like I've let them down. All of them. Even the ones in the wrong. Surely I should've seen something was happening right under my nose?"

CHAPTER SIXTEEN

BASTIEN

Bastien heard Rafferty's words as he wandered back to the bar, and his heart broke for the man. He was so kind-hearted; it was terrible that this had happened under his watch.

"You wouldn't have necessarily seen it, even if you had been looking for it," Logan said, flicking his gaze to Bastien's.

"Everything was done out of your eyesight, Boss," Bastien chimed in. "Not even I realised Nolan and Miles were in on it. As for Cassidy, well, let me just say, I'm not surprised."

Logan pulled Bastien close and fitted him between his knees, Bastien's back to Logan's front, facing Rafferty. "Cassidy is a spiteful piece of shit. I've seen that plenty of times during my visits here, but I wouldn't have thought he was capable of what we think he's done."

Rafferty shook his head and sighed. "I just don't know what to do."

"It all depends on whether you're able to trust them again after this or not," Bastien said. "They're good workers, but if they could do this once, maybe they could do it again? I don't know. Some people deserve a second chance; others don't. There's no wrong or right answer here. Trust your instincts, although I will say I don't know if I'd be able to work with them."

Bastien pulled away from Logan to wrap his arms around his boss's shoulders, rubbing his back gently.

"Thanks, B."

"Do you have another set to dance?" Logan asked him.

Bastien checked the clock and startled. "Oh, shit, yes!" He pecked Logan on the lips, then hustled to the dressing room. Quickly stripping off his outfit, he slid into the next clothes—forgoing his usual shower, unfortunately—and sat at the table to do his makeup. He had only enough time to make himself look presentable before he needed to get his music set up. Since Miles was no longer doing their music, each performer was having to set their music themselves, having been shown how to do it so they could take over should the need arise.

Lining up the song, he waited on stage in the dark until the necessary beat then began to move. He always started his routines in the same spot, give or take a little, because he loved being able to walk down the catwalk-like stage towards the pole. The audience always went wild during that walk, knowing what to expect when he got to his destination.

This time, though, he was dancing for one person and one person only. Logan. He'd chosen the sultriest song he could find, a routine he had not danced in a long time, but as soon as the beat hit, it was like his body was on automatic. His hands rose, his legs moved, his body swayed and curved and spun until there was nothing left of him to give. And when the music stopped, and he lifted his head from the resting position to stare into the roaring crowd, he locked gazes with the man he knew he loved.

Logan blew him a kiss, and Bastien simpered, rising from the floor to collect his tips. He was Queen Bee, and no one could usurp him. At least, for now.

By the time the club closed, Bastien was ready to take Logan home and devour him. He hadn't felt that horny in a long time, and having no respite due to

Cassidy's absence, meant he'd had to work harder and not see Logan as much, except in his periphery. After taking a quick shower and tugging on some more comfortable, but still in character, clothes, he headed to the main area, wanting to catch Cody before he left.

The man himself was talking to Rafferty, and Bastien had no concerns about interrupting, especially since both parties would benefit from his words.

"Sorry to interrupt…kind of. Cody, have you asked Boss Man about the music thing you were telling me about?"

He knew Cody had been taking classes at college for music, and having a job that was less dancing and more about creating music for the routines would be beneficial to him. Not only for his course evidence but as a safe continuous wage. The base wage for dancing was set, but the tips made it even better, although they weren't guaranteed, of course.

"No, he hasn't," Rafferty said, turning to the smaller man. "What did you want to ask me about?"

Cody flushed ten shades of scarlet and stumbled over some words that even Bastien had trouble understanding.

Bastien butted in again, "What he wants to ask is if he could have a chance at doing the music for the club. He's been doing music at college and wants to use it for his coursework and potentially as a shift in his job here." He patted Cody on the back, winked at Rafferty and left them to it.

Logan grinned as Bastien neared him. "Are you stirring up trouble again?"

"Possibly. Cody wants to do something with music, Rafferty needs someone to take over for Miles, even if it's just short-term, and as a plus, they look like such a cute couple. Who would've thought they both had the hots for each other and never had the guts to spell it out? They needed a little shove in the right direction."

"You're a little matchmaker, aren't you?" Logan wrapped his arms around Bastien, pulling him close and nuzzling his neck.

"That I am!"

"And you're not even ashamed of it!"

"Nope!" Bastien cupped Logan's face and took his lips in a kiss that was not suitable for the public. When they finally broke for air, Logan's eyes were glassy, his pupils blown, and Bastien was sure he was the same. "Home!"

"Yep," Logan agreed.

They shouted goodbye and headed out the door towards Logan's car.

"Have you heard any more from Kade or Joey yet?"

"Nah. I doubt we'll hear anything until tomorrow or even a few days after. They'll go through all the evidence first before coming to me because they know I'll be on their case if they haven't."

"Aww, give them a break. They've been good to us."

"They have, but they know that if it was the other way around, I wouldn't leave a stone unturned, and they will do the same."

"What about the stalker case? Did the man you arrested tell his secrets?"

Logan shook his head. "No, he's completely clammed up about it all. He's told us the bare minimum amount of information to show that he's cooperating, but it's nothing that helps us much. We have a lot of information to go through, though."

Logan pointed the car towards his house and reached over to Bastien. As per their usual routine, Bastien linked his fingers over the back of Logan's hands and threaded their fingers, ensuring Logan could still use the gear stick to change gears. It was a funny feeling and had taken Bastien a few attempts to be comfortable, but he loved that he didn't need to let go of his hand for any reason.

"Do you want to watch a movie to relax before bed?" Logan asked, a twinkle in his eye.

"If it's something I like the look of, sure." Bastien's eyelashes fluttered.

"I'm sure you'll like it."

Bastien stared out of the window, hiding his smile

as he watched the dimmed streetlights flicker past in the early hours of the morning while Logan's thumb brushed hypnotizingly against his little finger. The electricity flowing through his body had not diminished in the warm summer night air.

Bastien breathed through his nose when they pulled up to Logan's house, trying to cool his need, but it was no use. The minute he was through the front door, he wrapped himself around Logan and took his mouth—the height difference sorted by Bastien climbing up his body.

Logan spun them, bracing Bastien against the wall while he plundered Bastien's mouth, exploring every inch of it. Bastien rested his head back, letting Logan take control, willing to submit to whatever he wanted to do to him. An arm gripped under his ass and lifted him away from the surface, moving somewhere, though Bastien was too far gone to open his eyes to identify where they were going. He felt himself being lowered, and he tightened his hold, not wanting to be parted from the breath-stealing kisses Logan was providing.

Air was a requirement, though, and eventually, he had to pull back, panting. His eyelids flickered open, taking in the new surroundings of Logan's living room. The sofa was at his back, and Logan was at his front, kissing his way down Bastien's neck while he pulled at

Bastien's clothes. A sense of urgency took over, and they were naked before Bastien realised it.

"Need you," Bastien gasped into Logan's mouth right before their kiss was rekindled.

Several minutes later, Logan pulled away, Bastien whimpering in response. He moved Bastien around until he was kneeling on the cushions with his upper body resting on the arm of the sofa. Bastien glanced over his shoulder, watching Logan open a drawer in the small trestle table next to the sofa and removing a tube and wrapper.

With a smirk and a wink, Logan ripped open the wrapper and rolled the condom down his cock, Bastien following every movement, licking his lips. He felt the blood rush to his dick at the sight of Logan rubbing lube over his cock and pressing his fingers against Bastien's entrance. Prepping him quickly but sufficiently enough that the burn would only be seconds long, Logan rested the head of his shaft against the pucker. His hands slid up Bastien's spine, smoothing the goosebumps until he reached his shoulders. He gripped them tightly and drove forward.

Bastien's yell of surprise was lost to a moan, the heat of Logan's cock impaling him such a wonderful feeling. He rested his arms against the sofa, stopping his forward motion and giving Logan more traction.

"Fuck, yes," Logan growled, slamming his hips

harder and faster against Bastien's ass. "Round two coming soon."

Bastien was confused for a moment until he felt Logan's hand circled his cock and stroke hard. He had no time to prepare as his orgasm tore through him, his mouth opening on a silent groan of satisfaction while his muscles clenched. Hearing Logan roar behind him, he dropped his head, gasping.

He felt Logan retreat, but he didn't open his eyes. Even when Logan repositioned him on his back, and he grimaced at the feel of his release now coating his spine, his eyes remained closed as the aftershocks made his nerves twitch. Logan lifted Bastien's legs and settled between them. When he heard a snick, he blinked his eyelids, seeing Logan with a fresh condom, a slick shaft and a grin.

"Round two."

Logan pressed inside without fanfare, the sensitivity of his passage making Logan feel bigger than usual but also sent a tingle to every part of him.

"Oh, fucking hell," Bastien breathed, arching his back.

Surprisingly, when Logan was seated fully, he stopped, leaning down to cover Bastien's body with his own and sliding his arms under Bastien's back. When he grimaced, Bastien giggled.

"Yeah, should've thought about that beforehand," Bastien joked.

"Oh, well." He leaned down and took Bastien's mouth, sipping at his lips and licking along the seam before slipping inside. This kiss was as sensual as the first was carnal. Logan touched every part of him. Slowly, then fast, then slowly again until Bastien was writhing beneath him. His legs lifted and encircled Logan's waist, giving him something to brace against while he thrust his hips.

Logan began withdrawing in small increments, then pressing forward repeatedly while Bastien was going crazy. His head was being held still as Logan's kisses increased in fervency. Bastien clawed at Logan's back, wanting more, wanting everything Logan could give him.

Pulling away, Logan leaned their foreheads together and whispered, "You're mine, Bastien. No one else can have you."

Tears leaked from the corners of Bastien's eyes, and Logan kissed them away. His emotions were front and centre as Logan took him higher and higher, even though he'd just come.

"Mine, Bastien. You have to believe it." Logan kissed him again, and Bastien's tears came harder at the thought that this man might be everything he ever needed in life. "Mine. I love you, Queen Bee."

Bastien cried as his climax drew closer, and Logan held him through it all. He knew there was no denying it. They both knew how Bastien felt, but saying the words was difficult. Until he realised he'd already said the words with his actions. Logan knew what Bastien struggled to say, and although he knew he didn't have to return the words to him, Bastien wanted to.

As Logan's hips snapped faster, reaching for that release, Bastien pulled him closer, sucking his earlobe into his mouth, and whispered, "I love you, Logan."

After a one-second pause, Logan held him tighter and pounded his ass. Within seconds, Bastien flew over the edge with Logan not too far behind. They stayed entwined for many long minutes despite the uncomfortably sticky situation. Bastien didn't care. He had Logan. All of him.

Once they had showered and cleaned up, removing the soiled sofa cushion to be washed, they headed for bed, tangling themselves together.

The following three days were pretty normal for Bastien. He would be escorted to work, he'd dance, he'd be escorted back again, he'd spend time with Logan and his family, he'd eat, he'd drink, and so on. It was a little tedious, but Bastien understood the precautions, especially as they hadn't heard from Kade or Joey yet. Logan had called them for an update, but they had put him off, saying they were working on something and he needed to be patient. Bastien had laughed at that, earning a spanking and a fuckfest straight after.

He'd made a mental note that laughing at Logan ended with a sexy side-effect.

When Kade and Joey finally darkened their doorstep, Bastien thought Logan was going to throttle one of them; therefore, after preparing drinks for everyone, he sat on Logan's lap to entice him to be kind.

"What's the verdict?" Logan asked into the silence, tension tightening his body.

Bastien curled closer but kept his gaze on the two detectives.

Kade blew out a breath. "We've questioned four men for working togeth—"

"Wait! Four?" Bastien sat upright.

Kade nodded patiently. "All right, long story here. Miles told us that he'd taken a liking to you when he first started working at the club. He'd kept it completely to himself because he was too nervous about approaching you." Kade smiled. "His words were, 'He's so gorgeous and confident, how could I ever talk to him in that way? He'd think I was immature or something.' I think you'd have been flattered but..." He shrugged. "Anyway, apparently, it was only on a few occasions that he took a video recording of your routines. He said it was something to do with you using his songs. Does that make sense to you?"

Bastien nodded. "Yeah. He provided me with a CD that had some mixed-up music he'd created. I'd used several in my new routines."

"Okay, that confirms what he said, although it doesn't make it right, especially as there was a no recording clause in the employee contracts as well as a rule at the club." Kade glanced at his notepad. "As for Cassidy, he'd caught Miles recording one night and promised not to tell but told Miles that you liked him, too. Miles said that Cassidy had told him you were scared because you thought someone was following you around."

Joey took over, "It appears Cassidy put the idea into Miles's head that he was doing you a favour by following you and making sure you were safe. Miles doesn't seem to relate what he was doing as stalking because Cassidy made it seem like he was helping you, and you knew about it."

Bastien inhaled. "Yeah, I can see that working. It's why I was so surprised by it being Miles. He's so gentle and kind, wouldn't hurt a fly kind of person."

"Moving onto Nolan," Kade said. "He wanted Cassidy, and for more than the fling he'd been given. Apparently, the two of them had slept together on several occasions, but Cassidy refused to go for more. But from what Nolan has said about the man, Cassidy kept him hanging on a hook by flirting and making suggestions about getting together, which Nolan desperately wanted. Cassidy persuaded him to doctor the drink, saying he wanted Logan to be incapacitated and out of the way while Bastien was hit on by Miles. Nolan asked him why he didn't wait until Logan wasn't there, but Cassidy explained it away. Although Nolan didn't understand his reasoning, he didn't decline, thinking it was his way to get Cassidy to be with him."

Bastien frowned, and Logan said, "So, let me get this straight. Cassidy wanted Bastien scared, so he coerced Miles to stalk him. Nolan wanted Cassidy, so he tried to drug me to get me out of the way to give Miles a chance with Bastien, although Cassidy really wanted to fuck with me to get back at Bastien. Is that right?"

Joey grinned. "Pretty much, yes."

Logan rubbed a hand over his face and squeezed Bastien's hip. "Right, what else?"

"Cassidy, as we all surmised, hates Bastien and wants him gone. He found a…friend who had similar feelings." Kade looked at Bastien. "Deacon."

Bastien dropped his head into his hands and closed his eyes. "All this time, I thought he'd let it go. I haven't heard anything from him since he dragged my name through the mud and people dropped me. I assumed that was all he'd planned to do, which was bad enough." Logan rubbed a hand over his back, and Bastien nestled in again.

"Deacon has been brewing this up ever since you had him arrested. When he visited the club one night, he got to talking to Cassidy, and they found their mutual grievance. Deacon didn't have to work too hard to persuade Cassidy to be the middle-man and arrange all this," Joey explained.

"What did Deacon get out of it?" Logan asked.

"Bastien being discredited, losing his job, losing his house. Everything really. Cassidy wanted you gone, end of. What you may not have known is that Deacon is out of business. Ever since his arrest, people have stopped employing him. He says it's all your fault, which, of course, it isn't."

Logan tucked Bastien under his chin, holding him tightly. "Why can't people leave me the fuck alone?" Bastien murmured into his chest.

"All four of them spilled what they knew about how the others were involved. Only Cassidy knew about Deacon and vice versa, but both were willing to drag the other under the bus. We have arrested Deacon and Cassidy, and with the amount of evidence against them, they'll be spending time in prison. It's your choice whether you want to press charges against Miles and Nolan," Kade stated, sitting back and sipping at his coffee.

"All right. We'll have a chat and let you know in a

couple of hours," Logan said.

Kade and Joey stood, waving at Logan and Bastien to remain seated when they went to move. The officers left, Kade telling them he'd lock the door behind them.

As the noise around them settled down to a slight hum of the heating and not much else, Bastien sighed and stared out the window. He watched a squirrel dart along the top of the fence before climbing a tree, and he wished he had that freedom. Although maybe now that the four of them had been figured out, he would have that.

"What's wrong?"

Logan's quiet words sliced through his musings, and he slid his head up until he could look into the other man's eyes.

"I was just wondering if this meant it was over and I could get back to some sort of normalcy."

Logan quirked the corner of his mouth. "I don't see why not. Once we decide about Nolan and Miles, we can give our final statements to the police, and it should be finished. At least until the potential court case."

The idea of having to deal with that made Bastien's stomach churn. "What should we do with them?"

Logan pressed his lips to Bastien's forehead and spoke against his skin, "Personally, I think we should not press charges against Miles. From what information Kade and Joey provided, he seems to have been coerced into doing it. I think he's harmless. Nolan is less so. I'm on the fence about him, but maybe he needs to deal with the consequences of his actions."

"What about Miles's job, though?"

"That's really up to Rafferty. I would like to think he wouldn't be working at the club anymore, but it's not our decision at the end of the day. Rafferty needs to make the best decision for him and the club."

"I don't know if I could work alongside him if he stayed." Bastien's words were truthful, but he felt awful for it. He was all for giving people a second chance, but Miles followed him without saying anything, scaring the life out of him.

"Then don't. You have your jewellery and your makeup. Why not work on those and see what happens?"

"I would love to, but they don't pay the bills, unfortunately. I still have to afford rent and the bills to keep a roof over my head."

"Not if you stayed here, you wouldn't," Logan murmured, holding him tighter.

Bastien blinked, frozen in place. "You'd want me to stay, even though the stalking is over?" he asked hesitantly.

Logan pulled back, moving Bastien so they could see each other better, and cupped Bastien's chin. "I would love for you to stay here. Indefinitely. I love having you here to come home to after a shitty day. I love being able to watch you work when you're so invested in your gems, you don't know I'm staring at you—which I know is a bit creepy. I love it when you fall asleep and wake up in my arms. I would love nothing more than for you to stay, but only if that is what you want."

Bastien's eyes filled, and he felt his heart racing. "I love you," he whispered, tears spilling down his cheeks.

Logan smiled. "I love you, Queen Bee."

Leaning down, Logan captured Bastien's mouth in a fierce kiss, pressing him backwards until his head was resting on the arm of the sofa. Lifting his lips away with a whimper from Bastien, Logan said, "Stay with me?"

"Forever and always."

They settled in to watch a movie, and Logan sent a message to Kade, explaining their decision to press charges against Nolan but not Miles. They would have more to worry about when things started progressing with Deacon's and Cassidy's cases.

They lay on the sofa, Logan at the back with his arms tightly encircling Bastien in front of him. Bastien wasn't watching the movie; he was concentrating on their reflection on the TV screen and the occasional kiss Logan pressed on his head or neck. It had been a long time since he'd felt this happy like he had a home and family.

Maybe he wasn't that lost little boy anymore.

CHAPTER SEVENTEEN

LOGAN

"**D**ad, can I have a word?"

William Taylor glanced up from the folded newspaper, his glasses perched on the edge of his nose, pen in hand as he attempted the crossword puzzle. "Of course," he said, putting the paper, pen and glasses aside. "What do you need?"

Logan settled himself on the sofa, leaning forward with his elbows on his knees and fingers linked between them. He didn't know where to start. Everything had been perfect between Bastien and him for the past few weeks.

"You're thinking too hard. Start talking. You'll get to what you need to say eventually."

That was his dad. Ever the optimist. "I guess I'm still hung up on what happened with Casey and Bastien. I can't seem to protect those who mean the most to me. I don't know what that says about me, but—"

"It says nothing about you and a lot about the situations you were facing. You're not the only one beating yourself up about what happened with Casey. We can all say we didn't know what happened to him. We can all say we wouldn't have known any better had someone not brought it to our attention. Sometimes, life just gets away from us, and we don't keep in contact as much as we could. That's how things go. Everyone's lives take different turns, and you're not in each other's pockets like you used to be. No one was to blame except that asshole who did it."

"But I'm a police officer. I should be able—"

"Able to what? Read people's minds and know what they're planning? Look into the future and see what could potentially happen to each and every one of us? You're not a god, Logan."

"I should be able to help!" Logan stood, pacing back and forth in front of the fireplace.

"You do. Listen to me. The last case you solved—I know you can't give me too much information—was the outcome happy or sad?"

Logan thought for a moment about the missing girl who'd been returned to her family after three days of being locked in an abandoned house by a woman who had wanted the girl as her own daughter. "Happy with bits of sadness."

"But the overall result was that it was resolved and happy, yes?" Logan nodded. "And who made that happen?"

"The police."

"You."

"It wasn't only me. There was a team of people working on it.

"You."

"What about the others?"

"You, Logan. Yes, the others did their part, but you made it happen just as much as they did."

Logan paused in his pacing, staring at the floor with a frown. "That's different from keeping the people I love safe."

"Yes, it is. But that's not your job, Logan. It's a nice benefit that you're a police officer, but you are not the police officer for your family."

"But how can I help them?"

"By being a brother and a son. Being present. Helping others to get what they deserve. Keeping yourself safe." His father stood, coming over to him. "I was a postal worker. Does that mean I can't take care of my family? No, it doesn't. I can't fight, but you damn well know I would do everything in my power to fight if I needed to. Keeping someone safe doesn't always mean you need to be the strongest or bravest or most resilient. It means you love them no matter what. It means you help them when they need it, whether they ask or not. It means you lean on them when you need to. You don't need to be a police officer to be able to keep someone safe from harm. You just need to love them enough to be willing to do whatever you can for them."

Logan let that sink in, realising what his father was trying to tell him. He finally understood that he was not responsible for the safety of his whole family. They had their own lives, and those lives will take them somewhere where Logan couldn't always be. He wouldn't be able to keep them safe if they were in another country. What did it matter if they were living in the same city? If he was not with them at the time something bad happened, then there was nothing he could do about it.

"Thanks, Dad."

"You also need to remember that we can keep ourselves safe, too."

Logan turned to the doorway, seeing Bastien standing there with tears in his eyes. Logan's father left Logan with a squeeze to his shoulders, stepping over to Bastien and pressing a kiss to his temple before leaving the room. Bastien moved closer, wringing his hands in front of him.

"I have a lot of learning to do," Logan whispered.

"So do I," Bastien agreed, "but we can learn together. But not on your birthday."

Logan wrapped his arms around Bastien and

nuzzled his head into Bastien's neck, inhaling his unique scent. After several minutes, his body released the tension it had held onto for weeks, or maybe even years.

He lifted his head, cupping Bastien's jaw and joined their lips in a brief caress. As his thumbs smoothed across Bastien's cheek, he asked, "Did you sell any more jewellery?"

Bastien chuckled, a flush seeping into his cheeks. "No, but your mother has managed to get me several orders."

"That's amazing."

Bastien hesitated, staring into Logan's eyes. "What do you say to me still working at The Bone Yard?" He bit his bottom lip as he waited for Logan's answer.

Logan tilted his head. "I would say that if it is what you want, then I would be happy for you."

"Good answer. I'm only going to do one or two nights, though. I love the dancing, but I don't necessarily need to do it now." He paused. "I'm sorry that Miles was let go, but I feel happier working there, knowing he's not."

"If you'd still like to dance, then do it. I'll support you no matter what you decide. You know that. And I agree. Do you know what he's doing now?"

"No idea. Rafferty hasn't said, and I've not asked." Bastien glanced at him. "The same goes for you, you know? I will support you through thick and thin. If you ever need to talk about anything, I'm here."

"Thanks, Queen Bee."

Logan slid his arm around Bastien's shoulders and veered him towards the kitchen where his mother was finishing up lunch.

"Do you need any help, Mama?"

"No, thanks, sweetheart. You go and enjoy the time with your friends; it is your birthday after all. Liam and Alice will be in shortly to help take the plates out to the tables."

Logan gave her a kiss on the cheek, then guided Bastien outside. The large garden had been set up with several long tables and chairs, bunting, balloons, a barbecue sizzling away in the corner and several tables hosting different drinks. There was also a small area with garden toys for the little kids who were currently running around chasing after Casey and Asher.

"Hey, Logan! You have presents over here! Aren't you going to open them?" Claire shouted.

"Hmm, this is reminiscent of Casey's party," Logan mumbled.

"Why?" Bastien asked.

"Because they got interrupted, and then Claire came running back, reminding Casey he still had presents to open. She's so impatient. I would love to use her birthday as an excuse to not let her open her presents within the first ten minutes of receiving them. I'd make her wait and open one per hour."

Bastien elbowed him in the side. "That's cruel!"

Logan chuckled. "It would serve her right for all the hassle she gives us. We may as well give her presents on our birthdays. She's the one who usually helps us open them, especially if we don't want to. Like I said, impatient," Logan said to Bastien. "No, I'm not opening them. I'm taking them home with me!" he called back.

"No!" she screeched, practically running to them in her horror. "You can't do that! You have to open them now!"

Logan withheld his chuckle, but only just. "Why, dear sister?"

"Because…because there's something in there I want you to open." She crossed her arms over her chest.

"Even more reason for me to wait until I'm behind closed doors. I don't think I'll ever trust you lot after what Luke told me."

"What did he tell you?" Claire asked, frowning as she glanced around for the man of the conversation.

"Well, he enlightened me to the fact that siblings are very devious and often don't provide very… communally acceptable gifts for their family. I would like to reduce the chances of me opening something I would rather have kept personal."

"I would never…" Claire's denial froze on her lips, and she tilted her head. "Okay, maybe I would." She laughed. "I haven't, but it's given me an idea for next time. Thanks, Logan."

She skipped away, her happy buoyancy everlasting; Logan had no idea where she got the energy from.

"That's a really bad sign, Logan," Bastien whispered.

"What is?"

"That she has plans for next time. I'm no longer opening presents in public."

"Me neither."

They glanced at each other and laughed.

"Logan!"

He saw his brother waving him over and headed over to where he was manning the barbecue. "What's up?"

"Would you like the first burger of the day?"

"God, yeah. I'm starving!"

James handed him the cheeseburger, and Logan stepped to the condiments table. Filling the burger up, he held it in both hands and groaned as the flavours burst on his tongue. Barbecued cheeseburgers were the best.

"Enjoying that, are you?" Bastien asked with a twinkle in his eye.

"Only one thing better," Logan stated, winking at him, chuckling as Bastien's cheeks darkened. "I can't believe you're a stripper, and yet me talking about our sex life embarrasses you."

"Stripping is different. It's almost clinical in some respects. Our sex life…isn't."

"I can make it clinical if that's your fantasy, Queen Bee."

Logan grinned at the roll of Bastien's eyes. "Are you eating?"

"I'm waiting for your mother's stir fry." Bastien rubbed his hands together.

At that moment, Logan's brother and sister came out holding two steaming pans and placed them on one of the tables before his mother exited, holding onto a large cake. Logan's heart expanded at the thought of the love that would've gone into making it. Despite not liking cake—though he didn't have the heart to ever tell anyone—he ate a slice when it was given to him. When he bit into it, though, he found it was different than normal.

"What type of cake is this?" he asked.

"It's a gluten-free cake. I know you're not a fan of normal cake, so I thought I'd try this instead," his mother replied. "I don't mind if you don't like it."

"No, it's fine. You know I'll eat cake—"

"Yes, you've eaten cake for many years, even though you don't like it. I've never understood why." His mother smiled and shook her head.

Logan flushed and shrugged. "I didn't want you to

have to make something else because I didn't like it," he mumbled, lowering his head.

"Oh, Logan." His mother shuffled over to him and wrapped an arm around his shoulder, giving him a squeeze. "You're an amazing man, you know that?"

"Oh, stop telling him how good he is. He'll get a big head!" James complained.

"No different to you," Liam stated.

The siblings started bickering, and the rest of the guests laughed at their antics. Logan gave a small smile as he looked around at the people who had come to celebrate with him. Now that he was feeling a little more settled in himself, he realised his life couldn't be more perfect. Gazing at Bastien, who was in a conversation with Asher's niece, a seven-year-old who loved to dance, he honestly believed that if Bastien hadn't come into his life when he did, Logan would still be working all hours of the day and night, and a family-sized hole would have developed in his life.

He had a lot to thank Bastien for.

As they were sitting with conversations between friends and family surrounding them, Logan pulled Bastien closer, his front to Bastien's back—his favourite position—he realised something.

"Hey, when's *your* birthday?" he asked, pressing a kiss to Bastien's hair.

"Um...I don't really celebrate my birthday anymore. Ever since I was...left home," he amended.

"I didn't see the point in remembering something that linked me back to my parents." He shrugged. "I much prefer celebrating other people's birthdays."

Logan manhandled Bastien until he was sideways, then lifted his face with a finger beneath his jaw. "That doesn't tell me when it is, Queen Bee."

Bastien rolled his lips inwards and moved his chin out of Logan's hand, turning his gaze away. Logan didn't think he would give an answer, but he mumbled, "Tomorrow."

Logan was quiet for a moment, then said, "Seriously?" Bastien nodded half-heartedly, and Logan's heart broke. "Will you allow me to change your thoughts on celebrating it? I'd love us to start some new traditions. We could do something completely different from what you had growing up. Forget them. You have us now."

Bastien tucked his head under Logan's chin, sliding his arm around his waist and holding onto him. When Logan felt him trembling, Logan gripped him tightly, holding the back of Bastien's head against his chest, hoping he knew how much he meant to Logan. Instead of hoping, he said, "I love you, Bastien. More than anything in the world."

Bastien held him tighter, then lifted his tear-stained face to Logan's. "I love you, and I would love to make new memories and traditions with you and your family."

"Our family."

A tremulous smile appeared on his face. "Our family," he croaked.

"Logan Antony Taylor! What have you done to him?"

They both glanced at Logan's mother, who was marching towards them, a fierce expression on her face. Logan felt his face drain of blood, but Bastien chuckled beside him.

"You better not laugh, Queen Bee, or I'm taking you down with me," he hissed. "I haven't done anything, Mama! We were talking about something sad. I've been trying to cheer him up!"

Christine stopped in front of them, pointing a finger at her son. "That better be the truth, my son, because if I find out you've hurt him, I'll tan your hide. You're not too old for it."

"No, but he might like it now that he's older," James coughed into his hand to try and disguise his words, but they were clear as day. Their mother pivoted to face James, and his face paled before she turned back.

"What's the matter, sweetheart?"

"I'm all right, Christine. I promise. We were just talking about family, that's all." Bastien tried to placate her, but Logan knew she wouldn't leave it until she knew exactly what they were talking about.

"I'm sure it must be difficult being around all of us when you had no one, but we're here for you, too. All this," she waved her hand around, "is now a part of you." She smiled, and Bastien began crying again. She shushed him and held him in her arms, rocking him back and forth like she always did when each of her children was upset.

"We were talking about his birthday. We would like to begin some new traditions and need help thinking of some," Logan announced with a louder voice, including the nearby guests in his words.

"That's a wonderful idea," his mother said, pulling back from Bastien and wiping under his eyes. "New traditions are so important, but such fun to figure out. When is your birthday so we can figure out something new for you?"

Bastien glanced at Logan, and he could see him begging for help. As much as he knew Bastien, he instinctively knew he wouldn't want some huge party thrown for him; therefore, he leaned forward to whisper in his mother's ear.

She smiled at Bastien and nodded. "How about a cake for starters?" she mumbled to him with a wink. "We'll start small."

"Thank you, Christine."

"You're very welcome, precious boy." She ran a hand over his hair, then stood, heading over to Logan's father.

"Sorry," Bastien said, wiping at his eyes again. "I

didn't mean to ruin your party by making it about me."

"Hush! You didn't make it about you. You gave me something I really appreciate."

Bastien frowned at him. "What?"

"Your trust."

"You've always had my trust."

"Maybe, but you showed it by giving me a piece of you that had been hidden away for years. By shining a light on that part of you, you gave me more trust than ever before."

He kissed Bastien, unable to do anything else. When the wolf-whistling started, he held up his middle finger despite the reprimand from his mother and continued kissing Bastien until they both needed air.

"I think," he panted, "the first tradition should be a dance with the birthday boy. What do you think?"

Bastien licked his lips, smiled shyly and nodded. They stood, and holding hands, Logan shouted across for a slow dance song. When *I Get to Love You* by Ruelle came on, Logan smiled.

"Perfect."

Bastien nuzzled his head into Logan's chest and wrapped his arms around his neck while Logan encircled his waist. He closed his eyes as the words and music covered them in a little bubble, the sounds of the guests retreating until he was only aware of his and Bastien's synced breathing.

After the song finished, he blinked his eyes open to see them surrounded by their friends and family, smiles all around. He glanced down at Bastien.

"Not a bad start to our new traditions."

"Not a bad start at all," Bastien replied.

"How have things been going?" Amanda asked, crossing her legs and resting her hands on her knees.

Logan blew out a breath. "Really good."

He had seen Amanda every week since the first mandatory session, and he was glad of it.

"I'm glad. How is your relationship developing with Bastien? The last time we spoke, you said you were going to talk to him about your visits to the club when he didn't know you were there. Did you do that?"

He nodded and sighed. "He took it better than I expected." Amanda smiled at him, silently prompting him to continue. "He told me that it was a bit creepy, which I can understand now that I can see things clearer. At the time, I was worried about him." He frowned. "I didn't feel like he was safe anywhere, even with me around, but I also couldn't not be there in case something happened."

"When you say he wasn't safe anywhere, what do you mean?"

Logan slumped forward, staring at the floor. "Well, anyone could get to him at the club and his apartment. There was no security at all there. If something had happened, there was still no guarantee I would be able to help him. Despite him not being safe anywhere, I couldn't live with myself if I didn't try to protect him."

"Do you think he should've been involved in the decision about that protection?"

"Now? Yes," he said with a chuckle. "At the time, I knew I needed to do whatever I could, even if he didn't like it."

"Was that why you tried to get him to move in with you?"

Logan nodded. "Don't get me wrong, I wanted him there, too, but it was more about him being safer than where he lived."

"He is safe with you, you know." Logan lifted his gaze to Amanda's and held it. "How are things going with the stalker murders?"

"We finally managed to nail Brooke to the two women's murders, and then we were able to tie him to several other murders in various cities around the UK."

Amanda raised her eyebrows. "I bet that felt good."

"It did. The tech guys did a great job figuring out the last letters of the code on the bags of hair were related to the letters of the alphabet. It spelt out part of the town the murders happened in." Logan shook his head. "If he wasn't a killer, I'd think he was smart. He's going away for a long time. I'm happy."

He glanced down at his hands again.

"You're not going to hurt Bastien by being with him, and you won't hurt him when you're at work. You are not the cause of bad things happening in your life, Logan."

He closed his eyes and swallowed hard. "I want him to have a better life than what he had before," he whispered.

"He does. And it has nothing to do with how safe you keep him. It has to do with how much you love him and how much he loves you."

FIVE MONTHS LATER

BASTIEN

Bastien still struggled on occasion with the size of Logan's family, especially when throwing in the friends as well. After being alone for a long time, it was difficult to get into the habit of having so many people care about his wellbeing.

As for this particular day of the year…he hadn't celebrated it for sixteen years, so he believed he had a right to feel a little nervous. He had no idea what to expect.

So far that morning, Logan had woken him with a very nice blowjob, followed by a fuck in the shower, followed by a rimming in the doorway until he came over the floor. His legs were trembling like he'd been dancing for hours on end without stopping.

Once they finally descended the stairs, Bastien gasped.

"When did you do all this?" He held a hand over his mouth and stared around the living room, which had transformed their usual furniture into a winter wonderland. When they had gone to bed, there had been minimal Christmas decorations, including a tree and a few ornaments, and that was about it.

Now, though, the room contained a new and improved tree, heavily decorated with ornaments and tinsel; garlands covering several surfaces; red and green throws covering the sofas and different Christmas characters hanging from the ceiling. The windows had been frosted, there were 'snowy' footprints by the fireplace, and a huge pile of presents underneath the tree.

Bastien felt Logan's hands sliding around his waist, and he leaned back, still shocked by the change.

"We wanted you to have a special first Christmas," Logan murmured, nuzzling against Bastien's neck. "Casey, Luke, James and Claire came over last night to do it."

"I didn't even know you'd left the bed!" He twisted his head to see his boyfriend.

"I didn't. They messaged when they got here and let themselves in when I gave them the go-ahead."

Bastien faced the room once more, unable to believe they had gone to this much trouble to make it special for him. Tears pooled in his eyes, and he blinked, letting them cascade down his cheeks. No one

—not even his parents—had ever gone to this much work for him.

"Thank you." His voice cracked even though he whispered the words.

Logan held him tighter. "You're very welcome, Queen Bee. Shall we open some presents?"

Bastien's face split into a grin. "Yes!" He danced forward, dropping to a cross-legged position in front of the tree.

"Do you want a drink or something to eat first?"

"Nope!" Bastien picked up a present and put it to one side, then repeated the action with another gift. He went through each gift, putting them into two piles, then glanced over his shoulder at Logan. "Aren't you going to join me?"

Logan smiled. "I was leaving you to your fun. I wasn't sure I was allowed to interrupt."

"Come on!"

Bastien was so excited, he could hardly contain himself. He'd bought a few presents for Logan and his family, but he hadn't expected anything from them. If this pile of gifts was any indication, he had plenty.

Sitting beside him, Logan slid an arm around his shoulder, pulling him closer and pressing a kiss to his head. "Okay, let's do this."

Bastien lifted a gift from Logan's pile, then passed it over, waiting for him to tear the paper off the present from Claire. Nestled inside a purple box was a large purple dildo.

"Seriously, Claire!" Logan sighed, grabbing the easily eight- or ten-inch plastic dick and waving it in front of them.

Bastien covered his mouth, laughing out loud at the expression on Logan's face. If he'd had his phone with him, it would've made an impressive picture. "So, who gets that?"

Logan paused, then turned his head, smirking. "I think I can think of some ways for this to get some use after all."

Swallowing hard, Bastien focused on his pile, choosing a similarly purple-wrapped gift from Claire. "Why am I suddenly nervous about opening these presents?"

"Because you know my family well. Ever since we started getting involved with the Walkers, the present giving has become 'who can one-up the other.'"

Blowing out a breath, Bastien tore off the wrapper, smiling regardless of what was inside because it was the first Christmas gift he'd had in a long while. A purple box lay in wait, and he lifted the lid, uncovering two pairs of fluffy handcuffs complete with a key and a blindfold. He raised his eyebrows at Logan, whose pupils had dilated until he could barely see the colour of his eyes.

Bastien scrambled to cover the items, not wanting

to get distracted from the present opening. He shoved the box to the side and held out a hand, palm forward. "Not yet! Presents first!"

"But—"

"No!" He held his finger up in front of Logan's face. "Presents!"

Logan laughed. "Okay! Okay!"

They spent several long minutes unwrapping the gifts, and Bastien was overwhelmed by the generosity of the family. He'd not only received several vouchers for high-end makeup shops, but he'd received some gorgeous silk pyjamas, a pair of high-heeled, fur-lined boots, a silver glitter bag, a box of gems that would be perfect for his jewellery, and a guide to the Kama Sutra. They hadn't only been from Logan's family either. Some had been from their friends, which Bastien had expected even less.

"I can't believe there's so much," Bastien said, resting his hands on his cheeks and blowing out a breath.

"No doubt this is just the beginning."

Bastien stared at him. "What do you mean?"

"We're going to Mama and Dad's for lunch. I'm sure there will be presents there that they 'forgot' about."

"God! They can't give any more. It's too much!"

Logan pulled him close, and Bastien sank into the

embrace, closing his eyes and breathing Logan's scent deeply.

"They love you as much as I do."

As Logan predicted, there were more gifts when they arrived at the family home, along with more family members. Christine had prepared an enormous feast for them as well as enough food for each of them to take home as well.

After lunch, they all sat in the living room, playing board games and looking through the gifts they'd been given, generally having fun.

Bastien was curled up onto Logan's lap, thinking about how different his life was now. Deacon and Cassidy had both been given prison sentences, albeit short ones, and Nolan was doing community service for their parts in the events. Bastien was feeling more content than ever before.

He felt Logan tense and take a deep breath. "There is one more gift for you here." Logan reached behind him and put a medium-sized jewellery box in front of Bastien.

Bastien scooted upright. "What's this?"

"Open it."

He slid the bow off and lifted the lid, completely overwhelmed by the contents. Nestled in the ivory velvet was a bracelet set with several small different coloured gems, and in the centre, a white gold ring with a small heart-shaped diamond on it. Bastien stared at it, then focused on Logan, unable to say anything.

"I love you, Bastien. Ever since our first encounter when you were muffling your pleasure-filled screams, I knew there was something about you I couldn't ignore. You were a beacon to me. Someone who lit up my life when I hadn't even realised it was filling with darkness. You showed me how to remember to live instead of just survive. I don't ever want to be without you." He inhaled. "Will you marry me?"

Bastien nodded emphatically, tears streaming down his cheeks and blurring his vision. He wiped away tears when Logan took the box from his hands, then tried to steady his left hand as Logan slid the ring on his finger. Once in place, Bastien immediately straddled Logan's lap and kissed him.

"Yes! Yes! Yes!" he said in between kisses.

Logan cupped his jaw, holding him steady. "You have made this the best Christmas ever, Bastien Templeton."

"Bastien Taylor," Bastien corrected.

Logan's eyebrows rose. "You want to take my name?"

"I want nothing more than to be yours in every way I can be, including your name. I don't need to hold onto mine for any reason."

Logan's smile lit up the room, and they kissed

again, their bodies holding tightly to the one who meant the world to them.

Everything that had happened to him in the past was forgotten. He had a new family, a new beginning, a new future.

Have you read all of the Crush series? If not, why not start at the beginning—First Kiss

Sign up to my newsletter to get a free **BONUS SCENE** from Lawful Attraction and the Crush prequel short story, Love Conquers.

If you have a moment, would you write a review for Lawful Attraction please? Reviews help other readers decide whether they would like to read the book, and therefore, are also important for authors.

Can a tentative friendship wipe away years of loneliness?

When Dean was unwittingly outed as gay at his previous fire station, things became uncomfortable. So when he heard rumours of a station that welcomed everyone without exclusion, he jumped at the chance of a transfer. The trouble with moving was that he didn't know anyone, and he refused to become a pest by accepting daily invites from his Chief. Finding Nourris Moi was a stroke of luck, and soon became his haven.

Oliver's dream of owning his own restaurant had come true, and after three years, he was finally turning a profit. Nourris Moi was his life, and he had no time for anything else. Until a certain firefighter became a firm fixture at one of his tables. The quiet and reserved newcomer caught his attention despite his determination to focus on his business.

Can Oliver and Dean find a balance between their career needs and what their hearts are crying out for?

Pre-order here:
https://readerlinks.com/l/1817235

NEW SERIES ANNOUNCEMENT

Club Royal Series, Book 1

Welcome to Club Royal, where your kinks are no longer a secret...

Douglas is the spare heir, and he chafes at the restrictions placed on his extra-curricular activities. He wants nothing more than to lose himself in someone else, but too many people are out for what they can get from him, including a membership at the exclusive and highly confidential Club Royal.

Maverick was given the role of social media manager to Douglas as punishment for showing up his boss two years ago. Try as he might, he has not been able to get a transfer, though it could be because he is too damn good at his job. Despite being given the exclusive membership to Club Royal, he doesn't use it...it's just not his kind of thing.

When Douglas figures out Maverick's weakness, he wants to be the one to teach Maverick everything, and it sends them on a journey neither had anticipated.

Can Maverick trust his body to a man who can have anyone he desires?

***

Pre-order here:
https://readerlinks.com/l/1817165

ABOUT ELOUISE EAST

I am Elouise East but feel free to call me Elli. I write sweet and steamy connections in gay romance. I also touch on taboo stories under the name Elouise R East.

Books that tell the stories where friendship and family are the focal point - be it blood family or chosen - is very important to me. That's why I include a variety of personalities, talents, ages, situations and abilities as I believe a story needs, or a character needs. I want my characters to be real, to be relatable, to be free to have whatever views they tell me they have. And trust me, most of the time, I do not have *any* say in the matter!

My characters come to life on the page for me as well as my readers. Their stories unfold in front of me, and I have very little input into how they want to be shown. Just like real life, the lives of my characters change with every choice, every interaction and every conversation. And I wouldn't have it any other way.

I write books that are emotionally realistic, even if liberties are taken with other aspects of my stories. I don't know any other way to write. It comes from deep inside.

Who am I? A single parent to two children who make life worth living. An avid reader who still devours every book she can get her hands on. A student of learning about any subject that takes her fancy. An author of books she would read herself. And a romantic at heart who loves anything cheesy.

Who's in?

Stalk me here… ;-)
WEBSITE: https://elouiseeast.com/
NEWSLETTER: https://elouiseeast.com/newsletter
LINKTREE: https://linktr.ee/elouiseeastauthor

BOOKS BY ELOUISE EAST

<u>CRUSH</u>

First Kiss

Instant Desire

Primary Seduction

Deep Down

A Crush for Christmas

Life Support

Covert Strength

Love Scene

Lawful Attraction

<u>CLUB ROYAL</u>

Royal Firsts

Rogue Royal

Secretive Royal

Grieving Royal

Disowned Royal

Trained Royal

Awakened Royal

Commanding Royal

LOVE IN FLAMES

Out of the Frying Pan

Smokescreen

Breathing Fire

JUST A LITTLE CRUSH

Star-Crossed

He's Behind You

A Special Love (newsletter story)

DADDY

Love Me, Daddy

Soothe Me, Daddy

Spoil Me, Daddy

DARK & DIVERGENT

A Biker Make Three

Forbidden Temptation

Too Many Secrets

CHARMED

Treehouse Whispers

Rhythm Inside (Heard it in a Love Song Anthology)